BIRD

courtney collins

BIRD

hachette
AUSTRALIA

Extract from 'Thrush' by Louise Glück (*Averno*, 2006) reprinted by permission of Carcanet Press.

hachette AUSTRALIA

Published in Australia and New Zealand in 2024
by Hachette Australia
(an imprint of Hachette Australia Pty Limited)
Gadigal Country, Level 17, 207 Kent Street, Sydney, NSW 2000
www.hachette.com.au

Hachette Australia acknowledges and pays our respects to the past, present and future Traditional Owners and Custodians of Country throughout Australia and recognises the continuation of cultural, spiritual and educational practices of Aboriginal and Torres Strait Islander peoples. Our head office is located on the lands of the Gadigal people of the Eora Nation.

NATIONAL LIBRARY OF AUSTRALIA

A catalogue record for this book is available from the National Library of Australia

ISBN: 978 0 7336 5241 7 (paperback)

Cover design by Christabella Designs
Cover image (woman) courtesy of Shutterstock
Cover image (bird) and illustration (florals) courtesy of Dreamstime
Part page images (feathers) courtesy of Getty
Author photo by Jay Black @andthetreesphotography
Typeset in 12.2/17.4 pt Garamond MT Pro by Bookhouse
Printed and bound in Australia by McPherson's Printing Group

FSC www.fsc.org MIX Paper from responsible sources FSC® C001695

The paper this book is printed on is certified against the Forest Stewardship Council® Standards. McPherson's Printing Group holds FSC® chain of custody certification SA-COC-005379. FSC® promotes environmentally responsible, socially beneficial and economically viable management of the world's forests.

For Jude

'After many lives, maybe something changes.
I think in the end what you want
you'll be able to see—

Then you don't need anymore
to die and come back again.'

—Louise Glück, 'Thrush', *Averno*

PROLOGUE

Ten thousand strands of trouble, is what your father said.

He was laughing when he said it, and he was talking to his friends. He was referring to your hair. He was also referring to your life and all the lives you had not yet lived but he presumed would be full of misfortune – because you were born a girl. You had just turned fourteen when he said it. Your sister Mida was braiding your hair. You hardly knew yourself then, or what it was you wanted. But you already knew to doubt your parents and anything they said.

That first life, you had been born in a village with a wide river that wrapped around it and mountains in view. In your mind, the mountains promised the world, and the river is what separated you from it.

Your parents told you stories about the river, stories of newly betrothed village girls who had tried to run away and were drowned by the river – *because*, they said, *the river cared that the girls disobeyed.* They told you that in the river's rage, it boiled with their bodies as the fish ate them. *Because of their disobedience.* What the fish did not eat was washed up on the shore. They told you that the teeth of those girls littered the banks of the river like pearls. And they warned you to keep away.

You were twelve years old when you finally explored the river alone. You had just witnessed your parents arranging the marriage of your sister Mida to your neighbour Cho. Everybody in the village knew Cho to be selfish and cruel. Once, running past his farm, you had seen him kick his dog just because the dog was in his way. Whenever you heard that poor dog's yelp echoing through the valley, you knew Cho's boot was behind it. Your parents knew it too. So, you did not understand how it was that he came to be sitting at their table, negotiating what was a fair exchange for Mida, while she smiled on prettily, pouring them tea.

A moment in Cho's company and you could not stand one moment more. His eyes flicked hungrily over everything in sight. You ran through the field and out to the road, past Cho's farm, past your neighbours' fields, all the way to the river which was further than you had ever been. You searched the riverbank. But you could find no remnants of girls. You examined the mud, digging holes with your hands for what might be hidden. Nothing but grit caught your fingers, and you could find no bones or flecks of bone. You wandered up and down its bank and into its shallows, and nothing bad happened to you. You sat on its smooth stones, pushed your feet into its cool water and watched ducks skim across its surface. You understood with certainty then that the river would not punish you if you disobeyed your parents, or anyone. Because the river did not care. And you made a vow to yourself that one day you would cross it.

This place you began, this village with the river wrapping around it and the mountains in view, you are not there now. You have been carried further – to another life, another time.

You are in a hospital bed, so far from that place. But it is here you feel the river rising in you. You feel it break its banks and wash away the mud walls you have built over lifetimes, and all the other ways you have taught yourself to forget.

And it is here, strand by strand, you begin to remember—

1.

HIMALAYAS, UNKNOWN YEAR

A warm weather day. You stand facing a field. It is harvest time. The heads of the barley are heavy and drooping.

You can feel your mother's eyes burning into your back as she watches you from the house. You spin around to face her. She pretends not to see you as she flips and folds dough. She is making dumplings for the wedding you do not want to have, a mountain of dumplings you did not ask for.

Don't watch me. Watch him! you yell, pointing to your father, who is also avoiding you. He sits on a lump of wood behind the pigpen, swilling his homemade beer, as he has done every day since he announced your wedding at the harvest festival. He did not have the courage to tell you himself before you learnt, along with the rest of the village, that you would be married on the next full moon.

Travelling home, sitting on bags of barley that did not sell, you protested: *But there is no suitor! Who am I supposed to marry?*

Your father drove the cart on and your mother fixed her gaze towards a distant place, and neither of them would answer you.

In the village, when a daughter came of age, it was custom for the father to announce his intentions to find her a suitable match at a harvest market or a festival. Many moons later, if that was what it took, when the best suitor had declared himself and negotiations had taken place, the father would announce the wedding. This is how it was with Mida. Your father had stood on that same platform and announced his intentions to find her a suitable husband, boasting of her beauty and her virtues. Time passed and many suitors stepped forward and offers were made. So, you could not understand why Cho's offer was regarded as the best or why Mida chose to accept it. But she did accept it and you have not accepted anything.

Before your father steered the cart towards your farm, you leapt off the back and ran to find Mida. Since her marriage, she lived with Cho and his parents on their adjacent farm.

You found Mida in the kitchen. She made tea and waited for Cho to leave the house before she explained: *Since we've been married, Cho has been paying our father's debts. But now he refuses to pay. So what our parents are calling a wedding is an auction, and you are what is for sale. Debtors are threatening our father so there is no time to waste. On the night of the full moon, you are going to be sold off to the highest bidder.*

Harvest time. When the sky spills light on the field and the field glows back. It used to be your favourite season, when the crops grew way past your head and you could wander within them, hidden from them all. Now all that is left of your family's farm is this slim band of barley. Soon, your father will stumble out from behind the pigpen and slash it, but he will not see the rewards of that because he gambled away the takings in his last game of sho.

You had wanted to think all your troubles are because of him, that both of your parents could not have let you down so terribly. But this morning when Mida arrived to help your mother with preparations, you overheard them talking in the courtyard.

Will anyone want to marry her? your mother said. They were hanging lanterns. Dragging chairs.

Mother, forgive me for saying it, said Mida. *But perhaps this was not your finest idea.*

You have done your best to be terrible at everything your mother has taught you – cooking, cleaning, fetching, folding. She has made no secret of her wish that you had been born a boy and sometimes you have wished for that too, for the freedom it would have given you. Because as well as the tedium of chores, what she has tried to teach you is that a perfect daughter is one resigned to her fate, who does not ask questions.

How can you tell your mother that you do not want her life? That you want a life you cannot yet see? A life that the field, the mountains, the road, all seem to whisper to you – the road being proof that you can snake through the village and away.

The expectation you should want your mother's life, or accept whatever it is she tells you, creates a pressure in your body that only running can relieve. So, you run along the road whenever you feel it building. You have run since you were a child. But lately the neighbours, Cho included, have complained. They say you are drawing attention to yourself. They say:

Animals run. Not girls.

You stand at the edge of the field, your mother's eyes upon you. You pick up a rock and stare back at her. She shakes her head. She does not have to say a word for you to know what she is thinking—

Here we go again . . .

—as you aim a rock at the window.

I do not want to marry! you yell, and your mother closes the window shutter just as you pelt the rock. You yell loud enough for the whole village to hear, and then you stop. Everything is quiet.

You fling out your arms and turn your feet. You tip your head to the sky. You turn and turn until the world of house, pigpen, mother, sister, father, field, all disappear into a dull void.

But then you hear your mother's voice again.

Will anyone want to marry her?

You drop to your haunches and tear at the grass with your hands. You feel her betrayal as a pain in your chest. You are dizzy as you stand to face the field and you stumble as you run. But you do run. You run towards the road, and you do not care who sees you.

2.

DARWIN, PRESENT DAY

You wake alone in a white room. Your body feels heavy. You can hardly move. You are strapped to a bed. You push your legs against the straps, but it does nothing to loosen them.

Sunlight pulses around the edges of the curtains, so you know it is day. One of your arms rests above a sheet. The other is bent up in a sling. Your shoulder feels like it has been freshly bludgeoned, and your matted hair rises and falls as you breathe. It looks like a half-dead animal slumped across your chest.

You guess you are in a hospital. In the room there is a chair, a set of tall metal drawers, a table on wheels, and a machine with red and green lights blinking. A cannula is connected to your free arm.

You notice your nails are painted metallic green and a small *t* is tattooed on the inside of your wrist that is resting in the sling. Surely, it is not a cross, you think. Surely, you are not religious. You bring your wrist closer to your face. The way the tail bleeds looks amateur, like you may have done it yourself, though you can't remember doing it.

You can't remember much. Your head is full of fog and you want to ask someone how you got here.

Your mouth feels claggy, like it's coated with glue. You look around to see if there is any water.

A woman is standing by the door.

Good morning, Bird, she says. You did not hear the door open, and you do not know how long she has been standing there.

Who are you? you ask.

I'm your nurse, Margie. I'm just checking on you.

Why am I strapped to this bed?

You've been given a general anaesthesia and sometimes children come out of it kicking and screaming. It's called angry child syndrome.

Am I a child?

You are fourteen and nine months. The doctor was concerned about how you would come out of the anaesthesia, because there were other drugs in your system. Do you know what you took?

She is saying everything loudly and slowly, as if you wouldn't be able to comprehend otherwise.

You shake your head. *No, I don't remember.*

Can I pop this under your tongue? She is walking towards you holding a thermometer.

What day is it?

Tuesday morning.

And when did I get here?

Monday afternoon. Can you open your mouth for me?

With your mouth feeling the way it does, you do not want to open it.

Can you get me some water?

She pours water into a plastic cup. You sip it slowly.

Do you know how I got here?

I'm sorry, she says, screwing up her face. *I'm not supposed to say.*

A prickling heat comes over you.

Well, who can tell me?

She moves to the end of the bed and taps her pen against a clipboard hanging from the metal bedframe. The strip of sunlight from the window reaches her back. Some of her hair is growing vertically from the top of her head.

Can't you tell me anything?

She looks to the door and then back at you.

You tried to hold up a service station with a water pistol. Two police officers walked in and one of them shot you in the shoulder.

Why are you whispering?

Because there's a guard posted outside the door. And I'm not supposed to tell you anything.

A guard?

They're saying you're a flight risk.

Hah hah, you say.

Will you let me take your temperature?

You open your mouth. *Your tongue is still bright blue*, she says.

She watches you intently. Why would your tongue be bright blue? You want her to look away. You close your eyes until you hear the thermometer beeping.

How are you feeling? she asks as she takes the thermometer out of your mouth.

I don't know. I can't seem to remember very much.

You've been through a bit of an ordeal, haven't you?

Well, I only know what you've told me.

Apparently, you wanted a slushie.

A slushie?

That's why your tongue is blue. You drank it before you paid for it. Or didn't pay for it. Can I get you anything before I go?

One thing. Can you take off these straps? I can't move my legs.

She scans your face, looks into your eyes. *It seems like you've come out of the anaesthesia okay.*

Except I can't remember anything.

It will all come back to you, she says. *Just rest and wait.*

She unbuckles the straps from beneath the bed and then leans over you as she pulls them loose. But as she does, her legs seem to give way, and she loses her balance and falls on top of you.

Ouch! you cry.

I'm so sorry, she says, recovering herself. Her face suddenly looks grey.

Are you going to faint? you ask.

I shouldn't even be here, she says. *I should have finished my shift hours ago.*

Why didn't you? you ask, but she has already left the room.

With the straps off the bed, you attempt to sit up. Your whole body aches. You think about what the nurse has just told you. It makes no sense. Why would you hold up a service station? You do not know if you can trust her, but you do have a wound and by the pain of it, it could be from a gunshot. Though how would you know?

You pull back the sling. You can see your shoulder is covered with transparent tape and beneath the tape it is bound with gauze. You test the tape with your fingers, but you can't find the beginning or the end of it. So, you sleep.

3.

HIMALAYAS, UNKNOWN YEAR

You run to the charnel ground. As you step between two painted rocks that mark the entrance, a gust tunnels up and torn prayer flags whip above your head. Along with the river, this is another place your parents have warned you that you should not be.

You move slowly down the path, listening for monks and goats. Your friend Teshi, your only friend, has told you that monks will beat trespassers with sticks, and you know spooked goats will charge at anything. You continue, despite the risk, because you need to find Teshi. And soon.

You and Teshi met when you were small children. You had been building yourself a nest in the field, and he'd wandered in. Even before you asked his name, he was turning out his pockets – showing you coins and amulets like you had never seen. He told you his father was a body breaker, whose job it was to take care of the dead. It was a job that nobody wanted, he said, but his father had been born into it, and so had he. To help his father, he swept in after the vultures and picked out what was left. He told you he was an untouchable. But it was just a word to you then.

Teshi found you often playing in the field, and your games together became more adventurous. But the day your father saw you both running down the road, he came after you and demanded to know the boy's name. Your father towered over Teshi, but Teshi stood his ground.

And who are your parents? your father boomed.

You knew Teshi was afraid. But he spoke the truth of who his parents were, that they were untouchables, and then there was nothing more to say. Your father raised a stick above his head and chased Teshi down the road like he was chasing away a wild dog.

But your father's attention on you never lasted for very long and so your friendship with Teshi continued. You met in the tall grasses of your neighbours' fields or in the forest, where other villagers were afraid to go.

One day, as you emerged from the forest, you and Teshi met two monk boys who were carrying alms bowls. They were not much older than you. Teshi gave them the amulet he was carrying in his pocket and asked them where they were headed.

To the Pilgrim's Trail, they said.

And where does that lead to? you asked.

To the Holy Mountain.

You had heard people talk of the Holy Mountain, your mother included, but only in whispers not meant for your ears. You imagined it was another place your parents would warn you never to go.

And what happens at the Holy Mountain? you asked the boys.

They looked at each other for a moment, as if contemplating what to say. But then a brightness came over them. They nodded at each other and one of them said, *The Holy Mountain will purify your heart and show you who you truly are.*

Hearing the boys' words, and their conviction, you could feel your small world opening up. You could feel yourself grow larger.

What about an untouchable? asked Teshi.

Even an untouchable.

What about a girl? you asked.

Even a girl.

What you heard that day, and what you and Teshi have reminded each other of every day since, is that even if your heart is impure, it can be made pure, and despite your earthly limits – Teshi an untouchable, and you a girl – in the presence of the Holy Mountain you could one day discover the truth of who you really are.

The wind thrashes the juniper bushes on both sides of the path, twisting them right down to their roots. If you were to see a monk or a goat, these wind-battered bushes would not conceal you, so you slide between two boulders and climb down.

The afternoon light shifts quickly and confuses you. Where to place your feet? Cold air stings your face and your fingers. The truth is, even if you do find Teshi, he may not want to see you.

After your father's announcement at the harvest festival, you asked Teshi for a favour – to dress up in a dead man's suit and visit your parents' house, posing as your suitor. You wanted your parents to think that you were worth more than being sold off to a stranger. But if you had thought beyond yourself, you would have realised that Teshi's humiliation was inevitable.

When he arrived at the door, you saw him for the first time, not only as your friend but also as an entirely separate person. You saw him as you hoped your parents would see him – a handsome young man in fine clothes, carrying a posy of herbs for your mother. You welcomed him, and when he crossed the threshold, it was into an unreal world where you were both acting out your parts. Believing Teshi was a wealthy travelling trader, your parents welcomed him too. Your father offered him beer. Your mother offered him food. They were so impressed with his manners and his attire that they did not recognise him as the same boy your father had chased away with a stick so many years before.

It was Cho, your brother-in-law, who started asking questions.

You're a trader, he said to Teshi. *So, what is it you trade?*

Garments. Sometimes jewellery, Teshi lied.

And which route do you travel?

North-east.

North-east? Don't bandits block that pass?

Yes, Teshi said. *I have met bandits on the road. But in the end, they didn't cause me any trouble.*

What did you do to them? asked your father, intrigued.

Teshi ran his hands along his slim legs clothed in somebody else's suit. You felt your throat constrict as Teshi took a breath.

I told them I was a body breaker. An untouchable. Perhaps the bandits saw me as their own kind, or maybe they were afraid of me.

Cho slapped the table. *I knew it!* he said.

Your father stood up, rising to his height at the table. *Who are your parents? What is your name?* And time folded together.

Again, Teshi spoke his truth just as he had done when he was a small boy. But this time, he would not be chased down the road by your father.

Thank you for your hospitality, he said, collecting his coat and heading for the door. You followed him as Cho yelled behind you, *The butcher boy! I knew it.*

Teshi made long strides towards the road. You caught up with him and you wanted to say sorry, but instead you said, *Will you still run away with me?*

Right now is not a good time, Bird, Teshi said, his pace increasing. From the angle of his body, you knew that all he wanted was to get away from you.

What about the Pilgrim's Trail? What about our plan?

He stopped and turned to face you. *Bird, do not ask me to be someone I am not ever again.* Then he continued towards the road, and you watched the distance grow until you could no longer see him.

Searching the charnel grounds now, there is no sign of him. The earth is undisturbed, and the small hut Teshi and his father work from is ordered and empty.

You could wait for him inside the shut, but your father would come for you, or an angry monk might find you first. And on the eve of you being sold off like a sack of barley, haven't you already waited for Teshi for too long? He may not have forgiven you and perhaps he never will.

You make your way back to the steep path through the charnel ground, breaking off a juniper branch as you go, telling yourself that if you see a monk, you will hit him first, telling yourself that even the goats should be afraid of you.

4.

DARWIN, PRESENT DAY

When you wake, a plate of food has appeared on the metal drawers next to your bed. A lump of something orange and grey swimming in gravy. You can't bring yourself to eat.

At your hip you find a remote control that changes the angle of the bed. You press it until you are sitting upright. There is still a cannula releasing painkillers into your good arm. Your other arm is still in a sling. Again, you examine the splintering ink of the *t* on your wrist and you wonder if you made the mark yourself, and if you did, you must be left-handed.

You stare at the *t* for a long time, as if it will unlock a memory.

And it does, but only when you close your eyes again.

A hand appears. A hand holding your wrist, another hand holding a sewing needle. It is your friend, T. He is dipping the needle in ink, then tapping it against your wrist as he traces the outline of his initial.

His hands are warm. You are sitting in his caravan. You feel calm as he tattoos you. There is no music playing. There is only the sound of his voice. He is telling you that you are a great artist. And all around him you can see so many of the drawings you have made. They cover the walls. You watch T's face as he works with great attention and you decide that you like everything about him. Except he wears too much deodorant. And as you have that thought, you sneeze.

Then T presses too much ink into your skin and the perfect tail he is making on his *t* splinters. He tries to fix it with baby wipes. But the ink has found a path in your skin. T is disappointed with himself.

Don't worry, you say. *I like it. It's got character.*

Whatever happens, T says, *even when we're really old, you'll remember me doing this.*

You open your eyes and the nurse from yesterday is standing beside you, too close to the bed. She is hugging a green shopping bag to her chest.

You're awake, she says, sliding a table over your bed. She unpacks three containers and peels off their lids.

Have you bought me takeaway? you ask, confused.

No, she says. *I made you some real food. I noticed you haven't been eating. I don't blame you. The food in here will kill you.*

She hovers nervously, waiting for a response. You try to remember her name.

It's Margie, isn't it?

That's right, she says, smiling widely. *Your memory's not too bad after all.*

She has made rice paper rolls. You can see basil leaves overlapping beneath the translucent skin of the rice paper. In another container, she has fanned out slices of grilled banana, like a blossoming flower, on a pillow of red rice in coconut milk. And there's a small container of sauce.

Sweet chilli and lime, she says. *But not too hot.*

Is this all for me?

Yes. Eat up. Before I get in trouble.

You watch as Margie walks to the door. A word is forming in your mouth but it's too late for her to hear it.

Thanks, you say.

The rice paper roll is cool and sticky between your fingers, not long out of the fridge. Who is this woman, Nurse Margie? Is there something she wants from you? Your guts feel strange but you feel obliged to eat, just for the trouble she has gone to.

The rice paper roll snaps and squeaks in your mouth. Soft and chewy. You taste the basil and mango. Sweet and tart, it clears your mouth. As you eat, your appetite grows. You taste the fried banana. Buttery and warm. You spoon it into your mouth with the rice and coconut milk, wishing you didn't always doubt people's kindness.

Soon, Margie returns to the room. You look closely at the ID tag pinned to her pocket. Nurse Margie Shapiro.

Margie Shapiro, you say, *the food was really good.*

She looks happy as she collects the containers into her green shopping bag.

You must have been hungry. You've eaten everything.

You are wide awake now, energised by the food and by remembering your friend T.

You could open up a restaurant, you say.

But I'd have to deal with customers. I'd be bloody awful at that.

You think Margie looks better today. She's got her colour back, as your grandmother would say. You think for a moment of your grandmother and hope for her sake it is not true that you have held up a service station.

Do you think I could have a bath, Margie?

How much are you prepared to pay?

She says it with such a straight face, you do not know she is joking until she winks. *It's on my list*, she says. *Let's do it now before someone buzzes me.*

Margie disconnects the cannula and you swing your legs over the side of the bed. You are unsteady as you try to stand. She offers you her arm to balance on, but you want to do this yourself. She offers it again.

I can manage, you snap, and seeing her hurt face, you wish you hadn't.

Slowly, you step towards the door. You are suddenly aware that you are wearing a nappy.

How embarrassing, you say, as you try to pull the gown around you. *Can you see my bum?*

All good, Margie laughs. *I've got you covered.*

Just outside your door, a guard is leaning back into a chair, talking into his mobile, his feet stretched out in front of him. Margie scowls at him and he slides his feet in so you can pass.

I'm bathing her, says Margie. *You can follow us down to the bathroom but obviously you can't come in.*

The guard nods, grunting as he hauls himself out of his chair.

I think they wheeled that one out of retirement, whispers Margie.

You laugh, but it hurts. Walking is a challenge, requiring all of your concentration. As you shuffle along the corridor, your shoulder throbs. The squeak of the guard's shoes follows closely behind. You hold on to your ribs to keep your arm in a position that is less painful.

On the left, you notice a kitchenette. Further along, four rooms with patients, then a lift, a series of closed doors and an exit. The whole corridor smells like gravy.

They've put you in the geriatric wing, says Margie.

Well, thanks.

Best views in the house, she says.

In the bathroom, there are two toilets, two shower cubicles, and one cubicle with a bath. A pain rips across your abdomen, but when you go to the toilet, nothing passes. You dispose of the nappy in a large bin and try not to look at the contents.

All the painkillers you are on will make you constipated, says Margie, as if anticipating your question. She's inside the cubicle running you a bath. *I can give you something later to ease that.*

While you wait for Margie to fill the bath, you clean your teeth. You spit blue-tinged foam into the basin and rinse it away. You look at yourself in the mirror. You wonder if anyone else at fourteen and nine months has ever felt so old.

Margie emerges from the cubicle, her face flushed pink from the steam.

Do you believe in reincarnation? you ask.

Wow, you go straight to the big questions. I've never really thought about it, to be honest.

Do you think if you were reincarnated you would have the same face again and again?

God, I hope not, says Margie. She looks at her own face in the mirror, pulling up her chin with both hands. *Is that what you believe?*

I'm not really sure, you say.

Can anyone really be sure?

You shrug.

Doesn't it have something to do with how good you were in your past life, and your karma – if you come back as a dog or cockroach or something? Margie says, and then returns to check the bath.

How long did you say I've been in here? you ask.

You were admitted on Monday and now it's Wednesday.

Other than waking up to Margie, you don't know what happened to the rest of Tuesday.

You said I was given a general anaesthetic, but did they give me something else? Something to make me forget?

I was the nurse on duty when you came in, and you were given a general to explore your wound. It seems you're experiencing a touch of amnesia, which is common. And you may also be forgetting some things due to shock.

Is that what happens?

It can be a way of protecting yourself from memories that are overwhelming.

Margie takes off your sling. She helps you out of the hospital gown and wraps cling film around your bandages.

I'm sure it will all come back to you eventually. But maybe not all at once.

What if I don't want to remember?

Maybe sometimes it is better to forget. Margie pushes open the door of the cubicle. *I'm assuming you don't want my help in there?*

Nope, you say.

Okay. No splashing. I want you to keep that shoulder of yours perfectly dry.

Yes, Nurse Margie, you say and close the door behind you.

You hold on tight to the geriatric railing as the steam folds around you. You stink. Poor Margie Shapiro having to stand so close to you. You step into the water and ease yourself down. You rest your back against the curve of the bath. Closing your eyes, you don't even have to search for it.

The sun slipping from the sky.

A feeling of dread.

5.

HIMALAYAS, UNKNOWN YEAR

It is Mida, your sister, who comes to you in the morning and retrieves you from your bed. Her expectant face reminds you what day it is. Because in sleeping, you had tried to forget.

She tugs at your blankets.

Don't touch me! you say, pushing your back against the wall and tucking the blankets between your knees. *If my feet don't touch the ground, this day cannot begin.*

Don't be such a baby, Mida says, grabbing hold of your ankles and pulling you off the bed. You try to kick her. *Pathetic*, she says as she moves towards the door and drags in a heavy tub.

What are you doing?

I'm going to wash you. I'm going to make you presentable for the wedding.

I'm not a child.

But it seems you are. Mida stands over you with her hands on her hips.

You strip off your nightdress and throw it.

What is wrong with you? she says.

What do you think?

It is what has to happen, Bird. People will be arriving soon and I can't send you out there stark naked.

You step into the tub, crossing your arms over your chest.

Maybe I'll take holy orders, you say. *I'll become a nun. And never have to marry.*

Mida snorts as she ladles water and tips it over your head. *You know they starve the nuns up there.*

They do not.

Bird, everybody knows the monks only feed the ones they want to have sex with.

You try not to listen to Mida. She pretends to know about the world. But she agreed to marry Cho and she's hardly travelled further than his farm.

Through the window, you can see the field is now a messy patchwork after your father's drunk harvesting.

I don't want to go through with this.

I know, says Mida, softening. *But it won't be as bad as you think.*

How do you know that?

Because I've already married the worst of them.

Mida moves around you, her hair swaying in one lustrous piece. Her eyelashes so long they could catch insects. Everyone in the village says she is beautiful. But what good has it ever done her?

How long since you've had a bath? Mida asks, ladling the water which has turned the colour of tea.

I can't remember.

That's disgusting. She tips more water over your head and then drags a comb through your hair.

Ouch! you yell. *Can you be gentle with me for once?*

You tuck your knees into your chest so you can fit in the tub. Mida pours jasmine oil into her palms and rubs it through your hair. She hums as she twists tendrils around her fingers and massages your scalp. Her hands, her humming – for a moment, all the whirling matter inside of you settles. She scoops hair from the nape of your neck and twists and pulls, making your whole head tingle. She combs your hair straight, smoothing it down your back.

Stand up, she says as she steps back to examine you. *You know, you could be pretty if you tried.*

But I don't want to be pretty.

Mida laughs. *A piece of advice, little sister. When you're married, you will need to care if you're pretty or not. And you'll need to learn to shed a tear once in a while. But not too often if you want your husband to actually feel sorry for you.*

I don't want anyone to feel sorry for me, least of all my husband.

I promise you. You will.

You hear the sounds of relatives arriving and dress slowly as Mida hurries you along. When you are done, she gifts you her wedding jacket. You know you are supposed to be grateful, but you do not want any of it.

She takes your hand and leads you into the courtyard as if you are a small child again. You do feel small, sitting on the high stool your mother has positioned so that all the female relatives can eat cake and gawk at you. Your mother serves tea while Mida braids your hair, weaving in the gifts of ribbons and silver amulets.

As they pass through the courtyard, your father and his friends stop to ogle you, because now you are the official spectacle.

And that is when he says it:

Ten thousand strands of trouble, and the men laugh, jostling each other as they walk away.

At a table in the corner of the courtyard, your father sets up his round leather pad and shells for another game of sho. You would have thought he'd had enough, now there is nothing left to gamble. The men sit down, and some of the women deliver them dumplings and beer, but they are not invited to play. Since you were a child, you have watched your father from the sideline of such tables, and every time he held the dice cup above his head you prayed that the game would go in his favour.

But it hardly ever did.

And there is the sun slipping from the sky, and the wedding guests closing in. Your father and uncles sing a song about your hair and then the orations begin. An aunt you have never met presents you with a brick of tea to which your mother instructs you to say: *I am so happy with this gift.* You repeat your mother's words, and add, *Though I'd rather you gave me a beer.* The guests laugh because they think you are joking.

You sit through the performances of more drunk relatives. Their singing is loud. When you hold your hands up to your ears, people think you are making another joke, and they laugh again. Watching them gorge on food, you would like to cover your eyes as well.

Smile, your mother says to you. *At least look like you're enjoying it.*

In the courtyard, torches burn and a goat turns slowly on the spit. Faces grow blotchy with barley wine and shouts rise from the corner. There are too many people gathered around the sho table to see your father now, but you recognise his voice, rising desperately above the others.

Your mother ushers you to a low padded seat and bangs a gong. On cue, all the village boys and single men line up, each carrying an offering meant to woo you. But it is all for nothing because you will have no say in it. You can already see some of their parents placing bids with your mother.

One by one, the boys and widowed men push their gifts into your lap. When a village boy presents you with a chicken, Mida hits him across the head.

Do you really think you can win over my sister with a chicken?

The boy walks away, and you search the long, jumbling line. There is no sign of Teshi, not as himself or in any disguise.

The standards are very low, sister, says Mida. *I need a drink.*

Can you get one for me? you call after her.

With Mida gone, you ignore the boys and search the crowd again for Teshi. You allow yourself to imagine he has forgiven you, that he has infiltrated the party and when the time is right, he will tap you on the shoulder and you will escape together as planned.

You take the gifts and pile them on a table behind you. Some are wrapped and tied with string, but you don't bother opening them.

When Mida finally returns, her hands are empty and her face is ashen.

Where are the beers? you ask.

She looks stunned.

What's wrong with you? you say. *I'm the one being sold off.*

Our father has lost you in a bet.

Lost me? How can he lose me?

He's done it right there at the table. But it's even worse than that.

How can it be worse than that?

Because he's lost you to Cho.

Your Cho?

Mida nods. *He's lost everything. He's lost the house, and he's lost you.*

Whatever happens now, you know your life will not be the same. Your body has decided. Your limbs are already lurching from the seat.

Come with me, you say to Mida.

I can't, she says. *I'm pregnant. But I'll cover for you as long as I can.*

You hardly breathe as you move through the crowd of reddened faces, doing your best not to attract the attention of your mother or your father, or to turn back in your desire to save Mida.

As soon as you are outside, you run. Now there is no field to fold around you and offer you protection. There is only the long grey road, lit up by the full moon.

6.

DARWIN, PRESENT DAY

You sit up too quickly, splashing water over the side of the bath.

Are you alright in there? yells Margie.

All good, you say. *Just having an existential crisis.*

Must be catching, says Margie. *I had one earlier myself.*

You push your hand into the centre of your chest to try to calm yourself.

Call out if you need me, says Margie.

Ta.

There is a small square of soap in a crinkly packet and you tear it open with your teeth. You wrap it in a washcloth, rub your legs and your feet. The water clouds up quickly, like milky tea. *How long since you've had a bath?* The voice floats inside your head.

What if you do let yourself believe that you have lived another life, or other lives, and as you piece your life together, this is what you are remembering now?

You rest your head against the wall. Pipes wheeze from behind it. You sway your knees from side to side, the fine hairs on your legs collecting tiny bubbles.

You take three deep breaths, and then take three more, but you still feel panicked. Because what if you discover that this life you are in just repeats and repeats?

You step out of the bath and wrap yourself in a towel. When you open the door, Margie is there, waiting. She offers to wash your hair over the sink. In the mirror you can see there is still blood crusted to the ends of it, so you let her.

When Margie is done, you wipe the fogged mirror with the edge of your towel. Your eyes look clearer. Margie gently tugs at your knots with a brush.

I've bleached the life out of it, haven't I? you say.

Isn't that the fashion? says Margie.

Your mother's face comes to mind. Mia. Even with your bleached blonde hair, you don't look much like her at all.

Have I had any calls? Any visitors? you ask.

No, you haven't. We've been trying to get hold of your mum but she's not picking up.

You remember Mia's note, on the kitchen table.

She's at a yoga retreat.

Really? Do you know which one?

She didn't say.

What about your dad? Do you have a number for him?

No. I've never met him.

Margie takes a moment before she asks, *Do you look like your mum?*

No. She's blonde. A natural blonde. Anglo. Pale. She says I've got my dad's skin.

Do you know what his heritage is?

She says he might be Indian. Like, from India.

Might be?

Well, Mia – that's my mum's name but I never call her Mum – she said it was just a fling. She said it could have been an Indian man she met in Puna or a South American man she met in Nepal. She was backpacking at the time.

You could get a DNA test, send away for one of those kits. That's if you don't mind a company owning all your data. Not great if you want to pursue a life of crime.

I don't want a life of crime.

I'm happy to hear it.

Would you do it?

A DNA test? I've already done it. I spat into a little tube and sent it away. A few weeks later I found out I've got DNA from every continent except Antarctica. Margie laughs, and the shadows disappear from beneath her eyes.

Looking at Margie's face in the mirror, you imagine how you would draw her. Her high forehead, her cheekbones, her wide smile.

You look back at your reflection.

Do you think I'm pretty? The words escape your mouth and you're immediately embarrassed you've said them. *I'm sorry. Please don't answer that.*

Margie rests her hand on your good shoulder and looks at you in the mirror.

You look to me like a girl who should start taking better care of herself.

You look back at Margie's reflection and remember the state she was in yesterday.

You and me both, Margie Shapiro, you say.

Margie walks you back to your room in silence, and the guard with the squeaky shoes follows behind.

In the room, Margie helps you up onto the bed then moves towards the curtains.

Open or closed? she asks.

Open.

Sunlight fills the room. You stretch out your clean body and Margie covers your legs with a sheet.

Do you mind bringing me a clock? you ask. *I'd like to keep track of the time.*

Margie scans the walls. *There really should be one in here*, she says. *I'll sort it out before I finish my shift.*

Margie walks towards the door and you think she is about to leave but instead she collects the green shopping bag she left there earlier and brings it back to the bed.

Is there more food in there? you ask.

Her hand rattles past the empty containers and she pulls out something wrapped in a plastic bag.

I found this in your satchel, she says. *I thought it might help you remember.*

Margie pulls away the plastic bag and hands you a sketchbook. It is your sketchbook. You recognise it.

You raise your knees and prop the sketchbook against your thighs as you turn the pages. Every page is filled with pencil and ink drawings of five girls. In most drawings, they are standing shoulder to shoulder, under a full moon.

I can actually draw, you say.

Yes, you really can. I hope you don't mind but I had a look through it earlier. Margie leans over you. *You do seem to like to draw these girls a lot. Though I did find one drawing of a boy.*

Margie flicks through the book and finds the drawing.

Oh, that's my friend T, you say.

Does he go to your school?

No, we go to different schools.

You turn the page to another drawing of the five girls.

Are the girls your friends too? asks Margie.

You look at the page. They must mean something to you, you think, to have drawn them over and over. But a fog settles in your mind.

I don't know who they are, you say. You close the sketchbook and lean back into the pillows. *I'm sorry, Margie, I think I need to sleep now.*

I'll leave you be, she says.

Alone in the room, you close your eyes and wait for the girls to come to life, to step out of the fog or the infinite place where memories live, and reveal who they are and where they are from. But your drawings keep floating behind your eyes and remain just that. Pencil and ink on a page. Silent.

You remember Margie's words. *Just rest and wait.*

The panic you felt in the bath has passed.

You fix on one drawing in your mind. Silver and blue. Five girls standing shoulder to shoulder under the full moon. You can see them slowly turning their heads.

Speak to me, you say.

But they do not speak.

Not yet.

7.

DARWIN, FRIDAY LAST

Mrs Whitehead, your art teacher, is pushing your sketchbook across her desk. She is saying, *Bird, I want you to try to shift yourself out of the familiar and move a little further into the unknown.*

It is not the first time she has said this. But you are still not certain what she means.

As well as teaching art, Mrs Whitehead doubles as the school counsellor. You presumed you had been called to her office because you had fallen asleep in class again – a consequence of you sneaking out at night and painting murals in the street. But she doesn't mention it.

They're all wonderful drawings, she says. *But it wasn't what I asked. The assessment task was to draw or paint a series of portraits of yourself.*

But you have never drawn yourself. Until you met T, you had only ever drawn the five girls.

You want to say something clever to Mrs Whitehead. To challenge her idea of what a self-portrait is. You remember a visit to the Art Gallery of NSW with your grandmother in Sydney.

You had both stood transfixed in front of a work by the artist Del Kathryn Barton. She had painted a self-portrait which included her son and her daughter sitting between her legs, each body connected to the other. Your grandmother explained it: *Having a child completely changes who you think you are.*

But it's a Friday afternoon and you want to get out of Mrs Whitehead's small, grim office as quickly as you can. She looks exasperated with you already, running her hands through her hair, massaging her sunburnt forehead.

Bird, do you have anything to say?

You shake your head and Mrs Whitehead sighs.

I want you to start playing by the rules, she says.

The rules?

Isn't that what we talked about last time?

You don't remember what you talked about last time. The way these visits usually went was that Mrs Whitehead talked in inspirational quotes and you tried not to feel doomed.

You've been at this school for a year now. You are no longer the new girl. I think it's time you started making an effort with your peers.

You roll your eyes at the mention of your peers.

The truth is, Mrs Whitehead continues, *I think you are drawing these girls over and over because you have no real friends at school.*

When Mrs Whitehead calls you to her office, you turn up as part of the bargain where she gives you access to the art room at recess and lunch. Being called to her office doesn't always mean you are in trouble. Sometimes she tries to teach you mindfulness techniques or gently questions you about your home life with Mia. It seems you are her 'special case'. You know these sessions are over when she says, *Well, Bird, we can't always cross the chasm in one leap.*

You wish she would say it now.

Instead, she says, *If I can see you making an effort, then we'll discuss you getting back into the art room in a few weeks.*

Your hands begin to tingle. Your head and neck prickle with heat. The art room is your sanctuary. And you always leave it spotlessly clean. Why is Mrs Whitehead taking away what she gave so freely?

But I thought you said that art can teach us something about ourselves?

Yes, says Mrs Whitehead. *I believe it can. I believe your artwork is telling you to go and make some real friends.*

You have always drawn the five girls. The first memory you have is running screaming after Mia's car and then your grandmother taking you into her arms and sitting you at the kitchen table. She makes you an orange cordial and lays out your coloured pencils and a big, clean sketchbook. *Draw me one of your beautiful pictures, darling,* she says. Then you draw each girl, standing shoulder to shoulder, while your grandmother sits beside you and feeds you biscuits. When you finish, she asks you to tell her each girl's name.

That's Cleo, Dev, Kai, Reya and Bambi. Bambi's my favourite, you say.

Drawing every day since, you have learnt that art can fill a void. But you have also learnt that art cannot stop the void from opening. When your grandmother died last year and you were sent to Darwin to live with Mia, the void had never felt so vast. You found yourself in an uncomfortable, lonely place, the dimensions widening between how you wanted your life to be and how it actually was.

Mia was newly single when you arrived. Her inheritance from your grandmother allowed her to buy a two-bedroom bungalow that you felt grateful for. It was freshly painted in black and white, and had a tropical garden that attracted many birds. Its kitchen, flooded with light, reminded you of your grandmother's and was the perfect place to draw. For six weeks or so, you and Mia settled into this new nest, and even though you missed your grandmother, you felt her presence in the gift of a house. Mia seemed happy to have you with her and she gave you her attention, not so much like a mother, but more in the way of a big sister. And that had to be enough.

Before she died, and knowing that you would be sent to live with Mia, your grandmother enrolled you in a private school in Darwin because the school had a new art room and a good reputation. She set up a trust fund that paid your school fees directly, and paid Mia an allowance. Soon Mia was encouraging you to skip classes at your new school and then whole days to go shopping with her. She decided she wanted to furnish the bungalow in a 'bohemian luxe' style, which meant trawling expensive homeware shops and looking for things that were white or woven or silver. Afterwards, you would get your nails done. But it was not how you wanted to spend your days. You would have preferred to be in art class at school.

But then Mia met Jerome and suddenly there was this strange, brooding presence in the house. And you felt like you were the flatmate they were trying to ignore. Though if you were Mia's flatmate, you would have banged on her bedroom wall and complained. Because all Mia and Jerome seemed to do was have loud sex and cook lavish meals and never clean up after themselves.

You started escaping through your bedroom window at night. You walked the streets looking for deserted places, with an idea to paint the five girls larger than you had ever painted them before. You needed clean walls in places that felt safe enough, or at least allowed you an escape if anyone hassled you. You would draw the girls in your sketchbook first, and then transfer them to the walls using spray paint that you bought from an office supplies shop. The cans were portable and allowed you to paint the girls faster and larger.

The first time you painted the five girls on a wall in an industrial area of the city, you felt their force magnified. Cleo, Dev, Kai, Reya and Bambi – protecting you from all that wished to harm you.

Mrs Whitehead does not end the session like she usually does. She says, *Bird, think about what I've said and come and see me again on Monday.*

You slip out the door before she can squeeze your arm or give you a condescending pat. The problem with Mrs Whitehead is that she thinks she knows your story. It is a story where you are the victim of loss and a wayward mother.

But you want your story to be so much more than that.

After school, you walk a route you have not walked before. The humidity in the afternoon is suffocating. Locals call this time the 'build-up', pre-monsoon where clouds tower over the city but do not break. You call Mia three times but she does not answer. You text her but she does not reply. You need to know if she is at home with Jerome tonight because this afternoon you cannot bear the thought of seeing him. You walk until you find an underpass you think would be good to paint on, then your hunger gets the better of you so you walk home.

Standing out the front of your house, you see that Mia's car is parked in the driveway and the kitchen light is on. Jerome works as a security guard and you hope the absence of his car means that he's been rostered on the weekend shift. Tonight you and Mia can order takeaway and Mia can choose a soppy movie to watch, and you can move freely through the house without having to avoid Jerome.

Once, he opened the door on you as you were getting out of the shower and then he stood there and smiled while you screamed. And whenever Mia wasn't looking, his eyes would float over your breasts. You started wearing jumpers and hoodies until the build-up weather made the layers unbearable.

Last weekend, you were hanging clothes on the line when you caught him at it again. He was cooking a barbecue on the back deck, turning sausages, and staring blatantly at your chest.

Will you stop! you yelled.

Mia, fetching Jerome a beer, came outside. *What?*

He's staring at my breasts again!

Mia laughed. *Breasts! Birdy, there's nothing there to stare at.*

Living with Mia, you often think of the self-portrait you saw with your grandmother. You remember clearly what your grandmother said that day but also what she did not say: that having a child can change a person, but it had not changed Mia.

You find your house key in your bag and let yourself inside. The house is quiet. The kitchen is a mess. You call out for Mia, but there is no answer. You bang your fist on her bedroom door and bang again because the last thing you want is to catch them having sex. You open the door a crack. The bed is unmade, clothes are strewn across the floor. You cover your mouth and nose because you can smell Jerome.

In the kitchen, you stack the dirty dishes and the pots. It looks like they cooked a banquet and then vanished. The fact your grandmother's money bought the house makes you think of the house as hers, not Mia's, so it offends you when Mia makes a mess of it. Wiping down the kitchen table, you see a note from Mia propped against the fruit bowl. The fruit bowl is the place where she likes to leave notes for you, her childish handwriting scrawled across envelopes.

Birdy! Me and Jerome have gone camping. Back on Sunday. Here's some money for takeaway. Have fun with T. xo

She's left you three hundred dollars.

You do not know why she could not have told you earlier. Why she could not have called or texted you, like any other mother would.

You wash the dishes and the greasy pots and put away the food that has been left on the bench without lids. You turn on the oven and take two fish fingers out of the freezer and put them on a tray. You peel a potato, cut it into small pieces and boil it on the stove. This is the meal your grandmother would have made you when she sensed you were in a bad mood. She called it Flying Fish, and she would cover it in lemon and salt and parsley – parsley because she insisted you eat one green thing with every meal.

You mash the potato with butter and spoon it onto a blue plate like a cloud, with the fish fingers sticking out of it. You douse it in lemon and salt. You can't find any parsley so you cut up a cucumber from the fridge and arrange it in a way that would please your grandmother. You sit down at the table and wish she was sitting beside you and that you could lean into her soft body and tell her about your day.

You scoop potato onto your fork. When you bring it to your mouth your bottom lip begins to tremble. But no tears come. Because they never come. Even though you feel them forming, they quickly turn to ice and slide down the back of your throat and then it hurts to swallow.

You hold your throat and eat what you can. Then you take Mia's note and a red pen, and you begin to draw your fist, and then your fist flipping your middle finger.

When it's dark outside, you grab your satchel and a can of spray paint from your room, and you walk back to school. Before you cross the street and enter the school grounds, you pull on your hoodie and a surgical mask and then you run to the art room. You take the can of black paint from your satchel and recreate what you drew earlier on the envelope, only bigger. Black paint on the red art room door. Your flipped finger for Mia, for Mrs Whitehead, for everyone who has let you down and should have known better.

Friday night. You walk. The air feels slick, like grease. You call T. He tells you he's with the boys near the footbridge at the estuary. You agree to meet him there.

Crossing the footbridge, you can hear music rattling from a portable stereo, and further up, you can see the boys, their bodies lit by flames. They're dousing strips of fabric with kerosene, lighting them and throwing them out into the middle of the creek.

You walk slowly across the wet sand. You want to see T, but you are not sure if you want the company of the boys. T has spotted you already. He's walking towards you. He's waving. And soon he's hugging you. You hold on to him. His body feels like water, which is how it feels when he's stoned.

T takes your hand and leads you to the small fire the boys have made out of driftwood, not for warmth but to keep the mosquitos and sandflies away. T feeds the fire with eucalyptus leaves so it smokes up around you. All the boys are now sitting around the fire. They are grinning stupidly at you. You stretch your legs out onto the cool sand and T stretches his legs beside you. Jokes roll around and you laugh along, not because the jokes are very funny but for the relief of laughing together. One of the boys passes you a joint and you smoke it until something inside of you ungrips.

Two of the boys stand up and peel off their t-shirts, dousing them, setting fire to them and throwing them into the water. You watch the flames float downstream. Then all the boys, T included, are standing up, pulling off their shirts and setting fire to them. Someone turns the music up and the boys begin to dance and hug. They beat their bare chests to amuse each other. They wrestle on the sand. All the boys at the edge of the creek, protecting each other from loneliness, preparing each other for the battles ahead.

You wonder if you will ever have friends like these.

A police siren sounds in the park on the other side of the footbridge. Someone kicks sand on the fire and the party breaks up before it's broken up. You walk with T, your arm resting against his spine, his hand holding tight to your hip.

Can I stay at yours tonight? you ask.

I was hoping you would, he says.

You kiss, and then walking back to his place you tell him about your day, and you realise he is the only person in your life who listens to you, and in listening, always says what you need him to say.

8.

DARWIN, SATURDAY LAST

Early in the morning, you wake to T's mother Lyn banging loudly on his caravan wall.

Doesn't she know it's the weekend? you moan.

But T is already out of bed, opening the door.

Is she in there? you hear Lyn say and your stomach clenches at the way she says 'she'.

Mum, it's seven o'clock, T says, shutting the door behind him. But you can still hear everything they say.

I've told you I don't want her sleeping over. She's only fourteen. She's –

She's fourteen and nine months, interrupts T.

You tune out of whatever it is they say next, dress quickly, fling your satchel over your shoulder. Your shoes are under the front step. You do not want the indignity of crawling around Lyn's feet so you pop out cheerily, say, *Morning!* and keep walking barefoot across the grass and through the bamboo garden.

You do not feel like going home and being alone. So you walk to the bus stop and catch the bus to the shopping centre. You find a cafe that is open and chat to the waiter about the weather while you wait for a takeaway egg and bacon roll.

You wander through the shopping centre searching for the right bench to sit on. A bench with no one on it. No chewing gum, no strange stains, no 'bohemian luxe' homewares in sight. You find a bench and sit and eat your breakfast, watching the shopkeepers open up for the day. In sight is the nail bar where Mia sometimes brings you for 'Girls' Day', as she calls it. You can see three women inside. But the closed sign is still across the glass door. The women are rolling out small mats, lighting incense and bowing to a statue of Buddha that sits propped between two orchids in the corner.

One of the women, who calls herself Cherry, flips the sign over. You finish eating your roll and push open the door. There's a jangle of bells as you enter.

Lucky first customer, says Cherry. *Sit there.*

You climb into the large leather chair.

Massage? asks Cherry.

Yes, please.

Cherry turns on the massage chair and begins to fill the foot spa with warm water.

Shellac or normal?

Normal, you say, your body shaking in the seat.

Shellac better. Lasts longer.

Okay.

Cherry hands you a swatch of colours and begins scrubbing your soles. She doesn't comment on how dirty they are, or the fact you have walked into her shop with bare feet.

You choose the metallic green.

Not too hot? she asks, swishing water over your legs.

It's perfect.

Cherry looks at you over the top of her glasses.

Are you Bird?

Yes, that's me.

I remember you. And your mother. Very pretty mother. Like a model. Where is she?

She's away this weekend with her boyfriend.

Ahh, Cherry nods. *You have boyfriend?*

Kind of. His mother doesn't like me.

Huh! You're probably too good for him.

No. She thinks I'm not good enough.

Don't you worry about her, says Cherry. *Mothers are crazy for their sons.* She starts massaging your feet.

Around the nail bar you can see more statues of Buddha, with fat bellies and beads around their necks, fresh flowers laid in front of them.

Are you Buddhist? you ask.

Clever girl, Cherry says sarcastically.

Do you believe in reincarnation?

Yes.

Who do you think you were in your past life?

A cat, says Cherry, clipping your nails. *Very fussy. Not liking humans very much.* She laughs.

Do you think you can be born as the same person or creature again and again, with everything always the same, repeating and repeating?

No, says Cherry, now filing your nails. *You are not fixed. You are not cement. More like a river. Just flowing and flowing.*

Cherry turns to the other women and says something in Vietnamese. They respond and Cherry seems to agree with whatever they have said to her.

There was a little boy in my village, Cherry says. *He kept going back to a house that was not his house, but he knew where everything was. And the old woman who lived there was convinced he was the son she lost – sixty years before. You hear stories like that. And some people just know things. Like I know I was a cat.*

After Cherry finishes painting your nails, she gives you a pair of thongs and an iced tea.

Lucky first customer, she says. You pay her in cash, put on the thongs, and for a short time you feel better for her care.

But wandering through the air-conditioned shopping centre, now filling with groups of teenagers, and passing by so many posters of frolicking girls with frozen smiles, you can't help but feel bad about your life.

You want to distract yourself from this feeling so when you see a make-up shop, you go inside and watch a bride-to-be getting her make-up done. She is sucking in her cheeks and the make-up artist is circling a brush along her cheekbones and turning them hot pink.

You still have most of the money Mia left you, and you decide you want to paint your face, like the woman is being painted in front of you. You search the display for an eyeshadow, something to match your nails. You sample some of the colours, making stripes on the back of your hand, until you find the right shade of glittering green. You buy the eyeshadow and a hot pink blush, and then you walk home slowly as the paper-thin thongs Cherry gave you disintegrate on the hot concrete.

The house smells like fish fingers because you left last night without washing the pan or your plate. You flick on the radio so you don't feel so alone, and then you open all the curtains and the windows and imagine yourself as a girl in a poster, a girl loving her life. You peel off your t-shirt and fling it across the room. No Mia. And even better, no Jerome.

You shower and then you raid Mia's make-up drawer. You apply some of her foundation to your forehead, but it's too light for your skin. You wipe your face clean with a face washer, apply moisturiser and suck in your cheeks. You find a round brush like the one the make-up artist was using and cover your cheekbones with your new hot pink blush. You paint your eyelids glittering green, with a little cat-eye in the corner in honour of Cherry. You're not sure how to use Mia's eyelash curler so you abandon it and swipe mascara over your lashes until they clump together. Then you lean in close to the mirror.

You could be pretty if you tried.

You take Mia's round mirror out of the bathroom, the one she uses to pluck her eyebrows, the one that swivels on a stand. You prop it on the kitchen table. Then you scatter your art supplies from one end of the table to the other and examine your face in the mirror again. You open your sketchbook and begin the first drawing of yourself you have ever done.

Eyes, lashes, cheeks, lips, nose. Maybe this is how you change your life – by looking at yourself and imagining you are worth drawing a self-portrait of.

You draw all day, adding ink and watercolour to your self-portrait, stopping to make yourself snacks. When it grows dark, you lock all the doors and windows except your bedroom window, because you can't sleep with it closed. You call T but he doesn't answer, so you put yourself to bed.

You are in a deep sleep when you are woken by someone rattling at the front door. You listen. Footsteps moving around the side of the house and through the garden, trampling the ferns. You try to think of something in your room to defend yourself with. A pair of scissors. A heavy art book. You grab a spray can from under your bed because it's close and then you position yourself next to your window. You can spray the intruder in the face and maybe even whack them with the can if they try to come inside. Adrenaline courses through your body and you are about to take aim when you hear –

Birdy! Birdy! It's Mia's voice. She is giggling. *I forgot my key.*

You open the front door to let Mia in. She is standing there with Jerome. You do not say a word to them. You head straight back to bed and slam your door. You try to fall asleep again but it's not long before they are having sex so loudly you wonder if they mean for you to hear them. You feel wired now. It's 2 am. It is impossible to sleep. You dress in black pants and a black singlet. You grab your satchel, fill it with spray paints, and as you climb out the window you realise you could just as easily have walked out the front door. Because Mia would not notice or care.

You walk back towards the underpass you found yesterday afternoon. Your satchel is heavy with paints and digging into your shoulder so you strap it onto your back instead. When you arrive, you discover the light is smashed. But the moon is full and illuminates the wall well enough.

You did not bring your sketchbook. You left it on the kitchen table. But your portrait is so fresh in your mind you recreate it easily, all the lines and shapes you discovered in your face.

You paint until the sun comes up and then you cross the road to get a wider view.

You have painted yourself pink and green and blue. Eyes closed. Arms wrapped around your body.

Are you floating or falling? You cannot tell.

Whatever it is, you have a feeling that your portrait is not yet complete.

9.

DARWIN, SUNDAY LAST

You let yourself in the front door. Walking home from the underpass, you picked up a small lamp from hard rubbish to add to your collection. One of your discoveries, walking the streets at all hours, is that people leave furniture they don't want on the footpath in front of their houses. You are not sure if lamps are out of fashion here or if they're too difficult to transport when people move interstate. But now you have six lined up on top of your desk.

In your bedroom, you peel off your shirt and pants. They are damp with sweat and smell of paint. It's still early in the morning. Jerome and Mia won't be up for hours. You collect your sketchbook from the kitchen table, and the pens and paints you left there. You hope neither of them saw your self-portrait. Even though you have painted it on the wall of the underpass for any stranger to see, you do not want their eyes on it.

In the bathroom, you push the dirty clothes basket against the door and take a shower. You scrub the paint stains from your hands and arms, wash your hair and wrap yourself in a gown. In the kitchen, you make yourself a bowl of cereal with banana to take back to your room.

You browse your bookshelves. When you moved from Sydney to Darwin, you brought your clothes, your art supplies, and the small library of books your grandmother had gifted you. Mostly they are books on women artists and their work. You pull down a book about the Italian artist Alice Pasquini.

You sit on your bed and take in Alice's murals, which she has painted in public places around the world. There are portraits, mainly of girls, so public, so large, but revealing something intimate and real to you. None of the girls are frolicking or wearing frozen smiles. They are contemplative. They are in their own worlds.

You open your sketchbook and tear out your self-portrait. You place it next to one of Alice Pasquini's. You wonder why hers is so much better than yours.

You turn the pages of the book and take her portraits in until you realise the difference. Each one tells her own story. So how can you ever complete a self-portrait when you know so little of yours?

Mia wakes you by knocking on your door. She has brought you a toasted cheese sandwich. She sits on the end of your bed and watches you eat.

Are you good, my little Birdy? she says.

Yeah, I'm good.

Thanks for cleaning up.

That's okay. Did you have fun camping?

Jerome took me to a waterfall. Amazing. But there were so many mosquitos, so we packed up and came home early.

Is he still here?

He's going to cook us dinner.

I wish you'd told me before you went away.

Oh Birdy, it was a spur-of-the-moment thing. I left you a note, didn't I?

You could have told me the day before, or you could have called.

Did you have a good time without me?

I went to the shopping centre and I saw Cherry. I got my nails done. You wiggle your fingers in front of Mia.

Cute.

Cherry says you look like a model.

I wish! Mia says and starts scratching her legs. You can tell she is lost in this fantasy of herself as a model.

What are you thinking? you ask.

That I need to shave my legs! she says, and then she is gone.

You call T again but he does not answer. You text him: U OK? Then you get out of bed and open the blinds. There is a dead dragonfly caught in the windowsill. You hope you didn't kill it when you crawled through the window.

You rest it in your palm, stroke its orange and black abdomen, count its legs. One leg is missing. Maybe that was the death of it, you think. Maybe that threw it off balance. You draw the dragonfly with all its legs, and then you draw it in flight. You search online and read about its life cycle, how it transforms from egg to larva to adult, how it 'weathers all storms'. You read that its common name is wandering glider and that it crosses vast oceans.

You sleep and draw and sleep again.

Mia knocks on your door.

Dinner's ready, she says. *Jerome has cooked fillet steak.*

You check your phone. It's almost 6 pm. There's a text from T: Mum's out 2nite. Cm ova?

In the lounge room, Mia hands you a tray with a small beanbag cushion beneath it. She bought these tray tables because Jerome likes a TV dinner. It's nothing your grandmother would have ever let you do, to eat in front of the television. But at least you do not have to suffer sitting at the table with Jerome.

Jerome wants to watch the 6 pm news. He and Mia take the couch, and you sit on a chair away from them. The steak is overdone so you make a performance of carving into it, of scraping your knife against the plate, but nobody notices. They're both staring at the television, shovelling food into their faces.

Turn it up, says Jerome, and you are embarrassed at how easily Mia takes his orders, the way she fumbles around the cushions searching for the remote control.

The local news headline begins with a story about the juvenile detention centre. *Girls riot*, the newsreader reports. *Last night, detainees turned on the taps in their cells and flooded the upper floor of the prison, causing an electrical fire . . .*

There is footage of girls and guards running, of firefighters pulling hoses. And then a lingering shot of five girls standing shoulder to shoulder, their silhouettes lit by fire and the full moon.

You place your tray on the floor.

The newsreader says that the girls will be relocated to an older part of the prison while the clean-up is happening. The story ends with a close-up of a firefighter holding a red canister, white clouds foaming out, disappearing the girls.

The newsreader moves on to the next story but you do not hear it. You feel dizzy. You sit back in the chair and grip the armrests.

When the waves of dizziness stop, you stand up.

I'm going to T's, you say.

Finish your dinner, Jerome says.

I can't eat it. It's overdone.

You walk to T's. He's in his caravan, composing music on his computer, drinking a beer.

Want one? he says.

No thanks. I've given up. Did you see the news?

What news?

The news about the prison. There's been a riot.

What's new about that? He's absorbed by something on his computer.

I saw the girls.

What girls?

The five girls I always draw. I saw them on the news.

What?

You search your phone for the news report to show him. You stick the phone in front of his face. *It's them*, you say. *It's my girls. Cleo, Dev, Kai, Reya and Bambi.*

T watches the footage but seems disinterested, unmoved.

Watch it again, you say.

He watches it again, reluctantly.

I suppose they look kind of similar, he says.

What do you mean 'similar'? They're the same.

Whatevs.

There's something different about T tonight. Something so cool. It could be that Lyn has finally got under his skin and this is the beginning of the end and that's why he's asked you over.

I'm going for a walk, you say. *Do you want to come with me?*

I'm just going to hang here and make some tunes.

Why did you invite me over then?

I don't know.

You feel a tear in your connection, his disinterest, his turning away, and you are furious.

You wear too much deodorant.

What? Teshi finally looks up from his computer.

But there is nothing more you want to say.

You return to the last mural you painted of the girls. The one you only finished last week. T had stood guard at the end of the alleyway at the back of the supermarket in the city while you stood on the bins and painted the girls standing shoulder to shoulder and turning their heads.

There is no one to guard you now. You sit with your back to the wall, replaying the news footage on your phone. You pause on the moment the girls appear. You hold your phone up and compare the image to your mural in front of you. You know it is them; you know they are not just similar, they are the same.

You have so many questions about your life. Questions you think only the girls can answer. How is it that they came to you as a child, fully formed in your mind, their names, their quirky behaviours? What secrets of your life do they hold? And how can you find a way for them to tell you?

10.

DARWIN, MONDAY LAST

You wake with no intention of going to school. You open your laptop and search the juvenile detention centre's website for visiting hours and conditions. You read: 'Children under 18 must be accompanied by an adult'. When Mia gets up, you will ask her to take you there. She never minds you skipping school and you think she will be happy you have made other friends, even if they are all currently in juvie.

You dress in shorts and a t-shirt. You think about making breakfast for Mia, cutting up fruit, setting the table, making her a cup of tea. You flick the kettle on. You take a banana from the fruit bowl and, as you do, you notice another note from Mia, written, as always, on the back of an envelope.

Birdy,
I'm off to a yoga retreat. Back next Wednesday.
Some money to tide you over.
Jerome will look after you.
M. xo

You take the money from the envelope and shove it in your pocket. You don't even bother counting it.

Why won't Mia ever tell you when she is going away? She could have easily mentioned it when she was sitting on the end of your bed yesterday, scratching at her legs. Or before the TV dinner. Does she think you will run after her car screaming, like you did when she left you as a child?

You take rice puffs from the pantry and pour them into a bowl. You notice she's mopped the floor. You reef open the fridge door, which makes everything rattle. The fridge is stocked. You wonder if she plans to come back at all. You fill your bowl with milk and when some of it splashes on the floor, you don't bother wiping it up.

You eat the rice puffs and imagine you are a girl living a different life. A life where your mother does not leave you without notice and the person she has trusted to look after you does not try to look at you in the shower or stare at your breasts.

The bedroom door opens and you get up from the table quickly. You want to avoid Jerome. You are rinsing your bowl and stacking it in the dish rack when you feel him leaning over you, reaching for a coffee cup from the cupboard above your head.

Morning, Tweety Bird, he says.

Why can't you use one of the cups on the bench?

Because I like this one.

There is nothing special about the cup he is holding. Just looking at him gives you an instant pain in your gut. He is dressed in the vintage silk dressing gown you found in an op shop last year and gave to Mia for Christmas. It hardly covers his front, and you know he is wearing it to spite you. You think his skin against the silk will ruin it forever, the same way he is ruining your life, and ruining Mia.

What time did she leave?

She was on the road by 5.30 am, he says, putting the coffeepot on the stove.

Why didn't she tell me she was going away again?

She knew you'd get upset.

You don't have to stay here, you know. Actually, I'd prefer that you didn't.

I'm happy, he says. *I'm happy with the situation as it is.*

And then his eyes float over your body, and you are a bird who has flown through an open window, to be trapped by this horrible man. Your heart feels too big for your chest. You search for an escape.

Why aren't you dressed in your school uniform? he says.

It's mufti day.

On a Monday?

Why not?

You grab your satchel and head out the front door. He follows you outside and stands behind you on the step as you shove your feet into your runners. You don't bother doing up the laces.

See you when you get home from school, he says.

Won't you be at work?

I'm taking a bit of time off, having a little staycation.

Here?

Why not?

How fucking convenient, you say.

You do not know where to walk, or what route to take. Your heels feel heavy. Tears are forming behind your face. You wish you could cry. Once, you borrowed Mia's Clear Eyes and flooded your eyes until fake, fat tears rolled down your cheeks – just to know what it felt like.

You pull out the money you shoved into your pocket, count out three hundred and seventy dollars. You wonder how many nights' accommodation that will buy you in Darwin. Even if the youth hostel isn't booked out with backpackers and you share a bunk with a stranger, it might get you to the end of the week, but then what would you eat?

You wish you could call your grandmother and return to her. You wish she wasn't dead. You wish you had a father who knew you were alive and could care for you now in India, South America or wherever he actually came from.

You call T.

He answers. He is on the way to school. He says he will meet you at the bus stop. Although things feel strained between you, you still need to ask him this favour.

By the time you arrive at the bus stop, he is the only person there.

Did you miss the bus? you ask.

Yeah.

Is there another one?

Not direct to school.

You sit down next to him.

Mia's bailed again.

Where to this time?

A yoga retreat.

Did she leave you any money?

Some. Not enough. Can I stay at yours for a bit?

You feel T's body stiffen beside you and he starts scuffing his shoes on the concrete.

You continue: *Jerome has moved in and I can't be in the house with him alone.*

A deep sigh comes out of T. He rubs his face with his hands and messes his hair.

What?

After you left last night, I fell asleep and Lyn came in and found all the beer bottles.

She wouldn't have liked that.

I told her they were yours.

Gee, thanks.

I'm sorry, Bird. I just can't stand to be in the shit again.

Then maybe don't get drunk in your mother's backyard, you say.

Sun beats into the shelter and no buses pass. You feel the void opening up, where everything is silent and separate and there is too much you do not understand about yourself and your life. People, plants, creatures, houses all whirling inside you – where is your actual life, the life you want to live?

You know T has almost reached his limit, as everyone seems to reach their limit with you before they abandon you. Like Mia who left you as a child. Like your grandmother who went and died on you. Even Mrs Whitehead had her limit. You wonder what it is about you that means you can be so easily given up on.

You fold yourself over your knees and wrap your arms around your legs. You want to empty out your body. You want to empty out your head.

You pick up a stick and begin to draw lines and odd shapes on the concrete. Then an idea comes to you.

It is not a voice, it is a vision, and you are seeing it all from above, a whole pattern of how things have always been and what must happen next if you are to change it.

But it relies on you asking T for one more favour.

You stand up and check the bus timetable.

Do you still have your fake ID?

Yeah, it's in my bag, T says.

Can you come out to the detention centre with me?

Why?

Because there are five girls in there and I don't know how I know them but I do. And I think they can tell me something about my life and how to change it.

T shakes his head.

You owe me, you say.

T sighs. *Alright, what do I need to do?*

You catch the next bus to the detention centre. T sees someone he knows at the back of the bus and sits with him for a while. You look out the window and think of the girls. Cleo's snorting laugh. Dev, so tall, unsteady on her feet. Kai, nervous and shy. Reya, always picking at her face.

But it is Bambi who is the most vivid. Leaning into you with her long hair sweeping around her face, you can see her taking your hands to read your fortune. She traces the lines of your palm with her finger. You can hear her laughing at what she finds. But what does she find?

The bus trip takes an hour. The driver drops you at the end of a long driveway and then you have to walk across a car park towards the prison gates.

People are lining up outside a glass booth. You join the line. You can see they are being issued passes which they must show to two other guards before they are let through the gates.

When it's your turn, you stand on tippy-toes to talk to the guard.

I'm here to see my friend, you say.

Who's your friend?

Her name is Bambi. B-A-M-B-I.

You need to be accompanied by an adult.

I am, you say, pulling T in front of the window. *He's eighteen.* You notice T is wearing his school uniform, and the guard notices it too. *He's in Year 12*, you say.

ID, says the guard to T.

T presses his ID against the glass.

Pass it through that slot.

The guard holds T's ID up to the light and slides it back to him.

Nice try, says the guard. *Come back with an adult. They'll need to make an appointment online. You can't just turn up. Next.*

You both step away from the booth.

I'm sorry, says T.

It's not your fault.

You make your way across the car park and T falls behind. *Come back with an adult,* the guard said. But there is no adult you can ask.

T catches up with you.

Did you say Mia left you some money? T asks.

Yep.

And you need more?

Yep.

I could buy some pills from Harry, the guy I was talking to on the bus. We could sell them and then you'd have enough to get a room somewhere while Mia's away.

Sure, you say.

You hand T the cash from your pocket, and he runs back to the car park where Harry is loitering.

You discover there won't be another bus for two hours. You start walking. T catches up to you.

Want to try one?

I suppose we should, if we're going to sell them.

T hands you a pill. You swallow it without asking what it is.

You and T walk in silence, cars and road trains rattling by. A mini-mart appears like a mirage, and you browse up and down its aisles just to be in the air-conditioning. You buy two ice blocks and a five-dollar water pistol from the sales bin.

What's that for? asks T.

A spritz, you say, filling it with water from the tap outside the mini-mart and spraying him with it.

Ouch! That water is hot!

Everything is hot in this place.

I wish we had a car, you say.

And then, crouching under the mini-mart awning, eating your ice block, you recall the YouTube videos you watched together one weekend showing you how to hot-wire a car. T must have had the same thought.

We could try hot-wiring, says T.

This is one thing you have wished for today that you think you can make possible. You head away from the mini-mart towards the suburban streets. You walk until you find an old Honda parked under a tree.

It's unlocked, says T. *And there's a toolbox in the back.*

It's you who says: *I think it's meant to be.*

T has his L-plates, but he says he can feel his pill coming on, so you drive. You think you have more driving practice than him anyway because when Mia is stoned and Jerome is working, she will often get you to drive her to the shops. She says you are an excellent driver.

The air-conditioner in the car doesn't work. It blows hot, dusty air. A tree-shaped deodoriser swings from the rear-view mirror, but the car still smells of mould. T winds down all the windows and turns on the radio. You do a few laps of the streets and when you turn onto the highway your only plan is to drive as far as the car will take you. But soon, you are both thirsty and sweltering in the heat. You regret not buying water from the mini-mart. You see a service station ahead and a sign with a big blue cup so you decide to pull over for a slushie. T reminds you that you are driving a stolen car and warns you not to park in the service station.

There'll be cameras all over it, he says.

You park the car in the adjacent lot and walk across another expanse of concrete. Everything is shimmering now. You don't know if it's the heat or the drugs. The glass doors of the service station open and a blast of cool air hits the crown of your head. You locate the slushie machine and as you fill two tall cups, blue ice pouring out, you imagine it is all the tears you have never cried. You sip on it. You sip and sip and everything begins to vibrate inside of you.

You walk towards the attendant and put the two slushies on the counter. You smile at him, and he smiles back.

Anything else? he asks.

Just this. You reach into your pocket and remember you've given all your money to T.

I'm sorry, you say. Because as you reach inside your satchel, you know what you are going to do next.

You pull out the water pistol. It is so light it almost flies through your fingers. You laugh as you hold it out in front of you. But the attendant does not laugh. His hands are already raised above his head.

You grip the water pistol with both hands, like you have seen on TV.

You think holding up a service station will surely get you sent to juvenile prison and reunited with the girls.

You hold the gun in front of you and turn your head from side to side, so the cameras can capture you at every angle.

You think you will walk out of the service station with two blue slushies, and you will drive T home. You will wait in a public place, and if the police don't find you, you will hand yourself in.

But what you have not counted on is two police officers driving along the highway and, seeing the sign with the big blue cup, deciding they want a slushie too.

You hear the glass doors slide open behind you and then you see the attendant's hands come down slowly. You turn. Two male police officers are both holding guns that look like yours – only their guns are real.

There is no slow-motion memory of the bullet travelling towards you. There is nothing to recall because you are out of your body, floating above it all.

You see yourself, face down on the yellow-tiled floor, blood leaking from your shoulder, and you think you are dying again.

You turn your cheek to the tiles to see a carousel tipped over, sunglasses arcing out like a rainbow. You smell petrol and sweets.

Two sets of legs in blue trousers and black boots step towards you. One of them kicks your water pistol. It clatters across the tiles and hits the wall. You try to raise yourself up, but the pain from your shoulder pins you to the floor. An acrid taste floods your mouth.

You watch your blood crisscrossing into the lines of the grout, and you have the desire to reach out and scoop your blood back towards you – as if this might change things, or reverse time.

But you have no such power.

The two police officers are already above you, reefing you to your feet. Explosions of air and spit hit your skin and their mouths move fast around you.

One of them locks his arms around your waist and another tips you up and over so you are horizontal in the air. You try to bite, but one of them pulls a hood over your head. The fabric is thick and smells of sweat.

There are voices all around you. Car doors opening. You are being laid out on a hard, cold floor. Doors slam shut.

You know you have been here before.

You listen out for the girls, for their screaming and howling to begin. But there is nothing.

You yell, *Bambi! Cleo! Reya! Kai! Dev!* But nobody answers back. There is only the sound of the vehicle moving and then you alone yelling, *LET ME OUT!*

Where are your girls? Have they abandoned you?

But then you remember. It was another lifetime. And it was you who abandoned them first.

11.

DARWIN, PRESENT DAY

Good news! says Margie, bursting into the room, carrying a white plastic clock.

You sit up and try to adjust to this reality. To Margie. To the room. You feel like someone has held you underwater for too long and you have come up gasping for air.

I thought I wouldn't see you until this afternoon, you say.

I'm covering someone's morning shift, says Margie.

So, what's the good news?

You're going to be released on police bail.

What does that mean?

Two police officers will come here and explain it all to you at 3 pm tomorrow. It means there'll be conditions on you like having to go to school every day, agreeing to drug testing, and probably a curfew. And then first thing Saturday morning you'll be able to go home with your guardian.

What guardian?

Social services got in touch with your mum. She's still away, but she's given permission for her boyfriend to pick you up and take you home. He'll look after you.

What if I don't want to? What if I don't agree?

Why wouldn't you? says Margie, hanging the clock on the wall.

You stare at it.

Do you want to see the clothes I found you? You wouldn't believe the things people leave behind.

I'll look later, you say. *What about my shoulder?*

You're healing really well. The doctor will put you on oral painkillers and antibiotics. And no more hospital food.

Is that the right time?

Margie checks her watch. *Yep. Ten past nine.* She walks over to your bed and puts her hand on your arm. *It's going to be alright, Bird.*

But she has no idea.

How about this, she says. *I have a tea break at 10 am. I can get permission to take you to the cafeteria and I'll buy you a piece of cake to celebrate. Although we might have to take old bugalugs with us.*

That would be great, you say, because you desperately want to get out of the room.

Alone again, you watch the clock and track the sounds of the movements around you. The minute hand seems to tremble with the weight of your watching. Whatever happens, you cannot go home with Jerome.

Margie is back at 10 am as promised. She's found you a hospital gown that doesn't gape at the back and has press-studs at the shoulder.

You can change in and out of it yourself, she says.

The security guard follows you, but when you get to the cafeteria he sits at a separate table, and you soon forget he is there.

The mud cake is very edible, says Margie. *Would you like a piece of that?*

Sure. Thanks, Margie.

Are you allowed to drink coffee at fourteen? Margie asks.

You laugh. *I'm allowed to do anything I want. Can I have a cappuccino with heaps of chocolate?*

Well, I can't say no now, can I?

The cafeteria has a gentle hum, and you take in the people. The nurses and doctors. The patients and their families. An old woman stares at you and you wonder if your story has made the news. If T has seen it, or Mia. You contemplate if you felt worse when Mia did not answer her phone or when, in finding out that you were in hospital, she chose not to come home. You would like to be free of this loop of disappointment that is Mia.

Margie sets down two pieces of chocolate cake on paper plates, and hands you a napkin and a wooden fork. You taste the cake.

Wow, you say with your mouth full. *It's good.*

Your coffees arrive. Margie takes a sip and screws up her face.

We're not in Melbourne now.

I've never been to Melbourne, you say.

The weather's crap. But the coffee is the best in the world.

Is that where you're from?

I'm not from there. But I lived there for almost twenty years. Until last year, when I had to escape.

Escape?

I broke up with my wife.

Why?

Margie looks taken aback by your question.

She just didn't like me anymore.

But you're a really good person.

You haven't known me for very long.

I did think you were a bit weird to begin with.

Margie laughs.

What did you first think of me?

I had your sketchbook so I thought you were a really talented artist . . . It seems she wants to say something else but she doesn't. You notice blotches forming on her face.

Do you get heat rash?

Margie presses her palms against her cheeks. *It happens when I eat too much sugar.* She looks at her watch. *My tea break is over.*

After the coffee and the chocolate cake, your energy has returned in a burst. Back in your bed, you kick off the sheets and swing your legs back and forth while watching the clock.

12.30 pm. A phone alarm rings and you hear the security guard sliding out the small esky from under his chair. You hear the squeak of his shoes as he walks down the corridor to the kitchenette. The microwave whirs and then dings at two and a half minutes. You count the seconds it takes for him to walk back to his seat.

You pace around the room.

12.51 pm. A meal cart rattles towards your door. You jump back in bed, pull the sheet right up to your chin and pretend to be sleeping. You hear someone place a tray on the metal drawers next to you, and you wait until you hear the door click behind them.

You eat the vegetables on the plate, gulp down a bowl of stewed apples. You walk to the window. You are on the seventh floor. You can see all the way to the edge of the car park to where the mangroves begin. You watch people come and go in the car park. When they open their car doors, silver halos bounce off and blind you.

You make a plan. After your bath this afternoon, you will ask Margie to cut your hair. You will tell her you want to make a good impression with the police tomorrow. You will collect your hair in a band, and when you pass the guard, you will make sure your head is wrapped in a towel.

Tomorrow, at 12.28 pm, you will lay your hair across your pillow. You will plump another pillow and cover it with the sheet.

Anyone who glances at the bed will think you are asleep. You will dress in the clothes Margie has left for you. And then—

You will run.

12.

HIMALAYAS, UNKNOWN YEAR

A power is unleashed in your legs as you run. The rhythm of your pounding feet quietens all other voices in your head – your mother's, your father's, Mida's and Teshi's.

Tonight, you do not veer from the road to the charnel ground. You run right past it. Your hair, braided and heavy with amulets and ribbons, slaps against your jacket as you run. So many layers of wedding garb constrict you. But nothing will slow you now – you have already waited too long.

You hold the river in your mind. Soon you must cross it and find your way to the Pilgrim's Trail and the Holy Mountain. There you'll be able to conceal yourself amongst the crowd. You look back along the road to be certain no one is following you, and then you tear out across a neighbour's field.

Mud clings to your boots as you run, clumping around your heels like a brick. You have the sensation that something is trying to shift you off course, trying to pull you back, and when your feet leave the ground and come down again, they do not land where you expect them to.

So, you run harder still.

You think of Teshi. How often you have imagined making this escape with him. He is the one who mapped it for you. He is the one who told you about the river crossing and the Pilgrim's Trail. But he is not here, and you are resolved now that he is not going to be.

At the edge of the field and the beginning of the undergrowth, you drop down. You crawl through a thick tangle of bushes until your head snaps back, your hair snagged by a branch. You stop to untangle your braids then twist your body through the tunnel of knots and thorns until you finally reach the river.

The river is glossy. You have never seen it at night, the way it drinks in the darkness, the way it drinks in the stars. You should have left long ago. You should have left the very same day you and Teshi hid the bundle that you search for now. But Teshi insisted you wait.

You find the bundle, tucked in the V of a branch, just as you left it. You are grateful it has not been torn apart or claimed by any creature. You shake it from its cover. A knitted cap and a set of monk robes Teshi stole for you. It will be your disguise on the Pilgrim's Trail.

You strip off your wedding clothes and pile them at your feet. You twist your braids around your head and secure them beneath the cap. You wrap the robes around your body, but they are too long, so you tie a knot where they drag on the ground. You know there is a proper technique for wrapping them neatly around the body and if Teshi was here he would show you.

You stomp on your wedding clothes until they are caked in mud. You pick them up and throw them out into the middle of the river. They smash against its surface. Nothing in these past weeks has given you more pleasure.

You scramble along the bank to find the crossing. The soil is loose. You try not to think of newly betrothed girls and their teeth littering the bank like pearls. It is just a story, you remind yourself. And there must be a better story – one where the girl escapes.

You search for a stick sturdy enough to balance you. At the crossing, you test the water with your hands. It is so cold it stings. You step out onto a rock, and your boot slips on the moss. You take your boots off, thinking your bare feet will allow you a better grip. You cannot risk falling into the water. You have nothing to change into. Rock to rock, you must take your time as the water grows deeper. Soon, you lose the feeling in your feet. You lean on your stick to balance yourself.

You reach the other side of the river and stop to dry your feet with the end of the robes. Even out of the water, the cold still shoots up your legs like darts. But there is no one to complain to. There is no one else to blame. Choices are yours to make and yours to bear. Because now your life is your own.

Your boots back on, you begin to walk, recalling the map that Teshi drew for you. A mile from the river, a herder's track. If you follow it, it will lead you to the Pilgrim's Trail. And then, after months of walking, you will arrive at the Holy Mountain.

The grass is high on both sides of the road, but soon you spot a pile of rocks and you take this as a marker for the start of the herder's track. Using your stick, you push through the grass. Teshi warned that you must keep a steady rhythm if you are to reach the shelter of the forest by sunrise.

You haven't even walked a mile when you hear rustling behind you. You freeze. Could there be a wild dog on your trail? A goat? A mountain cat?

You hear it again.

Bird!

You lie flat, your face to the ground. If it is Cho, you would rather be trampled by his horse than have him take you as his bride.

Bird! It's me.

It is Teshi's voice. You stand up. You are furious with him. You fall over yourself to get away from him. The grass slaps your face as you run.

Wait! He is running too, trying to catch up to you.

You stop and spin around to face him. *Wait?!* You throw your stick at him and he leaps off the track to avoid it.

What is wrong with you? he cries.

I did wait. I waited until I was about to be sold off!

Bird, I tried to get in there. I tried to reach you. But I couldn't get past your uncles who were guarding the door.

How was I to know that?

I knew you'd escape. And I knew you'd come this way because this is the route we planned on taking.

You knew that, did you?

Teshi steps towards you. He is also wearing a monk robe, only his is perfectly arranged. And he is carrying two bed-rolls – goatskins he has stitched together.

Come on. We need to keep going before they come after you, he says.

You pick up your stick and use it again to push through the grass. A bed-roll, you think, would be welcome on the trail.

You walk, and the harvest moon casts the clearest of shadows. You are nervous. With a moon like that, it is not a night for escaping. It is a night made better for hunting runaway girls.

When Teshi suggested it, you had imagined there would be many pilgrims on the trail and that, in your monk disguise, you would disappear easily between them. But there is nobody except you and Teshi. On both sides are cleared, flat fields. All you can think of is Cho riding up behind you and throwing you over his horse like a sack. And that would only be the beginning of how terrible your life would be.

Since their marriage, you have watched Cho enact his foul moods on your sister and throw tantrums when things don't go his way. How much worse it would be for you because, unlike Mida, there is nothing in you that wants to please him.

You walk until you are startled by a strange shadow on the road. It is your own. Your head is made too voluminous by your braids. If Cho or anyone were to appear on the trail, your lump of hair would surely give away that you are not a monk but an escaping girl.

We need to stop, you say to Teshi. *I need to cut off all my hair.*

He keeps walking.

We can't stop now, he says. *That would be foolish. We won't make it to the forest by first light if we don't pick up our pace.*

You walk. You blame Teshi for the full moon, for the empty trail, for your bad disguise. You wonder if there are better, safer routes than this one he has chosen. You resent him for his knowledge of the trail and all the tracks out of the village because it is knowledge that has been kept from you because you are a girl.

You both sink into silence. Except for the scraping of your boots on the road, there are no other sounds. No trees, birds or insects rustling or buzzing. The fields are lifeless. You console yourself that at least in this silence, you will hear Cho coming. And then you will do what you always do.

You will run.

13.

DARWIN, PRESENT DAY

Margie isn't sure what it is about you and why, out of all the patients she has nursed, you are the one she can't get out of her head.

She has seen other teenage girls in worse states – pregnant, addicted, as skinny as whips. But they all had someone, even if it was just a girlfriend or boyfriend wasted and draped over their beds.

Margie was the ward nurse on duty on Monday afternoon when you came in. But because of a staff shortage, she was called down to emergency. So she was the one to undress you, clean you up and bandage you when you came out of surgery.

That first day, Margie considered you lucky. Lucky because bullets don't always travel in straight lines, but this one did. You had been standing straight on to the police officer when he shot you, so the bullet entered the front of your right shoulder and exited the back, leaving no shattered bone or fragments.

And she thought you were lucky too because she was the one who tended to you. Bagging up your things for the police, she had found your sketchbook in your satchel. Knowing that when the police took it you would never get it back, she tucked it into her gym bag for safekeeping.

That first night, before she finished her shift, she had sat by your bed and stroked your hand.

You are a lucky, lucky girl, she said. *So whatever your life has been, from here on in, I know you can make it better.*

But when days passed, and no one called, and no one visited, she wondered if your run of luck was over, and if any girl had ever made her life better alone.

Margie turns into her street and hopes her neighbours are not out the front watering their garden. She really does not want to have another conversation about her palm trees dropping fronds onto their side of the fence.

She can already see their Doberman bounding down their driveway to bark at her car. It barks and cries all day and keeps Margie awake after her night shifts. Sometimes she dreams of killing it.

Margie's dog, Elsey, is a camp dog she picked up from the pound the day after she arrived in Darwin. Heading north, buying a house, adopting a dog – these were all things that were meant to save Margie.

Margie pulls into her driveway and idles her beloved orange Datsun 280Z. Elsey is already clawing at the gate. Out of the car, Margie puts her hands on her hips and attempts to conjure some authority. *Sit, Elsey,* she says. *Sit.* But Elsey doesn't sit. *On your bed now,* Margie raises her voice. *On your bed.* But Elsey is trying to climb the fence.

Margie has to wear long sleeves to cover the litany of scratches up her arms from these arrivals. Soon after she brought her home, Margie took Elsey to the vet to see if there was anything she could do to make her dog less anxious. The vet found Elsey was in excellent health but recommended a series of behavioural interventions. One of them was the command 'On your bed'. So, whenever Margie arrived home, she was to say this to Elsey to give her the chance to calm herself before Margie opened the gate.

Because when you open the gate, the vet said, *you are letting chaos in.* And then she recommended anti-anxiety medication.

For me or the dog? laughed Margie. The vet was not amused.

Margie did not want her dog on drugs so she dragged her out of there and determined that love and daily walks would be the fix. But watching Elsey now, almost twelve months on, Margie wonders if medication would have been the kinder thing.

Please sit, Margie begs as she inches open the gate. Elsey pushes past, hurtling into her arms. Margie gets Elsey to the ground to settle her. She strokes her belly and when Elsey is calm enough, she lets her jump into the passenger seat while Margie parks the car.

Margie hooks her gym bag over her arm and uses the railing to pull herself up the stairs to the second-storey veranda. Covering everybody's shifts is wrecking her. But she's single now and there's a mortgage to pay, and the six-foot fence she had to have built to keep Elsey in cost her all her savings. And she still owes Len, her mechanic, for servicing the car.

Elsey bounds up the stairs beside Margie and sprawls across the day bed. Margie turns on the fan, kicks off her shoes and collapses beside her.

Margie closes her eyes. She's in the habit now of trying to sleep whenever she can. Since leaving Melbourne, it's like there's another body within her body reaching for her. And just as Margie relaxes, she wakes herself with a start as she feels the other body trying to pull her down.

But a woman must sleep, she tells herself.

Elsey turns her head towards Margie and licks her face. Her tongue is coarse and her breath smells like sardines.

Stop! She attempts to hold Elsey's mouth, but Elsey's jaw is too strong and she continues licking through the web of Margie's fingers.

Fuck off, Elsey! She shoves her dog to the floor and feels immediately guilty. She heads inside, turns on the air-conditioner and sits on a stool at the kitchen bench in arm's reach of the fridge. She just needs a moment to cool down, a moment to herself.

Margie takes a beer from the fridge and tells herself that vitamin B is an essential nutrient at any time of the day and isn't it almost 5 pm anyway? She opens a packet of corn chips and a tub of guacamole. She crunches and sips and tries to remember what else she has eaten today. A boiled egg. A piece of chocolate cake with Bird. An awful milky coffee. She shoves more corn chips into her mouth and tries to block out the sound of the neighbour's dog, whose barking has started up again.

Margie fills her mouth with corn chips until the sharp edges begin to hurt her cheeks. She puts a peg on the packet and imagines what she would eat if she were a better person.

Elsey slumps against the glass door, her head on her paws. Margie didn't know that having a dog would be like having a mirror to your moods.

I'm sorry, she says, letting Elsey inside. Margie takes Elsey's mince from the fridge and gives her a large serve. Then she watches her eat for a while.

Margie finishes her beer and resolves to not drink to get drunk tonight, but just enough to fall asleep. She lies on the couch and browses the music on her phone.

Her music collection is a time capsule and she tells herself that she must delete it from her phone. She cannot go near her crate of records, the one she so carefully bundled up in her getaway. She'd like to fling all those records into space and never hear them again. She searches for new music, but she has no idea what to choose. Her algorithms keep pulling her back to her past when mournful country singers seemed to be her prevailing mood.

When Margie wakes, it is 8.15 pm. She's slept for almost three hours. Elsey is standing next to the couch with the lead in her mouth, nudging at Margie's leg with her nose.

Yes! says Margie. *Let's walk.*

Out of the gate, Elsey pulls hard on the lead. Margie keeps her close as they pass other houses with high fences and barking dogs. When Margie bought her house, she swore she would not create such a fortress. But then she discovered she had a dog who wanted to follow her everywhere she went and was probably part dingo and could jump any normal-sized fence.

Margie strains her arm to keep Elsey by her side. She must focus, she thinks, on the progress they have made. Margie has taught her to sit and now she comes when she's called, but 'stay behind' is not a command Elsey is choosing to comprehend. She's too old for puppy school, and where would Margie find the money and the time? Margie resolves that on her next break she'll watch more dog trainers online.

At the beginning of the park, Margie lets Elsey off the lead. Elsey springs across the long grass, zigzagging between the few trees. She makes a game of chasing at nothing. Margie picks up a stick and throws it to Elsey and thinks of your drawings again.

On Monday night, she brought your sketchbook home and sat on the couch studying it while Elsey sniffed every page. She had worked from 7 am to 7 pm that day, and half of it in emergency. But looking at your drawings, she forgot how bone-tired she was. The five girls transported her to another place and time, where mountains were tipped with snow, and girls wore cloaks with hoods and looked at the moon and danced in gardens. She guessed that this was a fantasy world you had created. And you had a good reason to want to escape your own.

But the one drawing of the boy looked to Margie like it had come from this time and this place. With his big eyes and strong jaw, he could have been a teenage soap star for all Margie knew. Though on Wednesday when she returned your sketchbook, hadn't you said that he was your friend, T?

Margie follows Elsey towards the creek and tries to remember herself at fourteen. It was around that time she first had sex. It was with a boy in her year on a school excursion. Her biology class was mapping sclerophyll forests on the mid-north coast of NSW. The teacher had split them up into pairs and given them one hour to identify all the tree species in a specific area. When no one else was around, Margie had suggested to the boy that they try another kind of biology experiment. Aside from the banksias spiking her skin, Margie can't recall feeling hurt or harmed by it. It wasn't until years later, in her mid-twenties, that it didn't feel like an experiment. When Margie came out to her family and friends, and sex felt like some deeper expression of herself, that's when she really felt harmed by it.

And now she is thirty-nine. It has been almost twelve months since her last breakup, this one more monumental than the rest. This one: a marriage, a pregnancy, an apartment. All lost.

Margie throws another stick to Elsey. She would prefer to think of herself at fourteen than her present age. Because at fourteen, she was probably at her best. She was brave and she was open. It was a time when art, a film, a song, could reach inside her and utterly transform her.

Margie smells something rotten in the grass. Elsey has already smelt it. She darts towards it and disappears. No doubt she is rolling in it and it is sticking to her coat like tar, and Margie will have to wash her when she gets home. Margie calls her and Elsey shoots out.

Good girl, she says. *Good girl.* Margie puts her back on her lead and steers her to the path.

Ahead, a group of boys are walking up from the footbridge. There's six of them that Margie can count. Elsey is already straining towards them and Margie attempts to pull her back. Elsey has a bad habit of jumping on strangers and trying to lick them as they pass.

Good evening, miss, says one of the boys as they approach, and the others giggle at his politeness.

She's friendly, Margie says as Elsey strains on the lead, pulling out towards them, but then Elsey leaps onto one of the boys before Margie can pull her back.

I'm so sorry. Sit, Elsey, sit.

The boys are laughing now. Elsey sits and pants happily as they take turns to pat her.

I'm trying to train her, Margie says. *I don't know if it's working out.*

It's okay, says the boy Elsey leapt on. *She's a real friendly dog.*

She is, says Margie, glancing at the boys who are all smiling down at her dog. *Good girl*, *come on now*, she says, pulling at Elsey's lead.

Have a good one, says one of the boys and then they continue walking along the path.

For a moment, Margie watches them walk, the way their limbs seem to be floating in liquid, the way they move around each other like a choreographed dance.

Elsey nudges Margie's leg and Margie takes off her lead. Under the lamplight of the park, Elsey moves ahead of her, her body rippling, her brindle coat like a tiger's.

There is still beauty, Margie thinks. And it can still reach her.

14.

DARWIN, PRESENT DAY

Friday, 12.30 pm. One eye to the glass panel of the hospital room door, you watch the security guard shuffle along the corridor to the kitchenette. Slowly, you turn the handle and push the door. It is silent. You are grateful. You desperately want to run, but you walk. You must not bring attention to yourself. Your shoulder throbs. You pass the kitchenette. Four rooms. Then you feel an instant, sickening panic as gears kick and cables whir from the lift ahead of you. Any moment now you expect a doctor or nurse to step out and ask you where you are going. You focus on the exit door. You keep your measured pace until you are pushing your good arm against the door. You turn back. No one has seen you. You brace your shoulder and run down six flights of stairs.

Outside, the sun is fierce. The asphalt scalds your feet. You run past the parked cars, all the way to the mangroves. You can hear a cyclist, wheels thumping over the elevated track that eventually winds back to the city. You slow to a walk again. The cyclist passes and you are suddenly aware of how ridiculous you look.

There's a unicorn on your t-shirt with sparkles coming out of its nose and your shorts are covered with palm trees. What was Margie thinking?

Before another cyclist can see you, you duck between the wire rungs of the fence and climb down into a tangle of stilt roots. The tide is out and there is hardly a clear surface to walk on, so many sharp roots jutting out of the sand. It will be slower this way, but harder for them to find you. And for one night you need not to be found, because there are things you must do before you go to jail.

You step through the shallow creeks and the water soothes your feet. Tiny fish dart around your ankles. The creeks will rise with the tide and then the water will not be safe to wade through. You move as quickly as you can.

You reach the Water Gardens and wait until it is dark, hiding in a giant nest of palms. When the sun goes down, you make your way to T's along Rapid Creek Road. A woman on rollerblades bumps your elbow as she passes, and then two more cyclists ding their bells as they veer around you, leaving the smell of cigarettes and alcohol in their wake.

For a while, you stand at the front of T's house, trying to determine if Lyn is inside. You can see no lights on, so you wind your way through the bamboo garden and around the side. Before you met T, Lyn had turned his bedroom at the front of the house into a beauty salon, and bought him a vintage powder-blue caravan which he restored and put on cement blocks in the backyard. Even with her bad feelings towards you – she has not liked you from the start – you have aways felt safe in T's caravan, a private universe separate to Lyn, nestled between the banana trees and the back fence.

You are relieved to see T's caravan lit up. You tap on the door. T probably has his headphones on. You press your hand up to the window.

He opens the door. He's in his boxer shorts.

Did you miss me? you say.

What the hell are you wearing? he laughs. *You look like you've escaped from some Christian lesbian cult.*

Are you going to let me in?

He hands you the tub of baby wipes that lives next to the door. *Only if you clean your feet.*

You are such a clean freak, you say, but you sit on the step and wipe your feet. This baby powder smell is something you will miss. Every surface in the caravan smells of it.

Inside, you notice he has taken down your drawings and hung up fairy lights.

You had a spring clean?

Mum bought me the lights to cheer me up, he says, sitting on the edge of his bed.

Did they cheer you up?

Not really.

Well, I've been having a great time in hospital.

I'm sorry I didn't visit you, he says.

I didn't think you would. There was a guard at my door, anyway.

That was not our finest hour, Bird. Stealing a car. You holding up a servo.

You move to sit next to him.

I know.

I don't want to go to juvie, Bird.

You won't.

T weaves your fingers into his and he kisses the top of your fingertips. You know this is his attempt at an ending.

Can we just lie down together for a minute? you say.

You lie down on his bed and take in the bare walls. It looks like he has already erased you. This is no time to be sentimental, you think.

You sit up and begin searching beneath his bed.

Your clothes are in a bag in that top cupboard, he says. *Where are you going to go?*

I'm going to meet the girls.

In juvie?

Yeah. I think they can tell me something about my life.

You pull the bag from the top cupboard and tip out the perfectly folded bundle. It's all you can manage with one good arm. You pick through the pile to find a black t-shirt and a pair of black jeans.

T holds his head in his hands. *Bird*, is all he says. He has reached his limit, you think.

You change into your own clothes. *Does Lyn know what happened?*

Yeah. I told her.

Everything?

Everything. She flushed the pills down the toilet.

What about the car?

She took care of it.

What did she do?

I think she drove it into the bush and burnt it.

Go Lyn! you laugh. *Your mother is a very surprising person.*

I can't ever see you again, Bird.

I know, you say.

Looking at T sitting on his bed, you understand perfectly why Lyn wants to protect him and why she would do anything for him. For the light in him, the kindness. For the sweet boy he is and the gentle man he will become.

Did I leave my shoes here last week? you say.

Mum threw them out, but I bought you some new ones. Have a look under the table.

How did you know I would turn up?

You always do.

You open the lid of the shoebox and peel back the bright orange tissue paper. A new pair of runners, like the ones T wears and keeps fastidiously clean with his baby wipes.

There should be socks in there as well, he says.

You put on the socks and the runners.

I need to take all the paints I left here.

T drags out a backpack from under the bed. It clangs with spray paints. He helps you adjust the strap over your good shoulder.

You lean into him. Your foreheads touch. You close your eyes and the first moment you met flashes before you – when you collided into each other on the footpath opposite the park.

I hope you find it, he says.

Find what?

The life you really want.

You too, you say, and you kiss the *t* on your wrist, and he kisses the *b* on his. Then you step out of his caravan, and he closes the door. You walk across the lawn in your new runners. They are so white they glow against the grass.

When you reach the side of the house, a light flicks on. Lyn is standing at the lounge room window. You stop, hold up your hand, halfway between a wave and a surrender. Whatever it is, you want Lyn to know you will not be visiting again.

15.

DARWIN, EARLIER THAT DAY

Friday, 12.45 pm. Fifteen minutes before her shift, Margie turns into the hospital car park and parks her Datsun 280Z. She pushes her face into the air-conditioning vent and side-eyes her gym bag. Again, she has not gone to the gym. She woke this morning with a hangover and a terrible feeling of guilt – that she should have given your sketchbook to you on the very first morning you woke, and she should not have taken something so personal home with her. And yet, in the day and a half she had it, it seemed to give something to her life she did not know was missing.

In front of her, all the parked cars look like they are melting from the wheels up. The hospital car park always brings to mind the apocalypse for Margie, and some days when she turns up for work, she wishes the apocalypse would just hurry on up. That all the life-sucking systems of the world would collapse and there would be nothing left to exchange except home-cooked meals and human kindness. But then she thinks of Elsey, how much her dog likes cold mince. And how much Margie would miss driving around in her 280Z.

This morning, with her hangover, Margie made you an eggplant curry because she thinks it will be the last opportunity she has to cook for you. She grabs the container from the back seat and walks across the carpark, thinking she should not wait for the apocalypse to become a better person.

In the lift, Margie checks her watch. Eight minutes before she has to sign in. She gets out at the seventh floor and walks down the corridor, doing her best to conceal the container.

The guard is at his post. He's dunking a biscuit into his coffee.

Just checking on the patient, says Margie.

The guard pops the whole biscuit into his mouth and nods.

Margie thinks you are sleeping so she quietly places the container on the drawers. But then she notices the strange way your hair spills across the pillow – the hair she cut off for you yesterday afternoon. She pulls back the sheet.

You are not there.

Margie tries to get her bearings. She walks from one side of the room to the other. She opens the toilet cubicle. She looks under the bed. She pulls back the curtain, as if you might be hiding there, as if you might be playing a joke on her. And then she looks down to the car park and has a panicked thought that you may have jumped. She tries to jimmy up the window and is relieved it is not designed to open.

Margie sits on the bed. She takes the tangle of hair that she watched you gather up and secure with a hairband. She smooths the rough ends, rolls it up, puts it in her pocket. She thinks to check the drawers.

Your sketchbook is in there.

Looking around the room again, she notices your hospital gown is on the floor and the bag of clothes she brought for you yesterday is empty.

She thinks of your face, how anxious you looked when she told you that tomorrow you would go home with Jerome. She had said, *Why wouldn't you?* which was hardly a question, and certainly, she realises now, not the right one to ask you.

Margie slides your sketchbook down the front of her shirt, picks up her container and opens the door. She walks straight past the guard without saying a word. She takes the lift down to the senior nurse's office and paces in the corridor, working out what she will say to her.

Hi Jay, she says, finally stepping inside the office.

Hi Margie. Signing in?

Actually, I feel terrible. I shouldn't have come in.

What's wrong with you?

Margie puts her hand to her forehead. *I've got a fever.*

We've all got a fever, Margie. It's called the build-up.

No, I think I'm going to be sick.

Jay sighs and turns to her computer to look at the roster.

I know you're overdue for a break, Margie. But I'm understaffed.

I've covered two shifts this week.

I know. I know. And I need you back on your feet. Take the weekend off. But please be better by Monday. I need you for a twelve-hour night shift.

I appreciate it, Jay. Here's an eggplant curry for your lunch. Margie sits the container on her desk.

Sure, I'll take bribes, says Jay. *Get home to bed.*

Margie does not go home to bed. She drives around, searching for you. Moving further and further away from the hospital, she dares herself to drive to your home address which she has memorised from your file.

She has already broken so many rules already. Why not one more?

Margie types your address into her phone. She's anxious about what she might find. Some depressing, dilapidated house, covered in mould, spelling your neglect and demise. But when she pulls up opposite your house, she is surprised to see a freshly painted black and white bungalow with a lustrous garden of ferns and palms. Pretty pink heliconias grow under the front window. A four-wheel drive parked under an awning.

Margie is sitting in her car, contemplating knocking on your door, when Jerome walks down the driveway. He climbs into his four-wheel drive, and it roars along the street in a way that a car does not need to roar.

Soon after, Margie is knocking on your front door. She yells out your name. She walks around the side of the house and notices a foot stool beneath your window. She stands on it and takes in your room.

A collection of lamps, shelves of books, your art supplies lined up on your desk, and your self-portrait tacked to the wall. But again, you are not there.

And then she is crouching beneath your window and she is clutching at her chest. She is breathless. She has no idea why, in looking into your empty room, she feels so struck with grief.

16.

HIMALAYAS, UNKNOWN YEAR

The night tips into day. Even with the ebb and flow of your fatigue, you and Teshi have kept each other's pace. You veer off the Pilgrim's Trail towards the forest. The fading moon hangs above the trees. You have never thought of the moon as your ally. It's not your sister, as some people say. You know why holy men schedule weddings on harvest moons – so they can see the bride and chase her down when she runs away.

The sun is rising fast behind you, revealing mountains to the north and east where you thought there was nothing. By the time you reach the shelter of the forest, the light is bright. You look at Teshi. His eyes are sunken in, and so are his cheeks. He seems to have aged years since you opened the door to him and he was posing as your suitor. You think of that warm, handsome face and wonder what has happened to him. You want to ask, but then you hear voices and movement from the forest.

Teshi staggers forward like he is sleepwalking. You catch his arm. You raise your finger to your lips and pull him down so you are both hidden by the thick trunk of a tree. A group of pilgrims are chanting as they head out of the forest back to the trail.

When you can no longer hear them, you move into the forest and find the camp site they have left. The fire pit is still smoking. You fan it with the end of your long robes until it flames up again.

Teshi rolls out his goatskin and lies down. The way he crosses his hands over his chest, the gauntness of his face, he looks like a corpse. You poke him in the ribs.

Hey, butcher boy, can you cut my hair?

Don't call me that, you know I hate it, he says, rolling over, fumbling through his pack. *I help my father dispose of dead bodies. I don't butcher them.* He hands you a piece of rolled-up leather tied with cloth.

There's a whetstone in there, and a blade. You can do it yourself.

Can't you do it for me?

Bird, he says. *I haven't slept in days.*

Now the sun is up, and you have made it to the forest, you feel impossibly awake. You have survived the first night of your escape.

Teshi closes his eyes and resumes his corpse position as you prop yourself up next to a tree and begin to slice off your braids one by one.

Careful, you think you hear him say, but when you throw a braid at him, it lands on his chest, and he doesn't even flinch.

You sigh as the weight of each braid is released from your head. You fling the braids away from you until you hear your father's words: *Ten thousand strands of trouble.*

How long, you wonder, and how far will you have to travel for his voice, for any unwanted voice, to no longer reach you?

You slice off every braid and when you are done, you stroke your head. The tufts that remain feel soft and downy. You feel new again.

Sunlight filters through the canopy. The grass shines gold and green. White lilies grow in clusters around rocks, and moss grows on every surface. You push into the moss with your bare feet. You arrange your body in a patch of sun. And when any voice intrudes, you answer back: *Trouble no more.* You repeat this mantra until there is only your voice in your head, disappearing all other voices.

In your separate patches, you and Teshi sleep like babies in the sun, your bellies rising and falling, your mouths wide open. The braid you threw at him earlier curls on his chest and when he wakes, he flings it off in a panic.

Bird! he yells. *Bird!*

He cannot see you. You have tucked yourself behind a rock. He is trying to follow the trail of your braids, but you have flung them out in every direction.

Bird! he yells.

You roll yourself up to sitting.

What is it? What's wrong?

He picks up one of your braids and stands over you. *You can't scatter your hair around like that.*

What are you talking about?

Your hair holds power. And it can be used against you.

By whom?

Hungry ghosts.

You laugh. *Hungry ghosts! Did you really wake me up to tell me that?* You sink back down behind the rock. *You're as superstitious as an old man, Teshi.*

Teshi is on his hands and knees, crawling through the grass, gathering up your braids.

Didn't your mother ever teach you? he says. *Didn't she teach you anything?*

Maybe I didn't listen to anything my mother said.

Bird, he says in that tone of his that infuriates you. *When are you ever going to grow up?*

You stand up. You do not want Teshi to pick up your braids. You do not want him to touch them. You will collect them yourself and not for his sake, but because looking at the braid he has dropped next to you, you are reminded that each one is threaded with a silver amulet and that is something you will be able to trade.

You collect a clump of braids and shake them in his face.

Look out, or I'll curse you!

It's not a joke, Bird, he says.

Your braids collected, you sit cross-legged, and wonder when Teshi became so humourless. You had resolved to escape alone, but now Teshi is here, and his bad mood feels like an imposition on your freedom.

You watch him put on his boots.

I'm going to find us some food, he says.

Take your time, you say.

The forest folds around him and you are grateful for the space it offers you. It may be that things are irreparable between you since the night of his humiliation at your parents' house. Now you have escaped the village, what you do not want is someone else reminding you of your limits and your failings, telling you how and what you should be. With your braids cut off, and your disguise improved, what you want is to discover who you might be, away from your parents and away from the village.

You break a lily from its roots and suck on the stem. It oozes a sweet liquid that tastes like honey. Saliva floods your mouth. You are much hungrier than you thought so you eat the whole stem. Then you eat the flower too.

When Teshi returns with handfuls of wild spinach and a few mushrooms, you are still sitting cross-legged, watching the sunlight splinter through the trees.

You haven't moved since I left? he says. *I've explored the whole forest.*

I've been meditating because I am a monk, you say.

Teshi looks at you and laughs. *Truly, Bird, you look deranged.*

You throw a lily at him and stick another stem in your mouth.

You shouldn't eat those, he says.

Why? They're delicious.

They'll give you hallucinations.

Is that another superstition of yours?

It's not a superstition. It's a fact.

I've already eaten four of them.

Teshi widens his eyes. *Things are going to get very interesting for you, Bird.*

You run your hands across your head. You cannot stop touching your scalp. But it has begun to feel patchy and strange. Teshi keeps glancing at you as he feeds sticks into the fire and you begin to feel self-conscious – something you do not want to feel.

After we eat, will you shave off the rest of my hair?

Only if you promise to never call me butcher boy again.

Teshi cooks the spinach and mushrooms in his small pot. He shares the food with you, and when you are done, he sharpens his blade on the whetstone.

You press your palms together and bow to him.

Why do you always want to mock me?

I'm not mocking you. I'm giving thanks.

Just put your head down, he says, and he places his hand on the back of your neck and scrapes the blade across what is left of your hair.

Where did you go, Teshi? You just vanished on me.

I'm sorry, he says.

I'm sorry too. I shouldn't have asked you to do what you did.

That's not why I vanished, Bird. I wanted to tell you, but I promised not to.

Promised who?

My mother.

What did you promise?

Not to tell you or anyone she was dying.

What?

I suppose I can tell you now because she's dead.

Teshi. You grab Teshi's wrist and pull him down beside you. Everything in your sight is shifting now: the fire, the rocks, the trees. Nothing will stand still.

Why didn't she want anyone to know? you say.

In case your mother found out. She didn't want her coming to visit.

Why would my mother visit her?

Don't you know?

What's there to know?

They used to be best friends. When they were children. Pema never told you?

No, you say. *Nobody ever tells me anything.*

You must wait until nightfall to walk again. Lying beside Teshi, his eyes are closed, but you are not certain he is sleeping. You try to take his hand, but it's limp beside him. You sense he is pretending to sleep so he doesn't have to answer any more of your questions.

You gaze up at the changing patterns of the trees and think of Lhakyi, his mother, and Pema, your own. How did you not know they were best friends? Why has Pema never told you?

You had only met his mother once, at the market when you were shopping alone. Her beautiful face is clear in your mind. And the way she seemed to recognise you. The way she regarded you for a long time without saying anything.

You look like your mother, she finally said, and then she linked arms with Teshi and led him away.

Later, you told your mother what Lhakyi had said, thinking she would like to hear it.

And what did you say to her? your mother questioned.

I said, 'Thank you, ma'am', and I bowed.

A rash bloomed across your mother's neck and face, the way it always did when she was angry or upset.

You must never bow to that woman ever again, she said. *She is beneath you.*

A wind turns over the camp site, and the forest shrinks in the darkness. It is time to walk again. You shake Teshi by his shoulders. He must have been sleeping after all because it is an effort to wake him. Eventually, he sits up, rubs his face and stares blankly into the dark.

You stand and roll up your goatskin.

Thank you, he says.

For what?

For asking me to come with you.

You'd miss me too much.

I probably would.

Did you tell your father where you were going?

I didn't tell him anything. He left a week before my mother died.

In silence, you gather your things, and head towards the emptying trail.

I'm so sorry, Teshi, you finally say.

We should stay quiet now, he says. *Your voice could give us away.*

What if someone tries to speak to us? you ask.

Just raise your right hand to your lips. We'll pretend we've taken a vow of silence.

The wind whistles past your ears. When it finally stops, you hear the rhythm of your boots and then something else that sounds like a creature struggling for breath. It takes you a moment to realise it is Teshi trying to suppress his sobs.

17.

HIMALAYAS, UNKNOWN YEAR

Pema is crouched in the corner of her house that is no longer her house, where she knows no one will find her. Last night, she crept away from the guests and hid behind the bottles and the shelves because she thought she would dissolve.

In one night, you have run away, and she has learnt the only friend she has ever known has died.

Pema balls up her fists and pushes them into her eyes until they ache and she can see stars. She wants to believe there is still some light left in her. How else can she go on?

She has waited all night for the wedding guests to leave, and now she moves out into the house and sees that some guests are still passed out under the tables. Some are draped over chairs. Torn paper lanterns hang from every wall and ants are already doing their work on the leftovers. The sight of it makes her laugh. She had been so intent on making this look like a celebration so that the neighbours would not gloat at her misfortune. She wonders why she ever cared.

You have gone and Lhakyi is dead.

Last night, she overheard her neighbours gossiping about her old friend, talking so coldly of her passing. She wanted to strike their faces right there, to say, *How dare you even speak her name?* All those women who had shown Lhakyi no kindness in her life. But more, she wanted to strike herself for the very same.

Her childhood friendship with Lhakyi had bothered no one until they turned fourteen. Then, Pema's mother warned her that Lhakyi was an untouchable and forbade her from seeing her ever again.

She will ruin your reputation, her mother said.

Until then, Pema wasn't aware she had a reputation, or that it could be ruined. Later, she told Lhakyi of her mother's warning and how she would not abide it. Lhakyi stared at the ground and said nothing for the longest time. The silence made Pema uneasy.

Finally, Lhakyi said, *I'm surprised your mother's warning hasn't come sooner. It's all true what she says.*

But I would give up everything for you, Pema said.

Lhakyi laughed at this. It was a cynical laugh, one that Pema had never heard from her. *I promise you, Pema*, Lhakyi said. *You would miss your status much more than you would miss me.*

Those words, once spoken, marked the end of their friendship as it was. Pema did begin to care what other people thought of her and she found excuses not to see her friend. She resigned herself to living her mother's life, the life that was expected of her – to marry well, raise children, tend crops and accumulate enough wealth to feed her ageing parents.

But it was Lhakyi who married first, sealing her fate by marrying another untouchable, a body breaker.

Even though Lhakyi and Pema lived in the same village, and the village was small, years passed, and they did not see each other until one day when Lhakyi was driving a cart towards Pema on the road. Pema pulled up. She had missed her friend so much and she had come to understand that no one and nothing could replace her. She wanted to speak, to apologise. Lhakyi stopped too, but a distance away. It was close enough for Pema to see a small child bound to her. Later, she would learn it was Teshi.

The two women sat in their carts on an otherwise empty road. Lhakyi had not changed. Pema ran her hand across her belly to show Lhakyi she was pregnant again, and Lhakyi patted her son with pride. Then Pema stood up. She wanted to get down from her cart and walk to her friend, embrace her. But Lhakyi quickly picked up her reins and drove away.

Pema did not have the will to drive. She called after Lhakyi, but Lhakyi did not turn around.

Years later, Pema could not believe that Teshi had been innocently wandering past the field and found you in it. By then she felt a bitterness, like a pit growing inside her. She could only imagine that Lhakyi had sent her son as some kind of revenge. But then it became clear to Pema that Teshi was your only true friend and would do anything for you. She knew such love and loyalty was nothing a mother could ever orchestrate.

The day before you were to be sold off, and before you began throwing rocks at the house, you had leant over your breakfast bowl and made a point of eating like the pigs. Then you left your bowl on the table and did not look at Pema or thank her as you left. It was something you often did. It made her feel like your unloved servant. And when Mida arrived, Pema said to her, *Will anyone want to marry her?* And you heard.

Pema has spent so much of your life trying to understand you. She's come to think of you like some strange flower that has bloomed alone in the dark. And as she crouched in the corner of the house and balled up her fists, she asked herself: where did she first go wrong?

For the briefest time as a baby, hadn't you seemed content? So why did it end so suddenly?

She remembers watching you crawl. Your hand met the door and then you pulled yourself to your feet. You wobbled and turned not towards her, but the step, which was steep. She imagined you toppling headfirst, and yelled, *Stop!* as she leapt to grab you by your arm.

You were mid-step. But she caught you in time. You screamed. Pema ran her hands over you. You screamed and screamed. She turned you over, inspected every part of you. No lumps, no bites, no bruises. And yet she could not soothe you. She offered you her milk, warmed water to soak you in a bath. She made teas and tinctures. Nothing could stop your screaming.

Three days later, in desperation, she called in the monks. They examined you and concluded your little body had been overtaken by a bad spirit, and then they drove it from you.

After their chanting and their rituals, you did stop crying, so wasn't that their proof?

Too often since, Pema has wondered if those monks didn't take something else from you. Because you never cried again.

Pema steps out of her house that is no longer her house, into her courtyard that is no longer her courtyard. She picks up a mallet, and with all her strength, she bangs a gong. The sound is high-pitched. It rings in her head, signalling that whatever is happening must now stop.

She watches the last of the bodies come to life and crawl out into the sun, and then she moves back through the house, gathering what she can.

She understands what her first mistake had been: to trust the monks, or anyone, with her child. And now that you are gone, she can never explain that all she ever wanted to do was to keep you safe from harm.

She packs her amulets, combs, a silk jacket, and every small precious thing she can fit into a bag that she will carry when she leaves.

But before she does leave, she kneels at her altar one last time. She lights a candle and prays that she will learn the lessons of this life, so she does not have to learn them again and again.

18.

DARWIN, PRESENT DAY

Parked in her driveway, Margie sits in her car until it is too hot to sit, even with the windows wound down. Elsey had jumped on Margie at the gate and leapt into her customary position on the passenger seat. Now she's scrambling to get out.

Upstairs, Margie fills Elsey's water bowl and pours herself a glass of iced water. She props herself up on the day bed and holds the glass to her forehead. Elsey drinks noisily, then slumps on the opposite side of the veranda, her back to Margie. Margie wonders if Elsey is instinctively avoiding her, if she can sense the bitterness Margie feels, like something toxic leaking out of her.

Margie lies back and stares at the traveller's palm in her garden. Its branches fan out in perfect view of the second storey. Some of its leaves have turned brown. She should trim them, she thinks. But she doesn't own any gardening tools that would reach that far, and she can't think of one person she could call to ask to borrow such a thing. Or anything really.

Margie had thought that relocating to a place she had never been and where she knew no one would be a chance to find herself. But all she has found is herself alone. She could come and go and no one would miss her, not even Jay. Soon enough there would be another nurse to replace her, fleeing whatever she needed to flee.

Margie does not even remember leaving Melbourne, other than packing her car. She had no awareness of where she was until she reached Port Pirie, and then had to find herself a cheap room. By then, she had been driving for eleven hours, which was eleven hours of cycling through her life and asking herself how it had come to be so broken.

The breakup with her wife had been preceded by two months of Margie sleeping on the sofa bed in the study because that is what her wife had asked of her. After her wife miscarried, she said it was space she needed. Space and calm. Margie made no demands because she knew her wife was grieving. And it appeared she was not.

The pregnancy had never been Margie's choosing and it was largely out of her control, so when it happened, and then did not happen, it had felt more like bad luck than some terrible loss. None of it had ever felt real to her. During these months of sleeping on her own and moving about their apartment trying not to do anything to further upset her wife, Margie consoled herself with fantasies of the two of them growing old together. In her mind, she fast-forwarded through thirty years and had them in a country cottage in Castlemaine, tending their overgrown garden, arguing, still arguing, about what music to play.

When she had met a friend for coffee before work and he asked her how she was coping, she surprised herself by saying she could imagine being happy again in thirty years. *Don't you think there's a lot of living to do before then?* he asked her.

Margie had tried to sip her coffee, but his question made her quake. She couldn't hold the cup and poured coffee down the front of herself.

And then it hit her, the sadness of it all. The loss. She began to sob.

With a child coming, the big questions of Margie's life – how best to spend her time, who to love – were all suddenly answered. She would keep the child safe, housed, loved. And when it could walk and talk there would be soccer and camping and parties and piano lessons and how easily she had given thirty years away to someone who wasn't even born. And now, without a child to fill those years, what would she even do?

In a cheap hotel room in Port Pirie, Margie fell exhausted onto the bed.

I don't even like you anymore, was what her wife had said. Her straightforwardness had been attractive to Margie when they first met. It was what got them into bed. But in a breakup, it was brutal.

Exhausted as she was, Margie's sleep was shallow, and by 4.30 am she was driving out of the hotel car park and turning onto the Princes Highway, heading north again. When the sun came up, the road turned red, and for hours she did not see another car.

She thought of their wedding day.

She had married her wife on 10 December 2017, the day after same-sex marriage was made legal in Australia. Until that day, she had thought weddings were gimmicky, that they were only doing it for the party because now they could. She did not realise how much the symbol of marriage would affect her. And that when they put rings on each other's fingers surrounded by their chosen family, she would feel that she was inside a circle, and that circle was love.

Somewhere past Lake Hart, she wound down the window to breathe in the desert air. She didn't even realise she was crying. The wind stripped her tears right out of her eyes. But then she couldn't see and she had to pull over to wipe the specks of salt that had collected on her sunglasses.

Margie drove in long, straight sprints. Melbourne to Port Pirie, Port Pirie to Alice Springs. But after Alice Springs, she could only manage to drive five and a half hours to Tennant Creek. Something like jet lag caught hold of her, like she had left her spirit behind, but she could not go back to retrieve it.

She checked into a hotel in Tennant and fell into another bed. When she woke, her stomach was a churning pit and she realised she couldn't recall the last time she had eaten. So she walked to the service station and bought an egg sandwich, which was a day out of date but all that was left in the fridge.

Initially, at hearing her wife's words, *I don't even like you anymore*, Margie had gone into shock. She had felt a tingling sensation down one side of her body, and then a numbness, and she thought she might be having a heart attack. She retreated into the study and sat on the edge of the sofa bed with her head between her legs while her wife banged on the door. She ignored her and sat there for a whole hour, measuring her vital signs. It was only that she didn't want to pee into an empty coffee cup that she came out to use the bathroom. Her wife ambushed her on the way back.

I'm sorry, her wife said. *You just shut down on me.*

But her wife had already said what she had said. *I don't even like you anymore.* There was no apology that could go near it.

That night, her wife went out for dinner. Margie packed her things into their middle-sized suitcase, not exactly sure where she would go. But she knew she had to go somewhere. She decided to take a sleeping tablet and drive as far as she could in the morning. Lying on the sofa bed, waiting for the drug to take effect, she remembered a conversation she'd had with a locum who said there was a shortage of nurses in Darwin.

Before first light, Margie was packing her things into her car. She loved her car. A more dependable girlfriend she had never had. She stuffed into her suitcase her records, a couple of artworks, a few books, but left behind her vast collection of leather jackets and winter boots because the only thing she knew about Darwin was that it was hot all year round.

Buying fuel in Mataranka, 420 kilometres south-east of Darwin, Margie saw a sign for Elsey National Park and then Bitter Springs. She could not resist Bitter Springs, purely for the name. She imagined the water would be muddy and ancient, and she could wallow in the memory of all she had lost. In the heat of the day, she would lament this midlife of hers as the mud hardened on her like a crust.

Walking along the pandanus-lined path, she discovered Bitter Springs was a series of connected turquoise pools. Tourists bobbed along between them on tubes of coloured foam.

The water was lukewarm, soothing. Blue and red dragonflies buzzed above its surface. As Margie floated on her back, the current carrying her along, something in her softened.

In the lower pool, an orb spider, her abdomen swollen with unlaid eggs, wove a web between pandanus trees on either side of the bank. Margie trod water, watching the way the spider moved so determinedly across this great distance, golden thread spooling out of her, creating a web so intricate and sturdy. Her courage took her breath away.

Margie sits up. Elsey is curled beside her. Margie must have closed her eyes, drifted off. She takes a sip of tepid water.

The courage of that orb spider. This is what she has lacked, Margie thinks. The courage and determination to create a new life with everything she has inside of her.

Come on my girl, she says, grabbing Elsey's snout. *Let's search.*

19.

DARWIN, PRESENT DAY

Walking along the foreshore at Nightcliff, away from T's, you stop to drink at a water fountain. You can see coloured lights are strung from the giant banyan trees and the park is full of well-dressed people sitting on fold-out chairs and picnic blankets. They are drinking wine and eating fish and chips.

You weave around their blankets and make your way to the track that will take you to the underpass. The track winds through the long grass and soon it is utterly dark. When you finally arrive at the underpass, you discover you are on the wrong side of it.

The backpack T gave you is weighing down your shoulder. You hold on to it and tip yourself over the railing and listen out for cars. There's a blind corner so you cannot see any cars until they are right in front of you. You leap out and cross the road before another car screeches past.

Since you were last here, the smashed fluorescent light has been repaired.

You line your spray paints along the wall, and you take in the portrait of yourself. How different you feel now.

You choose a colour and shake the spray can, thinking of all the gifts of your short life. The love of your grandmother. Meeting T.

And now Margie.

You welcome Margie to your mind and there she is – always standing too close to the bed or lingering near the door, wanting to say something else, wanting to say something more.

You find the right distance from the wall. Your good arm sweeps, and you reach and reach, thinking it is tendrils you will paint, so many tendrils spilling out of your body and disappearing into the blue – wherever memories live and then retrieve themselves.

And it is in this act of reaching that it comes to you. You are not a girl alone and floating in the ether. You are connected. And all the ways you are feel inexplicable and true.

You follow the track back to the park. You don't know what time it is or how long you have been painting for. But you think that the police will be there now, moving everyone along after 9.30 pm when the drinking curfew begins.

The coloured lights have all been switched off and the well-dressed people have gone. A few strange men loiter.

No police. Typical, you think. Never there when you need them.

You find two cardboard takeaway containers sitting on a bench seat, and almost a full serving of fish and chips. You sit and eat and look out to the pitch-black ocean.

Beyond seeing T, finishing your portrait and trying to get arrested, now you don't know what else to do. You wonder if anyone in a passing car has reported you painting the underpass.

When one of the loitering men approaches you, you run to where the apartments and houses begin. You will walk the well-lit streets and maybe the police will find you.

It is so humid. The tall beachfront apartments lock out the breeze. You turn corners, seeking a cool pocket of air, thinking that if you see a dark, empty house you will break in, just to lie down in the air-conditioning, drink some cold water and rest for a while.

But all the houses and apartments seem to be occupied. Cars fill the driveways. People smoke on their balconies and verandas, lights pulsing from their screens. There is no cool place to find.

You return to the park. The sprinklers are shooting out water in great arcs, which has moved on the loiterers. You run through the spray, all the way to the edge of the park where the grass meets the beach and there is an overgrowth of saltbush.

The sand is still warm and dry from the day. You smooth out a patch with your arm and uncover a large piece of cardboard. You hope that whoever has put it here does not plan on returning tonight. But in case they do, you take off your runners and tie the laces to your wrists. If anyone aside from the police disturbs you, you will whack them with your shoes.

You pull the cardboard over your legs to stop the sandflies and mosquitos from biting you. And then you let yourself rest. You are so sore, so tired. But soon the police will come for you. If they offer you bail, you will refuse it. Because you cannot be sent home with Jerome. And you cannot let another day pass without meeting the girls.

20.

HIMALAYAS, UNKNOWN YEAR

What is wrong with you? Teshi is saying.

He has been keeping a strong pace while you have fallen back, enthralled by what is appearing in front of you.

Bird! he is calling. *Bird!*

Even though you can see Teshi is now standing close, his voice sounds so distant to you. Why can't he see the girls? The girls who are stepping out of the road and walking towards you in long, straight strides?

You reach out to them. But they walk past. And then they disappear.

You wait. Another girl appears. Is it Bambi? You run to her, and you wrap your arms around her, but she is made of air.

You hear a murmuring from the side of the road, and you move towards it. You listen, kneel. Someone is speaking to you in a language you cannot comprehend. You press your ear to the ground and watch white lilies spring up around your head. The lilies are speaking to you. You know they have secrets to tell, if only you could speak their language.

You feel Teshi's hand on your shoulder. He is trying to pull you away from the lilies, trying to get you back on the trail.

We have to keep moving, Bird, he says. *Cho could be gaining on us right now.*

Shh, you say. *The lilies are speaking.*

And then he understands.

Bird, you are hallucinating, he says. *It's from the lilies you ate in the forest. What you are seeing is not real.*

You want to prove Teshi wrong. So you pull a flower from its stem, but it dissolves in your hand.

It's just your imagination, he says.

Teshi's words break the spell. And you see yourself, just as you are, on your hands and knees, pulling at a tuft of grass.

Teshi offers you his hand and helps you to stand.

Drink some water, he says, handing you his flask. *It will pass. But right now, we have to keep walking. If Cho finds us, he will string us up and drag us behind his horse all the way back to the village.*

You hold Teshi's hand and he pulls you along until you match his pace.

Real or not, you know the girls were yours to see.

21.

DARWIN, PRESENT DAY

The police officers find you with your feet sticking out from the saltbush, your toenails sparkling green in the morning sun. They don't handcuff you, because the running shoes T gave you are still tied to your wrists. But they do tell you that you are under arrest. You ride in the back seat of the police car and you don't say a word. The officers drop you at the police station. Then you are led by someone else to a small room where you sit by yourself drinking tea and eating biscuits. A female officer comes in and tells you that by escaping from the hospital you have made things much worse for yourself.

I know that, you say.

Another woman comes into the room and introduces herself. She's a child protection officer. *I'm here to make sure you're treated fairly*, she says.

The police officer continues. *We've been in touch with your mother. We've let her know that you've been arrested for holding up a service station. We have evidence in the form of CCTV footage, and we have a weapon. There was going to be an offer of police bail, but since you escaped and committed another crime in graffitiing a public space without permission, you are going to be held in remand.*

Do you know what that is? the child protection officer interrupts. *It means you are going to be sent to juvenile prison and you'll have to stay there while you wait for your trial.*

You nod.

The police officer says, *Although the gun taken into evidence was plastic and shoots water, you used it as if it were an armed weapon. Do you understand why you are being charged?*

I do.

Is there anyone you would like to call?

Would you like to talk to your mother? says the child protection officer. *She said she wanted to be here, but she couldn't. I have her mobile number.*

You shake your head. You have nothing to say to Mia.

The police officer takes the laces out of your runners and checks your pockets. She puts you in a holding cell where there is a bottle of water and a thin mattress covered in plastic.

Five stars, you say.

Outside the cell, people are speaking in low voices. There is no window outside, so you have no way to tell what time it is. You rest your head against the wall, and you must pass hours like this, because when you are led out again, it looks like it is the afternoon.

Two police officers drive you to the juvenile detention centre. On the way, you pass one of your murals, a painting of the five girls.

I'm coming, you whisper, and you imagine they have heard you.

There are two prison guards waiting for you when you arrive. They lead you along a concrete path until you reach a building that looks like a spaceship, and then you are inside it being led down corridors and into a waiting room.

The waiting room is small. An air-conditioning unit takes up half the wall. One of the guards tells you to sit down, but that is all he says to you. The guards sit on the two chairs opposite you and one of them shows the other something on his phone and she laughs. You focus on a framed print of a breaking wave that hangs above their heads. Written beneath the wave is a quote that is like something Mrs Whitehead would say: 'You are not a drop in the ocean, you are the entire ocean in a drop —Rumi'. You wonder why it is that you never understand inspirational quotes.

Bring her in. A voice from the other side of the wall. The guards lead you inside what looks like a locker room, where two people dressed in hazmat suits instruct you to take off all your clothes. When you have undressed, one of them removes the bandages from your shoulder and inspects your wound. You must lift your good arm and shake out your hair, and then you must bend over.

One of them hands you lice shampoo and scabies cream. You are told to shower and then rub the cream all over your skin.

But I don't have lice or scabies, you say.

Let's keep it that way.

After you shower, you are handed a pair of blue shorts, a blue singlet, a pair of underpants and an elasticised bra. You dress and ask if you can have your new running shoes back, but one of them tosses you a pair of thick rubber thongs instead. You slide them on. The plastic is hard and sharp. You can tell they are the kind that will rub between your toes and give you blisters.

From the locker room, the guards lead you to the infirmary where a nurse douses your wound with disinfectant and bandages your shoulder. She takes your temperature, a blood sample and two swabs – one from inside your mouth and one from inside your nose.

Usually, people cry when I do that, she says.

Not me, you say.

Then the guards walk you to your cell in silence. You pass other cells. They are all open and empty. You can hear no human sounds at all.

Where are all the other girls? you ask.

But the guards won't answer you. They give you a box of water and a tin cup and then they lock the door.

In your cell, there is a bed, a desk, a high barred window and a toilet in the corner. There is no tap, just a rough patch on the wall where you can see a sink once was but you guess has been torn out since the flood and the fire.

You check to see if the toilet flushes. It does.

You lie on the bed, run your hand over the wall. Everything feels hot to touch.

Someone arrives and slides a meal through a slot in the door. You can see this person's hand but nothing else.

No cutlery in the cells, the voice says. *You'll have to eat it with your hands.*

The food on the tray is nothing you recognise.

Is your name really Bird? the voice asks.

It is.

What kind of a stupid name is that?

Then you listen to their fading footsteps, a door sliding open, and a door sliding shut.

22.

HIMALAYAS, UNKNOWN YEAR

When you were born, the monk who had predicted you would be a boy arrived at your parents' house bringing arrows when he should have brought spindles. Discovering you were a girl, he was annoyed with your mother as if she had deliberately shown him up. Wanting to stay in his favour, she made butter tea so thick that everybody's face in the room shone. She scooped out all the glimmering fat and served it to him, which went some way to please him. Then she offered him a tray of diamond-shaped sweets, which he ate, one after the other, until he finally said, *Bring her to me.*

Your mother lifted you from your basket, unwrapped you and laid you down on a mat in front of the monk. You were sound asleep. The monk made some incoherent sounds and then – because he had come to rely on your family's donations, and proving himself not foolish – announced, *This girl child will bring you good luck.*

Your mother and father were relieved, your father especially.

And what is my good luck child's name? he asked, already thinking of how he could put your good luck to use – good luck he did not seem to be born with himself.

The monk took his time examining your face. He scratched around your scalp and turned you over, searching for blemishes and birthmarks. You woke then with a loud squawk, widening your eyes and pursing your mouth into a sharp little point. The monk loomed over you.

It has come to me, he announced. *Her name is Bird.*

Bird? your mother questioned.

Yes, Bird, repeated the monk. *Named for her long skinny legs and her curious, sharp features.*

Your parents had never heard of a child with such a name, but it was the monk's privilege to name you so they did not challenge him further. The monk finished the plate of sweets, and then he rode away.

You were six months old when your father decided it was time to test your luck. Your mother was at the markets with your sister Mida and your father thought it was a good idea to balance you in your basket on his horse's neck and ride to the village gambling den. Only men were permitted to enter the small, thatched confines to play their game of sho. But they made an exception for you – you were a child, after all.

And soon, they came to regret it.

Your presence, your supposed good luck, filled your father with a confidence he never had, and that day he won against every opponent. When he returned home, his pockets full, your mother agreed he could continue to take you to the sho den, like his lucky charm, on the condition that he only spend his winnings on repaying his accumulating debts. Your father agreed, and he rode to the den twice a week for three weeks straight, you in a basket on his horse's neck. In the den, he set your basket under the table and he kept you quiet with sips of beer. By sundown, he was collecting from his neighbours.

But by the fourth week, the other village men had grown suspicious of his winning streak. They doubted a girl child could bring such luck.

As soon as your father slid you under the table, they pushed their strongest forward to tackle him to the ground and empty out his pockets. But they found nothing.

It's in the basket, a neighbour yelled, picking you up and kicking the basket over.

It's on the child! another neighbour cried.

You'll find nothing, your father said, pinned to the floor as his neighbour took you by your feet, tipped you upside down and shook you until a painted dice rolled out of the pocket of your tunic.

By the time you and your father arrived home, your mother had already heard what had happened. She was standing on the stone steps with her arms folded and she would not let your father pass.

You have embarrassed us all, she said.

Out of my way, woman, he said, limping past her.

She snatched the basket with you inside. *You have put our child in danger.*

You weren't so worried when I was bringing home the prizes, he said.

Following that, they did not speak for months.

Did you ever feel your good luck, and then did you feel it change?

23.

HIMALAYAS, UNKNOWN YEAR

Your head clears. Roads intersect the Pilgrim's Trail, and more and more pilgrims appear. You confirm with Teshi that these ones are real. They are monks and nuns and everyday people. You tell yourself that you are safer now, folded in their increasing numbers, with each step moving away from Cho.

Between the two of you, you only have your bed-rolls, Teshi's pack and his cooking pot to carry. Your amulets are in a pouch inside your robe. And although you still think it would have been better to escape sooner than you did, you know the amulets will keep you both fed all the way to the Holy Mountain.

Stalls selling fruit and vegetables, cakes and tea pop up along the trail. There is money to be made from the pilgrims, and you can see the wealthier pilgrims paying porters to carry their loads. You hear them complaining that some of the porters have already disappeared with everything they own. You are glad for your vow of silence. How easy it is to raise your finger to your lips and not get involved in other people's dramas.

You walk. The pilgrims' chanting swells. Carts rattling. Horses and mules.

But then you hear someone cry out. The pilgrims' chanting stops.

Did you hear that? you ask Teshi.

He nods.

Another scream, and then the sound of pushcarts tipping over.

Teshi turns around.

Don't show your face, you say. *It could be Cho. He may be coming for us now.*

From the yelping and the reckless sound of the riders, you know there are bandits coming up the trail. You want to run but running will only draw attention, and even though you are fast on your feet, you know you cannot outrun bandits on horseback. You must do what all the other pilgrims are doing – covering their heads and scampering from the trail like mice.

With Teshi beside you, you huddle with a group of pilgrims as the bandits pass, shielding your face with your sleeve. You peer past it to see if there are any bandits you recognise. But beyond the first few riders, it is impossible to see their faces for the dust.

You don't have to see her to know a girl is being carried off against her will. You can hear her piercing screams.

After the bandits pass, the pilgrims brush themselves down and return to the trail, as if it were all some natural and unavoidable storm.

A whisper travels along the trail. *She was promised*, the pilgrims are saying.

We should have helped her, you say to Teshi.

What could we have done?

We could have done something. We could have thrown rocks. The pilgrims outnumber the bandits, but we did nothing.

You walk, keeping close to Teshi. The girl's screams echo in your head. You feel it, as if a sound can gather dust and matter, and sink inside of you. A pain locks around your hips. You continue, thinking you must walk through this pain. But soon all you can manage is a shuffle.

You do not know what is happening until you feel a gush between your legs. And then your sister Mida's descriptions come back to you. *Menses,* she called it.

You grab Teshi's arm. *We have to stop*, you say.

You think of Mida's bloodied rags and how bright they turned the water she soaked them in. You are worried your blood will drip behind you as you walk and expose you for neither being a boy nor a monk, and then you will be in more danger than you already are.

What is it? says Teshi.

We need to get off the trail.

You walk out into the field until you are far enough from the trail that no other pilgrim can hear you.

I'm bleeding, Teshi.

He looks confused. His eyes search your face, your arms, your feet, for any wound. You widen your eyes and look down.

Moon time, you say. And then he understands.

You head towards a copse of trees and curl up in the grass while Teshi collects wood and lights a fire. Sitting with your back to the flames, the heat soothes you. You have no other clothes but what you are wearing. It is Teshi's idea to tear strips from the ends of your robes and make rags. You tie them between your legs and around your hips, but it is not long before the blood soaks through them.

We can camp here until it's over, Teshi suggests. *You can rest, and I will forage for our food.*

But this is the first time you have bled, and what you did not ask Mida was how long this bleeding would last. The thought of waiting indefinitely in a province filled with bandits was like waiting for danger to find you.

We'll camp here for the rest of the day, you say. *And at night, we'll walk. If I bleed on the road, no one will know. No one will see it in the dark.*

But before the sun goes down, the place you have rolled out your beds, between the copse of trees, suddenly teems with midges and mosquitos, too many to wave away.

You gather your things and walk again, thick rags between your legs. Walking is uncomfortable. The rags, the pain, slow you. Teshi walks patiently beside you, and you cannot help but grow envious of his supple body, which never seems to bleed or ache or injure.

You walk into the night, until there is no distinction between earth and sky, until walking doesn't even feel like walking but bobbing on a great black sea.

24.

DARWIN, PRESENT DAY

You wake to the sound of another alarm ringing out through the prison. Welts cover your neck and your chest. Midges and mosquitos circle your bed. Your skin is so itchy that if you start scratching, you know you will not stop. You imagine this prison must be built on a swamp.

You roll out of bed and onto the concrete floor, seeking some relief from the itch, from the blood-boiling feeling that has taken over your body.

The concrete is cooler than the bed. You lie there, your arms and legs splayed out. You wonder, where are the girls now? Will they know you when they see you? What will they be able to tell you about your life?

The cell door flings open, and a guard is standing over you before you have a chance to get up.

What are you doing down there? they say. You recognise the voice. It is the person who pushed your lunch through the feeding window.

I'm trying to cool down, you say.

Were you expecting air-conditioning, love?

You stand up, which has you seeing stars. You have to sit down on the bed, and you lean over your knees to ward off the feeling you are going to faint.

What are you doing now? On your feet. Put your shorts on and follow me. It's feeding time again.

The guard leads you along the corridor, past cell after empty cell. You have no idea if feeding time means breakfast, lunch, or dinner. Or how long you have been asleep. You can hear other girls now, but they sound so far away. The guard opens a heavy metal door, and then you are walking along another corridor and through another set of doors. There is a high-pitched beep as they swipe a card that hangs from a ribbon around their neck, and then they are pushing their back against another set of doors and you are standing in a shed full of girls.

Fans as big as helicopter blades slice the air above you.

You cast your eyes around and it only takes you a few seconds to find them.

Your girls.

All five of them are standing together in a line, waiting to be fed. They are fanning each other with their trays. They are dressed as you are. Blue shorts, blue singlet, black and white thongs.

You feel the recognition in your body. You smile and wave, waiting for them to feel it too. But they look at you strangely and begin to laugh. They are laughing at you.

It doesn't matter, you tell yourself. It might take them more than a minute to realise who you are. You walk towards them, and their laughter suddenly stops. They are glaring at you, and you have no idea what to say. So you stand there smiling, waiting for them to recognise you.

You can't push in, Dev finally says, towering over the rest.

You have to get to the back of the line, says Cleo.

You search Bambi's eyes, but she only looks at you suspiciously. You want to take hold of her, and say, *Remember? Remember?*

But remember what, exactly? What would you say? That you seem to be recalling a past life where the girls appeared to you as phantoms on a road and then vanished in front of you? Or that in this life they came to you when you were a four-year-old child, and you have been drawing and painting them ever since?

What would they even make of it?

I'm not crazy, you think, and unfortunately you say it aloud. The five girls narrow their eyes at once and a chill goes through you. They turn their backs.

Looks like this one's got scabies, you hear Cleo say before you collect a tray, clutch it to your chest, and move to the back of the line.

The line moves slowly and the fans whir. Everybody in the shed is looking at you and talking behind their hands. You feel a dullness in your body, a pain lock around your hips and then the heavy gush of your period.

It is your turn to be served, but you are not concerned with food. You are concerned with grabbing as many napkins as you can to stem the flow before it drips down your legs and onto the floor.

You sit alone, as far away from everyone as you can. And with your back to them, you shove the napkins into your underpants and hope they don't fall out when you have to get up again. You eat the strange yellow food on your plate and wonder how many humiliations are ahead of you, how many failed attempts it will take to know the girls or for them to recognise you.

And then you wonder in how many lives you have died trying.

25.

DARWIN, PRESENT DAY

Saturday afternoon. Margie is doing laps around the shopping centre with your sketchbook under her arm, desperate to find you. This morning, she pored over your sketchbook again and concluded that the surest way to find you was through your friend T. So, she's following teenage boys around to determine if any of them are T. The girls, she decided, were something out of your imagination.

She follows a group of boys down the escalators to the food court, trying to get a good look at their features. None of them are T, so she joins a line at a juice bar. Two girls in front of her are deliberating over the Tropicana or the Bubble Tea.

Hi, Margie interrupts them. *I wonder if you can help me?*

The girls turn around. They have matching bobbed hair and kohl-rimmed eyes.

Sure, says one of them.

I've found someone's sketchbook and I really want to get it back to them. I think maybe they are your age?

Oh, yeah?

Do you know a girl called Bird?

The girls shake their heads in unison.

What about this guy? She opens your sketchbook to the drawing of T. *Do you recognise him?*

I wish, says one of the girls.

Do you think he's famous, maybe?

I don't think he's famous. We'd probably recognise him if he was.

The girls are called to the counter.

Sorry we couldn't help, they say.

Thanks anyway, says Margie.

Margie stays in the line, not because she wants a juice, but because she doesn't know what else to do. But now she is here, she thinks she should probably increase her intake of fruit and vegetables.

She walks away with a frothing drink called the Green Goddess, finds an empty bench seat and watches teenagers gather in the food court. Two boys sit next to her eating falafel rolls.

Hey, she says, sipping on her drink, trying to sound nonchalant, but not feeling nonchalant at all.

Hey, they respond with their mouths full.

I wonder if you can help me?

Margie slides your sketchbook along the bench seat.

I'm trying to get this back to its owner. I think someone's left it here by mistake. She flicks through the pages again to the drawing of T. *Do you recognise this person? I think his name is T.*

Oh yeah. T goes to our school.

The boy takes a bite of his falafel. Margie wants to throw her arms around him, squeeze out everything he knows.

And what school is that? she asks, doing her best to look poised.

Darwin High. But he's in Year 10.

He's two years above us, says the other boy.

Margie's mouth goes dry and she has to take a large sip of her drink.

You could take it to school and drop it at the office, suggests one of the boys.

But I can't do that until Monday, says Margie. *And whoever owns it probably wants it back. Do you know where T lives? Do you have his address? I could take it to him right now.*

As soon as she says it, Margie hears the desperation in her voice. The boys hear it too. They stand up, shoot each other a look.

Gotta go, says one of them, and they quickly walk away.

I'm just trying to help, she calls after them.

Margie closes your sketchbook. Could this get her arrested, she wonders, approaching children, asking for another child's address? She slips your sketchbook into her bag and makes her way back to her car. Moving from the blasting cool of the shopping centre and into a wall of heat, she feels disoriented. She can't remember where she's parked.

She chastises herself. Why didn't she just have a day off, drink a few beers and watch dog training videos at home like she wanted to? Whatever could be gained by looking for you?

Margie remembers her car is parked in the undercover car park, not outside. She finds her car and sits in it for a while. The problem, she tells herself, is that she does not have a life. So, she's grasping for one.

Margie drives into the city and parks. She searches for a lip gloss in the console. She finds one melted, smears it across her lips, and rubs some of it onto her fingertips to smooth down her hair.

She has parked one block from the only gay and lesbian bar in town she knows of. It advertises itself with a glittery rainbow sticker above the door. She has walked past it but never been inside. Since she moved here, she has not been out anywhere at all. In Melbourne, bars and restaurants used to be her whole life.

Inside, all she can see are straight people. But the light is dim enough to ignore them and now she is here she thinks she may as well have a drink. She sits at the bar and tries to channel something of her former self. Didn't Margie Shapiro once have swagger? Wasn't she even considered rakish in some circles? She rests her elbows on the bar, winks at the waitress and tries to pretend she is good with being alone and waiting for no one at all.

Margie drinks two beers, eats peanuts and resists pulling her phone out of her pocket. No one will have called her anyway. She's not in any casual texting relationships. After the split, her wife got all the furniture and their friends – the story was her wife was grieving and Margie just abandoned her.

Margie sits and tries to remember the last time she was in a bar. It was in Fitzroy in Melbourne with her friends after work. How very different her life looks now.

Is this seat taken? A woman has appeared beside her. Margie glances at her face. She is dark-eyed, beautiful.

I'm waiting for a friend, Margie lies.

Well, hopefully they won't turn up. The woman has an accent Margie can't pick. She sits down, swings herself around to face the bar.

What are you drinking? she asks Margie.

Margie holds up her almost empty beer.

That's a fancy beer, says the woman.

I'm very fancy, says Margie, wondering if any part of her remembers how to flirt.

Well, I could tell this from the other side of the bar.

And so it begins.

Margie and the woman swinging on their stools, turning to face each other, turning away, taking turns to buy each other drinks, taking turns to talk and listen. Soon their hands are brushing across each other's knees, and Margie learns the woman's name is Izzy and she is part of the touring Brazilian women's soccer team. Margie tries to keep her cool. If only there was someone to text. And now the Brazilian women's soccer team are waving Margie and Izzy over. Sliding off the seat and walking across the bar, Margie realises she is already drunk. Someone buys a round of beers and then Margie buys the whole team a round of shots to welcome them to Australia. And a couple more.

Izzy leans into Margie's ear. *Your friend didn't show?* The bar has grown noisy with people. Under the table, Izzy and Margie entangle their legs and Margie puts her lips to Izzy's ear.

I lied, she slurs. *I have no friends. No friends at all. Except my dog. Elsey.*

I don't believe you, says Izzy, and they kiss, and then Izzy pulls Margie onto the dance floor.

Margie's hands find Izzy's hips, and Izzy finds hers. She is spinning Margie in and out and then she is holding her close. Margie feels free and loved and her loose hair falls around her face. She is spinning and spinning. But then the spinning does not stop.

I think I need to sit down, says Margie, and she attempts to find an empty seat away from the soccer team and the noise of the bar.

I'll get you some water, says Izzy, and as soon as her back is turned, Margie is out the door. She is running down the street, running as if the entire soccer team are running after her.

Margie reaches her car and sinks into the seat. She looks in all her mirrors. No one has followed her. She grips the steering wheel, tells herself she is not too drunk to drive. Tells herself she must get home to feed and walk Elsey.

She waits for a long time for a break in the traffic before she pulls out. When she does, a car flashes its headlights at her. She has forgotten to turn on her lights.

Margie white-knuckles her way, driving too slowly, then driving too fast, stopping at a traffic light when the light is green because she is being overly cautious and at the same time not cautious at all.

Somehow, she makes it to her street without being pulled over by the police or causing injury. She stops short of her driveway, in front of her neighbour's yard, just in time to hurl herself out of the car and projectile-vomit all over their grass.

On her hands and knees, she is suddenly sober, or more sober than she was, grateful that the neighbour's dog sleeps inside and is not now running up and down the fence barking at her. She wipes her mouth with her shirt and stumbles to her gate. For once, she does not want to wake the neighbours, or get revenge for all the times their dog has kept her awake. She drives her car slowly into her driveway, and before she locks the gate, she leans out to see the puddle of vomit glistening under the streetlight. It is too risky to attempt to hose it away. She can only hope it will sink into the grass by morning. Or evaporate. Likely, the neighbours will think it was some drunk teenager anyway.

Margie is halfway up the stairs before she realises Elsey has not greeted her. She must be asleep, she thinks. It is late. She will be curled up on the day bed on the veranda. Margie will rub her belly and lie down beside her and sleep and sleep.

But Margie finds the day bed empty. She runs her hands over the coverlet and props up the pillows, an attempt to set things right, an attempt to pull herself together.

Elsey! she calls as if her dog is close, as if she is calling her in for her dinner.

Elsey, my girl.

Margie listens for the sound of her dog's paws skittering up the stairs, and when there is no sound, she thinks she might vomit again. She searches the house – the bathroom where Elsey likes to sleep on the cold tiles, under the bed, on top of the clothes. Margie opens every cupboard, even cupboards where Elsey could not possibly fit. She takes the liver treats from the top of the fridge and shakes the packet. Elsey always comes running when she hears that sound. But not tonight.

Margie sits on the top of the stairs and holds her head.

It is 11.35 pm. The street is quiet. She listens for the tinkling sound of Elsey's tag and collar, for her scratching in the backyard. But there is nothing.

She races down the stairs and searches for a head torch in the glove box of her car. She finds one under the seat. She straps it to her head and walks along the fence, checking for any holes or trenches where Elsey may have dug her way out. Standing back from the gate, looking at the impossible height of it, she would never have thought it possible if she hadn't seen those videos of dingoes jumping over six-foot fences. But it is possible.

Margie is out the gate. The beam of light from her head torch swinging from one side of the street to the other as she searches for her dog, as she pleads under her hot, foul breath: *Don't you dare be dead.*

Margie strides through the long grass, calling out. When she reaches the estuary, she drops down into the sand and searches for Elsey's paw prints. The sand is so soft. It's like silt.

She is crawling over the sand, following an impossible trail of divots, when she feels a bristling in the back of her neck. She senses a sudden danger. She looks around. There are no humans she can see, but she can feel something watching her. She trains her head torch across the water, and there it is.

Two fiery red eyes gleaming back at her.

A crocodile, only metres from the bank.

Margie stumbles, then runs back through the long grass all the way to her street. She stands safe in the circle of the streetlight and tries to wipe her mind clean of the image that is now playing on repeat: Elsey at the water's edge, the crocodile with its prehistoric jaws moving towards her.

Back at her house, Margie leaves the front gate wide open. She pulls a camp chair from the laundry. It is covered with spider webs, but she does not care. She drags Elsey's bed out from under the stairs and arranges it in front of the camp chair in the driveway.

Her heart is burning. She remembers the sixpack of beer in the downstairs fridge, collects it, hugs it to her chest. She opens a bottle. The first gulp is better than breathing. The head torch is still on her head, its beam reaching all the way to the gate. She drinks and drinks and the vet's words come back to her: *When you open the gate, you are letting chaos in.*

Did the vet really say that? Margie wonders. What a thing to say.

In no time, Margie finishes the sixpack, and the reach of her head torch shrinks and shrinks. There are more batteries somewhere in the laundry. But Margie has begun to think that if she gets up from the camp chair, the whole world will tip, and her dog will not return to her. And that if she sits and waits and does not move, not even to empty her bladder, she can make a better bargain with the universe, and her dog will eventually trot back through the gate. Elsey, her one true friend, will bound up to her and Margie will never lose patience with her again.

But then Margie feels herself tipping forward and there is nothing she can do to stop it. The camp chair collapses and she falls onto Elsey's bed. She is burying her face in Elsey's blanket and she is sobbing, because the only thing Margie is sure of is that love always leads her to chaos and chaos always leads her to loss.

26.

DARWIN, PRESENT DAY

You are in your cell, staring at the patch on the wall where the sink once was. You are imagining the girls, lonely and bored like you, turning on the taps, letting the water cascade just for the thrill of seeing so much water spilling onto the floor, seeping out under the door, connecting each cell.

Last night you got through dinner and back to your cell without the napkins falling out of your underpants or anyone else speaking to you. This morning another alarm sounded, and you do not know what to do, so you wait for a guard or anyone to arrive and tell you. You think they must be coming soon because you can hear the sliding of doors, footsteps getting closer, a guard shouting, *Keep in line.*

And then your cell door opens.

Stand up, the guard says. *Hands out. Hasn't anyone told you?*

You do what the guard asks you to do.

Nobody has told me anything, you say.

You have to be up, dressed, bed made by the time I get here. She is poking her finger into the air, punctuating each word.

Didn't you hear the alarm?

I did.

Hands out, she says, and she walks around you, sniffing. *I'll tell you something. You stink.*

You feel your body flush with embarrassment.

I've got my period.

The guard says nothing as she pulls back the top sheet, exposing a stain of blood. She frowns at you as she flushes the toilet. *No tampons down there.*

I don't have any tampons. Can you get me some?

Not my problem, she says. *Outside.*

There is a line of girls in the corridor and they are all glowering at you for taking too much of their time. You walk to the back of the line, hoping you have not already bled into your shorts.

Now walk, says the guard.

The line moves slowly and you do your best to match the pace of the girl in front of you. But she stops suddenly and you accidently step on the back of her thongs. She trips, falls forward onto another girl and then she is on the ground, pointing and screaming at you.

She fucking pushed me!

I didn't, you say, stepping away, keeping your back to the wall. *It was an accident.* But no one is listening.

Two guards pull the girl up to her feet and drag her to the front of the line. You take your place at the back of the line again as another guard leans into your ear.

Watch yourself, she says.

At the shower block, a male guard is waiting. He has plastic shopping bags draped over his arm. He is an oversized human, on steroids, you think. If you poked him with a pin, he would pop.

He hands a bag to each girl in front of you. You are the last in line. Your name is written on the bag in thick black marker and inside you can see a clean t-shirt, underpants, a towel, and a few toiletries.

Inside the bathroom, there is only one cubicle left. Each cubicle is separated by a wobbly partition and there is no door on the front, only a water-stained plastic curtain. Standing behind it, you understand why this cubicle is the only one left. It is in direct line with the open door outside, where the oversized guard is still hovering.

You turn your back to undress, remembering Margie's instructions to keep your shoulder dry. You tip out the contents of the plastic bag, and with your good hand and your teeth, you manage to tie the bag around your shoulder.

Standing under the showerhead you discover there are no taps, but then you hear a hiss from the pipes and water shoots out towards your chest like nails.

You rub soap under one armpit and between your legs. It is too difficult to wash your hair with one hand and keep your shoulder dry, so you settle for tipping your head back and rinsing it instead. Even after the mandatory wash with lice shampoo when you arrived, you can still feel grains of sand on your scalp. You start scratching at them, but then the water cuts out. On both sides of you, girls are yelling.

That was not two minutes!

Time's up! a guard yells back.

You wrap the towel tightly around you. It scratches your skin. You are examining the state of your shorts when a female guard pulls back the curtain and sprays disinfectant around your feet. The steam delivers the chemical straight to your nostrils.

You dress quickly. You need to find something to soak up the blood that is pouring out of you, and in the privacy of the toilet, you wind paper around your hand and stick a wad of it in your underpants.

At the sink, in front of the mirror, you run a small comb through your wet hair. Bambi steps out of the cubicle and stands beside you. You glance at her. You try to smile. She has the same plastic comb and she is tearing at a thick knot at the back of her head. You want to offer to help her when she says:

What is wrong with you?

You look at yourself in the mirror. The mirror widens. You do not see one reflection of yourself, but infinite reflections now. Whatever this life is, you cannot comprehend it – the truth of yourself or why you are even here.

You grip the sink. Bambi has already joined the line of girls outside. You can hear the guards yelling.

Bird! Get out here now.

The fainting feeling you have been warding off since you arrived, the dread that you have made a terrible mistake in getting yourself arrested and seeking the girls, finally overwhelms you.

You collapse onto the floor.

27.

HIMALAYAS, UNKNOWN YEAR

After months of walking, the Holy Mountain is now in view. Its peak holds onto the sun like a halo and soon the halo dissolves and colours the sky red.

Walking beside you, Teshi is looking in every direction except the Holy Mountain. The closer you get to the Mountain, the more his suspicions seem to increase. He has started talking of hungry ghosts again.

They are everywhere, he whispers. *Can't you feel them?*

You do not feel ghosts, or hungry ghosts.

How will I know one if I see one?

They've got tiny mouths and scrawny necks, and big bloated bellies.

But this, you think, could describe so many people on the trail.

More than hungry ghosts, you are worried about the danger of the pass in front of you. The wind tunnels up so fast, it is strong enough to strip bodies from the trail. You drop down on all fours, and you tell Teshi to do the same.

The wind dies down and soon the trail is calm again. On either side of you are fields of wildflowers and herbs. You pass nomads who are camped on the slope of a lower mountain, their plump children drinking milk straight from the teats of their buffalos. You offer the nomads one of your amulets for some of their milk and cheese. Nearby, you find a freshwater stream and you feast on the cheese wrapped in wild herbs.

Raptors circle above you. You breathe in the sweet, earthy smell of wild thyme.

Do you still feel the hungry ghosts? you ask Teshi.

Teshi shakes his head.

Do you think the wind may have blown them off the pass?

It doesn't work like that, Bird, he says.

But what if it does?

You pack up and return to the trail. So close to the Holy Mountain, the trail splits off in different directions as pilgrims navigate the safest way to pass through the range. Someone has built a rope bridge and strung it between the trees. It swings and creaks as you walk across it, but it holds.

On the other side, a woman is sitting on a rock, her legs folded under her. She is chanting, and she gestures for you to leave her some food. You place some cheese and herbs in the bowl in front of her, but instead of thanking you she breaks her chant to lean forward and say:

Watch yourself.

You walk, and a blue mist sinks around you so you cannot see the trail. You wonder why Teshi did not stop, did not offer the woman any food. You ask him if he saw the woman on the rock. He says he did. But looking back now, all you can see is fog.

The trail winds up the mountain and the air grows thick with the smell of wild marijuana. Untamed hedges butt onto the trail and pilgrims pick the buds and hang them from their packs to dry. You and Teshi do the same and soon you notice how all your pains have eased, how days seem to vanish and then it is night again and you are sitting at another camp fire staring at branches exploding into flames.

Some pilgrims walk and sing at the top of their voices while others labour to breathe. More and more, you notice pilgrims rolling their feet or twisting their ankles on loose rocks in their fatigue. There are so many pilgrims now whose legs or arms are braced with sticks and wound with cloth. You witness a couple pushing their cart right over a cliff, not able to distinguish the trail's edge in the fog.

The marijuana hedges give way to syringa and jasmine, and the wind carries the sound of chanting from monasteries at higher elevations. You reach a small village by nightfall, no more than a collection of huts. A group of women have set up a stall at the entrance, selling cakes and milky tea. You want to buy a cake but the woman who serves you says you can have it for free if you deliver her prayers to the Holy Mountain.

In the morning you continue walking and the trail opens out onto a plateau. Traders appear with parades of mules decorated with bells and tassels. They are selling rides to pilgrims too injured or tired to continue. The wind on the plateau is sharp, carrying sand and dust that stings your eyes.

You walk all day. The wind does not die down, not even by nightfall, so you and Teshi seek shelter with a group of pilgrims in an abandoned hut. You share what food you have with them, but you do not speak. You and Teshi keep to yourselves, sitting apart from them. If another pilgrim approaches, you signal your vow of silence, and they walk away.

To sleep in a hut is a novelty. Teshi snores gently beside you but you cannot sleep for the sound of the wind stripping pieces from the thatched roof. Soon enough, you are grateful for that stripping wind that has kept you awake when another pilgrim attempts to slide his naked body into your bed. You have seen him crawling towards you in the dark. As soon as his hand touches you, you are ready. You kick him against the wall. Teshi wakes in the commotion, and you leave the man crumpled on the floor, the other pilgrims stunned, as you and Teshi roll up your belongings and head out into the night.

The safer thing now is to keep moving, you think, even against the strong winds and the steep drops.

You walk, remembering the moment you crossed the river out of your own village. How you had always thought that crossing that river would mark the beginning of a new life, a new world. But what seems truer now is that your life is on a continuum, and people in the village and the world are just the same.

When Teshi starts weaving out in front of you, you realise he is sleepwalking again. You link his arm into yours and lead him towards a clearing. You roll out his goatskin and pull him down. Soon, Teshi is safely asleep, your arm linked into his so you can be sure he does not get up and sleepwalk off the ridge.

The sky is turning. You search for what remains of the stars, but they fade quickly into the pale morning. As the sun rises, you sit up and look across the plateau at the distance you still have to walk, asking yourself why it felt so important to leave your village and discover the world.

What was ever so special about you that you could not submit to being someone's wife and a life of servitude?

Because isn't that just how life is for most village girls?

28.

DARWIN, PRESENT DAY

Someone is sitting beside you, talking into your ear. They place a damp cloth across your forehead, rubbing a piece of ice over your bottom lip which you split in your fall. As the ice melts, water tinged with blood trickles down the back of your throat. You feel it entering your body like a cool stream.

Hot air turns over your skin. Some part of you is shaking, but you cannot tell which part. You feel it ricocheting through your teeth.

The room smells sterile. You are lucid enough to know you have a fever. But you do not know if you are back in hospital or still in prison.

You hear the person beside you talking to someone else. They are talking about antibiotics. Your wound is infected. They are discussing if you should be sent from the prison infirmary back to the hospital.

Just see how she goes, you hear one of them say.

Whoever is sitting beside you is wiping your face. Whoever they are, you are at their mercy and there is nothing you can do about it.

You wish the person beside you was Nurse Margie. You wish she was stroking your hand. You want to hear her say: *You are a lucky, lucky girl. So whatever your life has been, from here on in, I know you can make it better.*

Soon the person beside you leaves and you are sweating alone in this dark place. Heat moves through your body in waves. You cannot run now. You cannot even sit up.

A bright light comes on. The person has returned. They are lifting your head from the pillow, sticking a tablet in your mouth, pouring water down your throat.

You sleep and wake in this small room that smells of disinfectant. You realise it is the same kind the guards sprayed around your feet in the shower. When you wake, you move your arms and your legs, to make sure you still can.

You don't know how long you have been in this room. Or what it will take for you to get out.

In the dark, you make waves with your hands and let yourself imagine there is some line, some trembling thread, connecting your past to your present to your future.

And, you wonder, if you pulled on such a thread, could you now pull a different future towards you?

29.

THE HOLY MOUNTAIN, UNKNOWN YEAR

You walk all day with the Holy Mountain in view. Some pilgrims seem to float right past you and others walk like they have bricks strapped to their feet. You pass a man who looks like he has prostrated the whole way. Large wounds have opened up on his forehead and he moves at the pace of a snail, each sweeping movement seeming to cause him pain. You wonder why anyone would want to make the trail more difficult than it already is.

You are tired and hungry now. There will be nothing more to eat until you reach the Mountain. Every edible thing, even the weeds, has been picked down to their roots.

At the end of the day, you and Teshi roll out your goatskins on the hard flat plains, to rest and get your energy for the final length of the trail.

I'm so hungry, you say to Teshi. *I think I might faint.*

Teshi says nothing but pulls out a strip of dried meat he has been saving and shares it with you. You eat your ration quickly and then watch as Teshi makes his portion last and last, chewing each tiny bite loudly and deliberately.

Months of walking beside him has not brought you any closer. And now that it is safe for you to talk, flanked by so many pilgrims, you have nothing to say to each other. You have felt him disappear into his silent vow. He seems intent on sinking further into his sadness, like he doesn't want to find a way out. You consider what it would be like to walk this last stretch without him.

You fall asleep and Teshi is the one to wake you. *If we start walking now, we will reach the Holy Mountain by morning.*

You focus on the Holy Mountain, which is lit up by an almost full moon. You walk and imagine the world it might offer you. Growing up in the village, the world was anything beyond the lives of your mother and your sister – lives that never seemed to favour them. You watched them seeking solace through their prayers, in quiet corners of the house, working the fields. You think you are already far beyond their world.

The sun rises and you want to run these last miles. You reach for Teshi's hand and ask him to run with you, but he recoils.

I'm going to prostrate this final distance, he says.

Teshi's commitment to his suffering confounds you. You will not walk alongside him while he measures his pain in increments.

I'll meet you at the camp site, you say.

Teshi is already on his knees, stretching his body across the ground, forcing other pilgrims to step around him.

The trail is too congested for you to run so you fold into the stream of fast-walking pilgrims and keep your focus on the Mountain. With every step away from Teshi, you feel yourself grow lighter. Alone, you let yourself imagine without limit who you might become.

Soon paths branch off the widening trail like newly grown limbs. When you see a sign, unintelligible to you except for the word 'Bird', you take it as a personal invitation. The path is steep. Chickens peck on tufts of grass on either side of it. You walk until you reach a wooden gate where an old man sits collecting payment for entry.

Welcome to Bird Springs, he says.

Behind him, children are selling fresh eggs. Further in, pilgrims cook the eggs by dipping them in nets into a boiling spring. You buy two eggs from a small boy and pay him more to cook them while you find a place to swim.

There is a small spring with no one else in it. You set down your few things, roll up your robes and dip your toes in the water. You cannot resist the soothing warmth of it and soon you are sliding in up to your waist and then your neck. You tread water and giggle as your robes balloon up. You pull your robes around you and let yourself sink down until you are sitting on the bottom of the spring, gripping stones to anchor yourself. You hear the tinkling of sand as it settles around you. You tell yourself that here there is peace to find, and it is peace you have earnt.

But then something plunges into the water above you. A stick is coming for your head. You dart away from it, but it pokes you in the back, so you grab the end of it and you are pulled to the surface.

It is the old man who took your money at the gate. He thinks he has saved you from drowning and is expecting payment. You give him an amulet so he will leave you alone.

Stretching across the warm rocks, you soak up the sun. The small boy brings your boiled eggs. You peel them and eat them as you watch pilgrims spill out from the trail below. You wonder how far Teshi has travelled.

When your robes are dry enough, you make your way back down to the trail, weaving around caravans of people with their goats and horses and mules. So many people from so many places. In the safety of the Holy Mountain, you wonder now if you need any disguise at all.

Pilgrims yelp to signal their arrival to the Mountain and so do you. But as they pass beneath the prayer flags, they split off in so many directions and you have no idea which direction you should go.

Even after eating two boiled eggs, you still feel hungry, so you follow the smell of food. The first stall you come to is just a cart piled high with a kind of fruit you have never seen. Brown and scaled, in the shape of an apple.

Snake fruit, says the woman sitting on a stool next to the cart. *Here.* She hands you a piece.

Is it sweet?

Try it, she says.

You nibble on the edge of it and make a face. The woman cackles.

Just off the trail? she says.

Yes. Do you sell anything else to eat?

She lifts the lids from the other baskets. There is dried dung, incense, tea and herbs, but nothing you can eat.

She picks at the gap in her teeth with the edge of her knife, then points it towards a swelling mass of people.

You'll have to push your way through that crowd.

The crowd is larger than any you have ever seen.

Do you have a tent? she asks.

I have a bed-roll.

She shakes her head. *A girl shouldn't camp here without a tent.*

How do you know I'm a girl?

The woman laughs.

You've got money?

I've got amulets, you say.

Take this one, she says, reaching under the cart and handing you a roll of canvas, sticks poking out the end of it.

Will it fit two people? you ask.

It will, if you're happy to sleep close.

The tent is heavy, but you carry it through the camp site, your goatskin and a bag of snake fruit tucked under your chin. You notice that other pilgrims have painted letters and characters on their tents, and you think this is what you should do – write your name in large letters on the canvas to help Teshi find you.

You walk towards the last row of tents facing the lake and set up yours a good distance from the others. You take a piece of charcoal from someone's fire pit and write your name on both sides of the tent. You trace the letters until they are thick and dark, visible at a distance. Then you sit in front of the tent, eating snake fruit, waiting for Teshi.

Night falls and you wonder if Teshi may have wanted to get away from you too. You have begun to miss him. But you think it will be easier to search for him in the morning. You crawl into your tent. The air is cooler here, but the tent soon grows warm with your breathing, and you sleep.

In the morning, you peek out and see there are now tents on either side of you. Nuns and monks younger than you run from tent to tent delivering tea to their superiors. You decide to wander in search of food that will actually satisfy you before too many more pilgrims rise and the lines to the food carts swell.

The morning light around the camp site is pink and filled with smoke. The smell of burning hair and dung takes your breath away. You notice many old monks sitting cross-legged in front of their tents. They look well fed, but most of the old nuns look like skeletons.

Outside a tent pavilion, a young monk offers you tea and a crate to sit on. Two older monks are lecturing about the universe. You have spent your short life contemplating what the world might be, but never the universe. The monk describes it as specks of dust and whirling matter. And you can think of no better description for what you feel inside yourself.

You sip the tea and notice raptors circling above you. Three of them ride a drift, looking to feed. They are reading the earth, you think, reading the air, choosing their moment to strike. They circle one of the old nuns who already looks half-dead. She is focused on her prostrations towards the Holy Mountain and hasn't noticed them. She is so slight that you can imagine the raptors sweeping in and carrying her away.

You leave the monks and their talk of the universe and find your way to a stall selling flatbread slathered with something spiced and buttery. You stand next to the stall and eat the bread, watching many more pilgrims pour in from the trail. This morning, it is hard to tell where the camp site begins or ends. You wonder how you will ever find Teshi. In this sea of shaved heads and robes, how will you distinguish him?

You return to your tent. You think Teshi will see your name written in black against the canvas better than he will see you. You empty your pouch and count out what is left of your amulets, and in the bottom of the pouch you find a piece of hashish. You smoke it, looking towards the Holy Mountain and its reflection in the lake. A group of pilgrims trudge past your tent, packs on their backs, pots and pans rattling around their hips. You watch them line up along the shore and shout their names across the water. Then they wave their arms to the reflection of the Holy Mountain like they are waving down an old friend.

You remember the old woman who gave you cake and tea. You look at the Mountain and recite her simple prayer.

The pilgrims continue waving their arms and shouting across the water. You sit and stare at the Holy Mountain, wondering if silence is the better prayer, and if you did have your own prayer, what it would be.

You wait for Teshi all day. In the late afternoon, you return to the woman who sold you the tent and the snake fruit and ask if she has a hook and a line. You think fishing the lake will be a good way to properly feed yourself here, and Teshi. You will save what is left of your amulets and avoid the swelling crowds.

The woman digs into a box of trinkets and pulls out a tangle of things.

There'll be plenty of fish in there, she says, *because most pilgrims are too superstitious to fish.*

I'm not superstitious, you say.

She hands you a line and a hook.

Good luck then, she says. *If you believe in luck.*

You do not answer her.

You buy a piece of dried meat from another stallholder and weave your way back to the lake. You walk along the shore until the noise of the pilgrims fades. The crowd has begun to sound like bees swarming inside your head.

You take off your boots and let the tiny waves lap at your feet. You thread the dried meat onto the hook and cast it into the lake as far as you can. Concentric circles radiate across the surface, expanding until they reach your feet. Holding the line between your thumb and your forefinger, you can feel the tug of the currents beneath. You squat on your haunches and wait for a fish to bite.

In no time, something is swiping at the hook. It takes the bait. You let the line run through your fingers, imagining the size of the fish trying to escape. You tug the line hard and feel an impressive, fighting weight. You tug again, but then the line is running across your hand too fast. It feels like it will slice your skin. And then whatever was hooked is gone and the line is slack in your hand.

That fish, you think, could have fed you for days.

You wind in the line around a flat piece of wood, careful not to collect any kinks or knots. A flock of black-necked cranes flies overhead and their sudden honking sound startles you. They land further along the shore and begin their fishing too. You cast out again, but the hook snags on something submerged.

You tie up your robes so they are above your knees, and wade out. The water is clear until you stir up the silt with your feet. Then you cannot see what is beneath you. The line grows taut as you carefully wind it and get closer to whatever it is snagged on.

The water is suddenly deep. You cannot feel the bottom. You pull hard on your line. You don't want to lose it. You pull and pull and then a bright cloud rises up, air bubbles exploding on the surface. You reach out to this bright cloud and bring it to your body. And then you wade back to the shore. It is large, but pulling it through the water is no effort at all.

You drag it onto the sand.

It is the body of a girl, dressed in a wedding jacket, with braids like yours.

You run from the girl, from the lake, clutching your line and hook. You crawl into your tent, your robes dripping wet. You hug your knees and rock back and forth, as if the motion can wipe away what you have seen. Your teeth chatter, not because you feel cold but because you are afraid. You strip off, wrap the goatskin around you and hang your robes over your tent to dry. Inside again, you cocoon yourself and take comfort in the chorus of the pilgrims' singing and praying outside.

Only when the sun is sinking do you coax yourself out of the tent. You retrieve your robes, which are now dry, and wind them around your body. So many more tents have gone up in a day. If you were to go in search of Teshi, you are not sure that you would find your way back again. Everything is changing so quickly.

You fix your eyes on the Holy Mountain and try to focus your panicked mind on its peak. You think of the two monk boys you and Teshi met so many years ago, coming out of the forest. How bright their faces were when they spoke of the Holy Mountain's redeeming force. *The Holy Mountain will purify your heart*, they said, *and show you who you truly are.*

But already in its presence you have walked away from your only friend and his suffering, and run away from the body of a dead girl, leaving her to rot on the shore.

You fear that such a heart can never be transformed.

It is dark now. You realise you have left your boots beside the lake. You tell yourself you will wait until the morning to find them. You tell yourself that you are tired, you ate too much snake fruit, you smoked too much hashish. Perhaps you were hallucinating, as you have hallucinated before. You find comfort again in the distant sound of chanting from monks and nuns who never seem to sleep, and the constant noise of traders moving in. You tell yourself that in such a place of prayer and noise and people, you should not be afraid.

Finally, sleep takes you over. You dream you are walking back along the shore. Your boots are where you left them. The lake is blinking with stars. There is no disturbance on its surface until you throw a handful of stones. They make ripples that overlap, but then the ripples turn into waves.

You wake. The wind has loosened a guy rope and it is slapping against the wall of your tent. You crawl out to tie it down. The wind is cold against your back, and you have a sudden urge to empty your bladder, so you walk in search of a rock to squat behind. You look behind you to be sure no one is following you.

What you don't see are two horses strung together with rope. They are hitched to a wide wooden cart loaded with baskets, and between the baskets, two drivers sleep. Nearer to the rocks you are approaching, two watchers wait. They know that soon enough bodies will surface like fish around a full moon.

And you do.

They have watched you crawl from your tent and scramble towards these rocks. And now they watch as you pull up your robes and confirm what they were hoping.

That you are a girl.

They move in, thick arms wrapping around your waist. A gloved hand stuffing rags into your mouth. Your body turns limp as they tip you into a sack.

They carry you to the cart. You are bucking inside your skin, but your body will not obey you. You peer through the weave. There is a blurring light as pilgrims pass by with lanterns.

Why do the pilgrims not ask the watchers what they are carrying in their sack?

Why can't you cry out?

The watchers wake the drivers. One of them pulls you out of the sack and arranges you in a basket. He props you up and tucks your legs beneath you. He wraps your arms around your body and binds your hands. Although you cannot move any limb, you discover that you can make a muffled sound in the back of your throat, so you make this sound over and over.

Shut up, says the driver, squeezing his hand around your mouth. *Or I'll bind your tongue to your throat.*

You stay quiet.

You search through the gaps of the basket and see the watchers delivering five more girls. The drivers arrange them, as they have arranged you, then they secure the lids of the basket with leather straps.

You hear the drivers clicking their tongues. You feel the cart lurching forward. You imagine, as they steer the horses out of the camp, baskets swaying in the back, that the drivers must look like any other traders, and their baskets must look like any other trade.

For so many moons you have walked to reach the Holy Mountain. Along roads and trails, across river passes – for its redemptive force, its promise of the world. And now there is one cold voice in your head that says: *It was never yours to seek.*

Far from the camp and the Holy Mountain, you discover you can move your lips again, you can move your tongue, and so you spit the rag from your mouth. You hear another girl cry, *LET ME OUT.* And then another girl is yelling the same. Soon, you are yelling too. And not just yelling, but howling like a hurt dog. The sound coming from you all rises above the cart, glorious and terrifying. It is enough to spook the drivers. They pull up.

We'll let you out of the baskets if you promise to be quiet.

No one answers back. The drivers take the silence as agreement, and they unbuckle the straps, one by one, lifting you all out. They arrange your bodies three on one side, three on the other, tying your hands to the slats.

Another full moon. You look along the line of girls and see a repeating silhouette. The grim lines of your mouths pressed tight. The flashing of your eyes.

The cart lurches forward again, and with it your bodies. A shoulder presses sharply into yours. Someone's hand is twitching in your lap. Soon, the sun will rise and with it a terrible knowing – you are six girls whose lives will be forever linked.

30.

DARWIN, PRESENT DAY

Margie's phone rings in her back pocket. She has fallen asleep in her driveway, curled up on Elsey's bed.

She pulls out her phone, croaks, *Margie Shapiro*, and attempts to sit up.

Sorry to call so early but . . . are you missing a dog? It is the voice of a boy.

I am! Margie says as she struggles to get off the dog bed. *My Elsey.*

Yeah. I can see her name on her collar. That's how I got your phone number.

Is she alright?

Yeah. She's right here with me. Margie can hear Elsey's familiar panting through the phone.

Thank you. Thank you, says Margie. *Where did you find her?*

She was scratching at my door this morning. I've fed her some leftovers. She's pretty happy.

She's never run away before.

We only have a low fence so she's on a long rope in the shade. Do you want to come and get her?

I'll come right now. What's your address?

I'll text you.

Okay. Thank you, says Margie. *That dog means the world to me.*

The boy hangs up. And Margie kisses the phone as it pings with his address.

Five minutes later, Margie pulls up in front of the boy's house. She pushes open a jasmine-covered gate and steps along a stone path through a bamboo garden. Lush potted plants spill over the veranda. There are two cane chairs and a side table with a shallow bowl of frangipanis. A heart-shaped wind chime hangs between the plants. It looks to Margie like she's stepped into a resort, not someone's front veranda.

Margie knocks on the front door and it occurs to her that she has not even washed her face. She dips her hands into the bowl of frangipanis and does her best to smooth down her eyebrows and her hair. She's thinking she should have brought cash, some kind of reward for the boy. But in her rush to get here, she's left behind her purse. Of course, she could do a bank transfer. But with her bender last night at the bar, she's uncertain how much money is even left in her account. The thought brings on a sudden brutal hangover. She squeezes her head between both hands and takes a deep breath. She hopes she does not look as bad as she feels.

While she waits, she breaks off some of the jasmine that winds around the railings, crushes it between her palms, pats herself down – an attempt to disguise the stench of alcohol leaking from her.

She knocks on the door again, considers texting or calling the boy. Did he tell her he was around the back? Should she just walk around?

The door opens.

A short, muscly woman with a tea towel over her shoulder smiles at Margie curiously.

Hi, I'm Margie. You have my dog?

Yes! Come in.

Margie follows the woman along a breezy hallway.

I'm halfway through making pancakes, says the woman. *It's our Sunday ritual.*

The woman leads Margie into a sun-filled room that smells of butter and cinnamon. She is wearing open-backed overalls and her movements are elegant and precise, like a dancer.

Was it your son I spoke to on the phone before?

Yes, he's out the back with your Elsey. She just popped her head out from under his caravan this morning.

I'm so relieved, says Margie.

I bet you are, says the woman, and her face is so welcoming and familiar that Margie thinks she might cry. *Just keep heading that way*, says the woman, *then out the back door.*

Margie opens the screen door and Elsey bounds towards her to the length of the long rope.

Hello, my girl! says Margie, as Elsey jumps onto her lap. Margie wraps her arms around her. *Oh, my good girl.* Elsey licks Margie's face and Margie laughs, but then her laughter breaks into a sob.

That's one happy dog, says the boy, stepping out of a caravan.

Margie stands and wipes Elsey's slobber from her face, attempting to regain her composure.

Thank you, she says. *For finding her. For calling me. This is the first time she's run away.*

That must have felt awful, says the boy, untying the rope from Elsey's collar.

Why don't you join us for breakfast? the woman calls from the back door. *I've made a huge stack of pancakes. Much better for us if you share.*

I'd love that, says Margie, stroking Elsey.

You can bring Elsey inside with you, says the woman.

Margie tries not to feel overwhelmed. It's the first invitation she's had since she left Melbourne.

In the sunroom, Margie sits at the table and Elsey slides under her chair.

Sorry. Is there anything I can do to help? she asks the woman, who is gliding around the kitchen, looking like she has everything under control.

No, it's all done, she says. *Your timing is very good.*

Margie admires the artwork on the walls, the flourishing plants, the elegance and order of the place. She wants to ask the woman about herself, but she feels shy, tongue-tied, hungover.

This is a beautiful home you have, she manages to say.

Thank you, says the woman. *It's my sanctuary. My son finds it all too much, so I got him his own caravan in the backyard. Now he has a sanctuary too.*

The woman sits at the table with Margie, and soon the boy comes in. The table is set with napkins and there's mango and blueberries in a glass bowl.

Is this a special occasion? Margie asks. She's suddenly self-conscious, aware of what a mess she must look from sleeping on a dog bed. She looks at her pants. There's dog hair all over her.

Just a Sunday ritual, says the woman. *I think rituals are important in this day and age.*

Margie has eaten so many meals alone this year that she wonders if she can still use cutlery and not spill food down the front of her.

Coffee? asks the woman.

Oh yes, please, says Margie. The woman leans over her, and Margie tries not to breathe.

Margie gulps the coffee. *I'm sorry. I didn't catch your name.*

I'm Lyn, and this is my son, T.

Margie looks at the woman and her son. There is a strong resemblance. Large dark eyes, strong jaws. As Lyn and her son fill their plates with pancakes, fruit and yoghurt, it takes Margie's tired, hungover brain a moment to register.

Did your mum say your name is T?

She did, he says, cutting into a stack of pancakes.

Really? Margie says. She doesn't mean it to, but it sounds accusatory.

Yeah, really, says T.

Short for Teshi, adds Lyn. *But he doesn't like the name his mother gave him, so everyone calls him T.*

T? Margie repeats. And then she is aware that Lyn and T are both looking at her strangely.

It's just . . . I think I know who you are, says Margie. Their bodies straighten defensively. She continues. *This may seem strange, but do you know a girl called Bird?*

Margie's question is followed by a long silence. Lyn flicks her eyes to T, and T keeps his eyes fixed on his plate. Lyn puts her knife and fork down and pours herself another coffee.

I do, T says finally, wiping his mouth. *We hung out for a while, but we don't anymore. Do you know her?*

I do and I don't, says Margie. *I'm a nurse at the hospital and I treated her recently. Did you know she was shot by a police officer?*

Yeah, I heard that.

She was in hospital for five days and she didn't have one visitor. Not even her mother.

T nods.

She left her sketchbook at the hospital.

Where is she? asks Lyn.

She escaped.

Right. Well, as T says, he used to see Bird. But he doesn't anymore.

Lyn picks up her knife and fork, and Margie takes this as a signal that the conversation is over. She starts eating again.

But it is Lyn who continues, without prompting.

It's not that I don't like Bird. She's got enormous talent. But she's one troubled soul.

Mum, T says. *Can we not?*

Bird hasn't had much of a home life lately. Her grandmother died and she was sent up here to live with her mother who is quite young and has terrible taste in men. T wanted Bird to move in here, but I said no.

You said, 'Not on my fucking life'.

Yes, I did say that. Because I want more for my son than a young woman with a death wish.

She doesn't have a death wish, says T. *She just can't be in her home with Jerome.*

That may be –

Can I leave now, please? T interrupts Lyn.

One more pancake, Lyn says, and she slides her son the plate.

So, what do you do, Lyn? Margie asks, an awkward attempt to save T. *Aside from making delicious pancakes.*

I'm a beautician. I specialise in an anti-ageing face massage. My clinic is next to the veranda where you came in.

I've never been to a beautician in my whole life.

Lyn leans towards Margie and looks closely at her face. *You have good skin.*

Thanks, says Margie, immediately embarrassed, feeling far too seedy for any close inspection.

Everyone falls silent again.

Margie quickly finishes the food on her plate and the last of her coffee. *We should get going now. You've been very generous. Thanks for looking after us. T, thanks for finding Elsey.*

She's a really cool dog, says T.

She is, says Margie. *You know, I was going to post a reward, so I'd like to give you something to thank you for finding her.*

That's not necessary, says T.

But I'd really like to.

Honestly. I didn't find Elsey. She found me.

Lyn walks Margie through the bamboo garden and waves to her at the front gate. Elsey jumps straight into the passenger seat.

Looks like you've got a friend for life there, says Lyn.

Margie laughs and waves until Lyn vanishes from the garden. Then she turns to Elsey. Elsey looks like she is smiling too. Margie holds her face and kisses her nose.

You are a clever, clever dog, Margie says. She winds the window down so Elsey can sniff the breeze.

Margie pulls out onto the street. She cannot quite believe what Elsey has done. How is it that Elsey found T?

Driving along the coast road with the windows down, Margie inhales the salty air and feels her lungs expanding. A song she has never heard but likes the sound of is playing on the radio. She turns the volume up, takes in the emerald water, the palm trees, the handsome profile of her dog. She thinks of Lyn and T.

Cyclists stream past her and it occurs to Margie that this day marks twelve months exactly since she arrived here. The same cycling race was on the weekend she drove in. Twelve whole months of Margie licking her wounds. And what about this past day? She's danced with a beautiful stranger, lost her dog, found her dog, met Lyn and T.

At home, Margie cleans every surface and Elsey follows her from room to room. Downstairs in the laundry, Margie approaches the mountain of clothes she has been ignoring all week. She goes through the pockets because she is forever leaving tissues in them. In the pocket of her work pants she finds your hair, rolled up, pressed flat, bunched together with an elastic band. She stands in the laundry and holds it for a while. She will make a little altar for you upstairs, she thinks. A place in her house where she can light a candle and wish that you are safe.

When Margie has finished cleaning and hanging out the clothes, she feeds Elsey a kangaroo bone and orders home delivery for herself.

She sits on the day bed and eats two curries with Elsey sitting on her feet. She asked for extra chilli so she's sweating all over as she eats. She welcomes this cleansing and feels her hangover finally shift. She drinks two litres of water and puts herself to bed, with Elsey beside her.

All night Margie is up and down to the bathroom, but she does not mind this feeling of being flushed out, flushed clean. Each time she wakes and lifts herself from the bed, she has the sensation she is emerging from some deeper layer, some forgotten self. And all this time, it is what has sustained her.

31.

HIMALAYAS, UNKNOWN YEAR

Smash it as you go.

That must be another lesson of life, Pema thinks as she picks, pulls and destroys the gardens that now belong to Cho.

You are gone, and there is no sign of your father or Mida. She wonders why it did not occur to her to run away earlier herself.

She is wrecking whatever she can, to spite Cho. A small part of her wants to stay, to see Cho face the mess of it. But now her hands are blistered and her stomach aches and there's still one horse in the stable for her to claim. She's surprised Cho or some opportunistic neighbour hasn't already taken it.

She collects her bag and a blanket for the horse. In the stable, she saddles the horse and mounts it. Then she rides out. Past the house, past the patchwork of fields. She feels no sentimental thread pulling her back.

She rides in the direction of Lhakyi's house.

Now there must be no second-guessing herself. She must find a way to say goodbye to this woman she loved, even though it is already too late.

Past Cho's farm, past newly harvested fields, past the charnel ground, Pema finally approaches the rise to Lhakyi's house. She remembers them as little girls, climbing the rocky terrace, perching on top of the escarpment, dreaming of how much better their lives would be when they could spend every day together.

Pema dismounts, ties her horse loosely to the tree and discovers the house is deserted. She knocks on the door and wonders if the gossip is true – that in her dying days, Lhakyi's husband deserted her. She imagines Teshi has escaped with you, but she cannot imagine he would have left his mother alone.

There is no one to ask permission of, so she climbs the rocky terrace behind the house and sits. She recalls the very last time she and Lhakyi sat there. They were not talking about their lives together. Pema was, in fact, telling Lhakyi what her mother had said, that she was not to see her again because she was an untouchable. Pema only told her because she had thought it would unite them against the world, that it would bring them closer. Instead, it drove them apart.

Her feeling is the same now as it was then. Her heart shrinking inside her chest, the sorrow of the wrong words spoken at the wrong time, feeling their great unlived life disappearing from her sight.

Pema stands and takes in the view over the ridge. How much vaster it had all seemed when they were children. Fields blooming with every colour and every kind of flower. All she can see now are fields stripped by the wind.

She cannot believe her chance to be with Lhakyi never came again, when that was all she ever prayed for at her altar. She cannot believe that a future life that felt so vibrant, so real, could suddenly cease to exist.

So where did that life go?

32.

DARWIN, PRESENT DAY

When Margie wakes, Elsey is snoring beside her on the floor. Margie peels herself from the bed and tiptoes quietly to the door. Elsey raises her head and when Margie puts her finger to her lips, Elsey sighs and closes her eyes again.

Margie considers the public pool in Nightcliff the only safe place to swim in her area. She's surrounded by turquoise ocean, but she's only ever dipped her toe in. She cannot understand why any sane person would ever choose to swim anywhere knowing there are crocodiles and stingers in the water – that can kill you.

Margie pays the entry fee to the pool and ignores the sign, PLEASE SHOWER BEFORE SWIMMING. She wants the sensation of plunging in, a sheet of water meeting her skin, her temperature plummeting. She straps her goggles to her head and dives in. Laps of freestyle in the slow lane. She's halfway into her third lap when another swimmer overtakes her, kicking too close to her face. Margie duck dives beneath the lane rope and continues her slow laps in the open pool.

A heavily pregnant woman is paddling in circles, buoyed by two tubes of coloured foam that Margie has now learnt are called pool noodles, because they sell them at the counter. The woman's children are running on the concrete and bombing into the water. With yellow floaties around their arms and candy-striped rings around their middles, they look unsinkable. Their mother is making a game of paddling away from them. They squeal as they try to swim after her.

Margie attempts to swim around them but when one of the children does another bomb and his foot collides with Margie's, she realises she's not going to be able to do the slow, rhythmic laps she wants to.

Grabbing hold of the railings, Margie pulls herself out of the pool and then rolls out her towel in the shade. Sunglasses on, her head propped against her arm, she watches the pregnant woman and her children. Soon, the mother has had enough of the game and is wading to the edge of the pool. Heaving herself out of the water, she has a hand on each railing and torrents of water spill from her belly and thighs.

The great golden orb spider comes to Margie's mind, the one she saw weaving her web across Bitter Springs. Her spiderlings have hatched and are trailing behind her. And now she's buying them hot chips.

Margie lies back on her towel, puts her shirt over her head.

The life of a mother was never one she craved. Her wife, on the other hand, wanted it more than anything. So they found a donor – a friend who worked from home and lived in the same apartment block. Overnight, it seemed, their shared calendar, which had once been full of music festivals, friends' birthday parties and overseas trips, was taken over by red and green stripes indicating the different stages of her wife's fertility.

What followed was her wife weeing in cups, narrowing in on her ovulation time with little cardboard strips. Margie began to double-wash any cup she drank from. When the strip showed a bright line, one of them would ring up their neighbour and he would appear within the hour with a turkey baster wrapped in a pillowcase or a tea towel.

Margie would have preferred never to have to unwrap the baster or to touch it when it was warm. But she would do it if her wife asked her to.

There were so many unsuccessful attempts to fall pregnant, but Margie didn't feel crushed that they would not have children after all, that their life could return to normal. She began making plans for them to spend three weeks in Portugal. She even booked tickets and surprised her wife – on the very same day her wife peed on another strip and discovered she was pregnant.

Margie was flooded with guilt. How was it that she wanted to go to Portugal more than she wanted a child? She didn't tell anyone this, especially not her wife. She kept it to herself, sealed it up, but she was paranoid that she would somehow transmit this feeling to the unborn child.

They confirmed the pregnancy with a blood test and an ultrasound, and when they got home, they stuck the ultrasound image to the fridge and her wife drank her last glass of champagne.

Margie looked at the image every morning as she drank her coffee before work. She wanted to find a way to relate to it somehow, to form a connection. But the more she looked at it, the more it looked like a lost planet than an actual human life form.

Margie worked in the emergency department at the time. She felt constantly frayed and wanted to take some time off. But now her wife was pregnant, Margie would soon need to be the provider. At least for twelve months. She started taking on extra shifts and her wife talked her into cancelling their overseas trip so the money could go towards thoughtful adjustments to their apartment and their new organic diet, which was already costing them a fortune.

When they went for a scheduled ultrasound at fourteen weeks, there was no heartbeat to find. Her wife was disbelieving. But what Margie didn't tell her was that the night before the ultrasound, she'd dreamt of a bright full moon blinking out, and she knew that the life was now gone.

In the weeks that followed the miscarriage, Margie was as tender as she knew how to be. She made bone broths, put flowers in vases, bought the expensive lemon myrtle-scented candles her wife liked and ran her hot baths with magnesium salts. She gave her every gift she could think of. And time. And space.

But it wasn't enough.

Margie sits up, finds her phone in her bag, looks up 'Lyn anti-ageing face massage Darwin' and presses 'call'.

Hello, Lyn speaking.

Margie is suddenly flustered. She expected to leave Lyn a message, not for her to immediately answer the phone.

Lyn! Hi. I thought I'd get your message bank, says Margie, adrenaline coursing through her. *It's Margie. From yesterday.*

Oh, Margie. Hi. How's Elsey? Is everything okay?

Yeah. Everything is great. Elsey's at home sleeping in the air-conditioning. I don't have to be at work until nine-thirty tonight, and I'm thinking maybe I do need an anti-ageing face massage.

You're in luck. I'm booked out for the next three weeks, but I've had a cancellation this morning.

Really?

Can you be here in fifteen?

Or even less, says Margie.

Margie throws everything into her bag, gets into her car, and in six minutes' flat she is pushing through the jasmine-covered gate and standing again at Lyn's door.

Oh my god, you are made of knots, says Lyn.

Margie is face down on the massage table. From the moment she stepped into Lyn's therapy room, with its ambient music and salt lamps, she felt every muscle in her body clench. Lyn had looked at her face under a bright light and declared that what she really needed was a full-body massage. She mentioned something about her lymphatic system, but Margie didn't take it in. Face down, looking into a hole at a single frangipani floating in a bowl, she wonders what she was thinking.

How long will this take?

We've got one hour.

Okay, says Margie.

She tries to calm herself. Some people must find this soothing.

Margie flinches as Lyn wipes her feet with a hot, damp cloth.

So, you're booked up for three weeks? says Margie, trying to distract herself.

Yes. Take three deep breaths for me.

Margie breathes a shallow breath.

And again, says Lyn as she wipes down Margie's skin.

I have something to confess, says Margie.

That didn't take long.

This is my very first massage. Like, in my whole life.

Lyn laughs. *Don't worry, I'm very good.* Lyn presses her warm hands into Margie's shoulder blades.

I have no doubt you are, but have you ever tried massaging a plank?

Aside from the drunk dancing with Izzy the Brazilian soccer player, no woman or man has touched Margie in over a year. In fact, she can't even remember the last time someone has touched her as tenderly as Lyn is touching her now. What if Lyn begins to massage some part of her body where all her feelings are locked up? What if Margie falls to pieces in front of her?

They only met yesterday.

Talk, Margie thinks. Just talk your way through it.

Did you ever meet Bird's mother? Margie asks as Lyn runs her hands along her spine.

Mia, says Lyn. *Not much of a mother. She acts more like an irresponsible older sister from what T tells me. I tried to meet her. T wouldn't tell me where she lived because he knew I would want to interfere. So I followed him one night. Bird lives quite close to here. It was late, Bird was waiting for him out the front of her house and they kept walking, so I followed them.*

Like a stalker.

Yep, like a stalker. Do you know Bird goes around doing graffiti on the streets? That's her thing. I thought that's what they were up to and I was preparing myself for some sort of citizen's arrest. But they kept walking. I followed them into the bush. They ended up at a waterhole, got undressed and swam. I thought I was about to witness something awkward, but they just got dressed again and T walked her home.

A bit of an anti-climax, says Margie.

Lyn laughs.

The next day, I drove over there to talk to her mother about Bird sneaking out. T told me she studied yoga and sold jewellery online or something. I knocked on the door and the sleazy boyfriend answered. He looks like a pimp. I asked him where Bird's mother was and he said, 'Who's asking?' I said, 'Bird is a friend of my son's.' And he told me her mother wasn't available. Then he closed the door in my face.

That's weird.

He's not the kind of guy you would want in the house with your teenage daughter, let me put it that way. And then it dawned on me. Bird sneaking out was probably her way of getting away from this creep and whatever was going on between him and her mother.

But you didn't want her here?

Lyn presses her hands into the base of Margie's spine. *Take another breath. You won't break.*

Margie exhales.

No, I didn't want her here. She's not homeless. She lives in a lovely house, she goes to a private school, she's always got new art supplies. In some ways, she has more advantages than T.

You and T live in a lovely house, Lyn.

I work really hard for it, Margie.

Have you thought about reporting the boyfriend?

I asked T if Jerome had ever touched Bird in any way and he said no. He said he was a perv. I mean, can you report a perv? I know this sounds harsh, but I want my son to have a good life. I think Bird is troubled. And T can never say no to her.

Why? says Margie.

He thinks it's his job to protect her. And if something happened to her, I don't think he would ever forgive himself.

Lyn lifts Margie's shoulders off the table and wraps Margie's arms behind her back. Margie can feel her rib cage widening and she tries to focus on letting in more breath. She breathes as Lyn pulls, but then something inside her feels like it will split.

Okay, that's enough now.

But we're not even halfway there.

I'm done, says Margie, pushing herself up from the table.

Your body is incredibly tense. You could really benefit from massage.

Margie pulls the towel around her. *You wouldn't be the first person to say that.*

You did well, Margie. For your first time. Take your time getting dressed. I don't have another client for an hour. Come and have a cup of tea with me and tell me how you got all those knots.

Lyn closes the door behind her. Margie sits on the massage table, looking out the window to the garden. Everything is so well-tended, so perfectly placed. Margie dresses slowly. Her first massage. Or half massage. She got through it. Lyn touched Margie and Margie didn't fall apart.

And then she does.

Driving home from Lyn's, Margie forgets where she is going. And only through a series of automatic turns and surrendering does she finally reach her home. She opens the gates, but the gates themselves seem unfamiliar, like she is entering a stranger's house. Margie walks slowly up the stairs, still unsure of herself, of what is happening. She opens the glass sliding door, and Elsey is there, a familiar loving creature.

Margie lies down on the day bed, holding her dog, stroking her neck. And when Margie finally closes her eyes, memories flood her as a whole other life plays out.

33.

HIMALAYAS, UNKNOWN YEAR

Pema rides away from Lhakyi's house carrying a sharp, tight feeling in her chest, a feeling she has carried for most of her life, which takes all her breath.

She rides east out of the village, across farmlands and through swamps, and soon she feels the warmth of Lhakyi at her back, her chin resting on her shoulder. She remembers their first kiss—

On the first warm day marking spring, Pema knew Lhakyi would be raking the forest floor, collecting pine nuts. It was something they had done together when they were children. Pema's missing had become unbearable, so on that warm day she rode to the forest and waited for Lhakyi. Sure enough, Lhakyi arrived, but when Pema approached her, she froze, like she was caught in the sights of some dangerous animal.

Pema stepped back and began looking for the small seeds herself. They did not speak that day. But the next day when Pema returned, Lhakyi was there again. On the third day, they collected seeds side by side, and on the fourth day, Lhakyi allowed Pema's touch.

When they finally kissed, they discovered they could breathe together, that their chests could rise and fall as one. Standing in the sunlight, Pema traced Lhakyi's collarbones with her fingertips and they made a promise to meet there every spring. Collecting seeds would be their cover.

Then the cold weather came, and there was no safe way for them to be together, or to touch. Pema learnt to shift her body into the memory of Lhakyi's, and she wore it through the winter like a warm coat, and everything in her life seemed so much better than it was. She imagined their future – the two of them together in a stone house, working the fields, bone-tired, falling into each other's arms at the end of the day. Thinking of it brought blood to Pema's cheeks.

She began to live for the promise of the next spring, and fantasised about a time when they could finally weave their lives together.

When the warm weather returned, Pema rode to the forest again. But Lhakyi was not there. Pema returned every day and collected pine nuts, just as she had done the year before, just as they had planned.

But Lhakyi did not return.

Pema rides, watching waterbirds rise from the tall grasses. She speaks aloud as if Lhakyi is really with her. She tells her all the things she has wanted to tell her and should have told her sooner.

Soon the day signals its end and Pema pulls up her horse at the edge of a lake. She lies down. She can see Lhakyi lying beside her and she reaches for a flower to place in her hand.

This is her goodbye.

When Pema wakes, it does not hurt to breathe. She mounts her horse and continues riding east, but then feels certain of what this road will yield – a version of herself wandering forever. Pema asks for a sign because she believes in signs. She feels her horse begin to plod beneath her, and it is Lhakyi's voice she hears:

Go home. Go home.

The home that comes to Pema's mind is not the home she wrecked. It would already be taken over by Cho. Pema's wide, deliberate turning of her horse is towards the place she has dreamt of living in since she was a child.

Lhakyi's home.

34.

DARWIN, PRESENT DAY

Monday, 9.25 pm. Margie arrives at Jay's office to sign in for her night shift.

Wow, Margie, says Jay. *You look totally transformed.*

Do I?

Amazing what a few days off can do.

I needed it.

Okay, first things first. There's a couple of police officers waiting for you downstairs. They called earlier. They want to pick up Bird's things, take them in as evidence. Ask you a few questions. You were in emergency that night, weren't you?

I was. I tended to Bird before and after her operation.

Great, I'm hoping you know where her things are?

I do.

I can't find them. Can you take care of it?

Sure. Have they found her yet?

They picked her up on the beach on Saturday morning.

Margie feels overwhelmed with worry for you. She takes the stairs and attempts to steel herself before she faces the police and their questions. She finds them waiting near the reception.

Margie Shapiro?

Yes.

We have a few questions about the day of Bird's escape, the officer says.

Sure, ask away.

The guard reports that you were the last person to see Bird.

I don't know if I was the last person or not.

What time was that?

It was just before I started my shift, around 1 pm.

Was Bird in her bed when you saw her?

She was.

Did you check on her or try to wake her?

No. I saw that she was asleep, so I kept going.

Is it usual that you would check on a patient before your shift?

No. But I was concerned for her. She had no visitors. She seemed to have no one.

Right. We need to collect her clothes and her belongings. It's all evidence now.

Evidence she was shot? Margie says.

Evidence, the police officer repeats.

So she's in juvenile prison now?

She is. She's on remand.

No bail?

It wasn't offered.

Can you tell the prison nurses that Bird needs to be on oral antibiotics immediately? And probably painkillers too. Can you make sure you do?

The officer nods and begins to type a note on her phone. Margie leans towards her, to try to see what she is typing.

Could you go and grab that evidence for us now?

Just give me a few minutes, Margie says.

In the storage area, Margie climbs a ladder to reach the plastic bag she has tagged with your name and date of admission. She slid the bag onto the top shelf where no one else could find it. She wonders why she has this instinct to protect you, even your belongings.

Walking back to the police officers, she feigns a cool efficiency and hands over the bag. One of the officers holds up the bag and inspects what's inside.

Was there anything else? The officer who arrested her mentioned there was a bag slung over her shoulder.

It was a cloth satchel, says Margie. *It's rolled up in there with her bloodied clothes.*

Was there anything in it?

Her student ID card, a purse, a rolled-up t-shirt, a few pens, from what I can remember.

It's all there?

Yes, officer, says Margie.

Did you search the pockets?

Nothing in the pockets.

What about a phone?

Oh, the phone. Margie panics at the thought of the incriminating things you may have stored on it. *Yes, the phone is in there too.*

Thanks, nurse, the officer says. *We'll take your mobile number. You may be called up to give a written statement.*

Margie gives her number, watches the officers leave and admonishes herself for not thinking to take your phone as well. She could have thrown it in the creek and no one would have ever known.

Twelve hours later, Margie finishes her night shift. She drives home and lights a candle on the small altar she has made. On the altar she's placed your sketchbook and your hair, which she has plaited into one piece. She gets into bed and has the thought that the police won't be able to unlock your phone without a passcode and if they insist on it you can pretend to have forgotten. This puts her at ease. Elsey jumps on the bed next to her, and they both sleep a deep, restful sleep. Even the neighbour's dog does not wake them.

At 4 pm, Margie wakes, notices a missed call. It's the same number that called her on Sunday morning – T.

Thanks for calling back, he says.

Of course. What's up?

Do you really want to know about Bird?

I do. I mean, I think I do.

I want to tell you because I think you might be someone who can help her.

Margie is silent. There are too many conflicting feelings she can't explain.

Bird doesn't have anyone else, Margie.

Where are you?

I'm still at school. Can you pick me up? he says. *There's something I want to show you.*

Sure. My car is bright orange. You won't miss it. I'm on my way.

T is waiting at the front of his school. He waves to Margie as she pulls into the pick-up zone.

Cool car, he says, sliding in. Elsey licks his face from the back seat, and he laughs.

I love my fair lady.

What are we listening to? he says, making a face like the music is causing him physical pain.

The radio. I'm not even sure what station it's on.

Do you mind if I plug in my phone and play something else?

I would love that.

What do you like to listen to?

T, I really don't want to tell you. I'm trying to re-educate myself.

You're from Melbourne, right?

How do you know that?

Mum told me.

Did she? Margie feels her face flush.

T scrolls through the music on his phone. *Okay. I'll play you a band called Time for Dreams from Melbourne. I think they're your vibe. Kind of haunting and lonely and hopeful all at the same time.*

Margie wonders if this is really her vibe. A strange, sultry sound melts out of the speakers, and she decides that it is.

I like it, she says. *So where are we headed?*

Into the city. We'll try to park near the mall.

What's near the mall?

One of Bird's murals, he says. *It will help me explain some things to you.*

Margie and T travel in silence for a while and the song carries them along. How different Margie feels from only a few days ago when she was frantically searching for you and T. Now he is in her car, directing her to you, or something of you.

How did you meet Bird? Margie asks.

We crashed into each other – I mean, literally. T laughs. *She was walking along the footpath, probably thinking about what she was going to paint. She stepped one way and I stepped the same way, and then wham! We just collided in space.*

That sounds very memorable, says Margie.

Yeah. She is very memorable. She was carrying a roller brush and a tin of paint. I asked her what she was doing and she said, 'Something illegal.' So, I said, 'Can I come?' And she said, 'Sure.' We walked to an old factory building and I helped her paint an undercoat on an outside wall. She told me it helped the spray paint go on. And then we hung out for about the last nine months. I know nine months probably doesn't sound like a long time to you. But it felt like a long time to me.

What do you make of her mother, Mia?

Mia is a flake. Not really mother material. Bird was brought up by her grandmother. And when she died, Bird had to come up here and live with Mia because she's got no one else.

What about Mia's boyfriend?

That guy is a menace. Bird can't stand him and neither can I. Mia inherited some money from Bird's grandmother and I think he's taking her for a ride.

T points to a free car park. *You should take that one there*, he says.

Margie parks and puts Elsey on her lead, and T directs them through the mall. They pass people sitting at the front of cafes under big umbrellas. Margie wonders if anyone looking at them would think T was her son.

T leads them into an alleyway behind a supermarket. They pass a row of roller doors and industrial bins and then he says, *Here they are. The girls.*

Margie immediately recognises the girls from your sketchbook. Arms linked, their heads turned over their shoulders, they look intimidating painted so large. They seem to be glaring down at Margie, challenging her.

T points to the end of the alleyway. *I sat there for five nights while Bird painted, to make sure no one hassled her and we didn't get arrested.*

How did she manage to paint them so high?

We rolled that bin over and she stood on top of it. And when that wasn't high enough she'd stack crates on top of that.

Do you know why she always draws and paints these girls? asks Margie.

She told me she's painted them since she was a kid, says T. *She's convinced herself that they're real. She thinks she saw them on the news the other night. You know, the girls' riot in juvie? That's why she's there. She really believes the girls can explain some mystery of her life . . .*

As T talks, Margie isn't sure her legs will hold her. She leans against the wall. She needs to feel something solid against her back. Elsey tugs at her lead but Margie doesn't have the strength to hold her.

Do you want me to take her for a quick walk? says T.

Oh, she'd love that.

Just around the block.

Okay. See you in a bit.

Margie crouches down and watches T and Elsey turn out onto the street and disappear. She takes in the girls, searches their eyes, feels the gaps and mysteries of her own life opening up. She's felt this before – what you call the void, Margie calls the abyss – where there are too many feelings to fathom, or express. Under the gaze of the girls, she feels pressed to name what she has been avoiding in herself: who she truly is.

If it took her a second or a lifetime, she does not know, but in the alleyway looking up at your mural, Margie finally understands herself. Her ex-wife was right, she had shut down. She had shut down on herself and everyone around her. Because Margie Shapiro is afraid of life, and even more afraid of love. And she has always been.

35.

HIMALAYAS, UNKNOWN YEAR

You hear a crack, and the ceaseless moving of the cart comes to a sudden, jerking halt. Some of the girls are moaning in their discomfort, but any sounds they make are muffled by the cloth binding their mouths. For now, you remain quiet as the drivers launch from their seats and curse the broken wheel. They move along the cart, roughly untying the girls' hands roped to the slats.

They grab the first girl within reach. You don't yet know her name. You don't know anybody's name because no one has spoken. One of the drivers locks his forearms around her chest, while the other scoops his hands beneath her knees. Your body shudders. It is the same way they tipped you into the hessian sack.

They turn the girl out onto the ground and continue until each one of you has been arranged in a line beside her.

The drivers turn their attention to fixing the broken wheel. You attempt to stand, but your legs are like reeds in a river and they collapse beneath you. Seeing your attempt, another girl tries and fails. Another girl manages to get to her feet, but soon she is back on her knees.

The sun bears down. The girl beside you shields her face from it, but then her arm begins to spasm. She glares at it as if it is someone else's arm stuck on her body, as if it is a stranger's.

Pins and needles run up and down your legs. You close your eyes and do your best to breathe slow, deep breaths.

You don't want to see yourself as one of them. You don't want to imagine you are linked in any way to these girls who are whimpering and twitching in the sun. Wherever the drivers are taking you, whatever cruelty they have in store, you cannot accept this as your fate, even though you know there is no one to save you. No one even knows where you are.

The drivers fix the wheel and light a small fire to make a mealy porridge which they feed to you all, a spoonful at a time. The porridge is gritty, but you eat hungrily. The driver spills it down your chin and looks at you in disgust. The sun dries the porridge into a thick, hard crust. Meagre though it is, the porridge is sustenance, and it gives you energy to find some coordinated movement, enough to wipe your chin on your shoulder, but not to clean away the mess.

We need water, you say. You are surprised to hear your own voice. It sounds strong and clear.

You only had to ask, smirks one of the drivers before leaning into the tray to retrieve a waterskin. Resting it on his shoulder, he walks along the ragged line of girls, splashing water into their open mouths, and when he reaches you there is only a trickle left. But it is enough to wet your throat.

Where are you taking us? says one of the girls. But her question only prompts the drivers to bind your mouths again and load you back in the cart.

The wheels creak, and the cart jerks forward. You flick your eyes over the girls as you all sway from side to side. Their wide eyes hardly blink. They are afraid. The bind around your mouth is tied too tight. The cloth is cutting into the corners.

You wonder if they are thinking what you are thinking. That the life of servitude you were trying to escape has finally captured you, and you will be sold off as someone's slave.

You close your eyes and take yourself back to the Pilgrim's Trail. Only days before, you were walking with Teshi, arms linked, marvelling at the dust from pilgrims' feet, the way it caught the sunlight and streaked through the trees.

Then you see yourself back at the Holy Mountain, fishing the dead girl's body out of the lake. You are kneeling and examining the detail of her jacket. You are tugging on the red thread of the sleeve and trying to comprehend . . .

Had you travelled so far for your future to be revealed, and then, revealed, decided you did not want to see it?

36.

DARWIN, PRESENT DAY

Three days after you collapsed in the bathroom, you are released from the infirmary. Still, nobody will speak to you, only the guards on occasion to give you an order. You learn quickly that to do anything in here, you must join a line, and you are careful not to get in anyone's way again or cause any more trouble. So you wait, each time, to be the last in line.

The nurse in the infirmary has deemed the antibiotics she gave you effective. Your shoulder is healing and you are well enough to work. You are assigned to what the guards call 'easy work' – wrapping pretty tissue paper around toilet rolls with a group of other girls who won't speak to you either.

At breakfast, lunch and dinner you are marched to the shed, and you sit far away from everyone. You wonder how long you can survive this pattern on repeat. You wonder if anyone outside is thinking of you or misses you. As far as you know, you've had no letters or calls.

You think about what Margie told you in hospital, about people not remembering things as a way to protect themselves from memories that are overwhelming, that sometimes it is better to forget.

It is clear from the blank looks the five girls have been giving you these past days that you are a complete stranger to them. They don't recognise you at all.

Remembering what you have remembered, that you were all kidnapped from the Holy Mountain, is nothing anyone would want to remember or be reminded of. What would you say? *You think your life is bad now . . .*

Your very reason for being here, your instinct that the five girls might be able to tell you something about your life, or hand you some missing piece, now seems desperate and deluded. Why did it ever seem so important to solve the mystery of yourself, of the void you carry, when each remembrance feels like another load of trauma?

In wanting to solve the mystery of yourself, you have sabotaged the education your grandmother paid for, the generosity of Mrs Whitehead, the chance of a relationship with T.

You wonder if that is all there ever was to discover. That in the end, you are just like Mia – always ruining a good thing.

Another lunchtime in prison and you feel yourself growing invisible. You have sat down alone again, far away from anyone, and realised you have forgotten to collect a plastic spoon. The simple act of collecting one seems epic and not something you can muster the courage to do – to walk across the room of girls who don't seem to see you or want to acknowledge you.

You tell yourself you have only yourself now and that you must focus on the things that are in front of you, the things that are real. So you eat the food with your fingers, concentrating on the warmth of it, on the feeling of mush in your mouth. And as you watch the food disappear on the tray, you take it as some proof of your existence.

You tear up the slice of white bread and push pieces of it into your mouth. You chew loudly, like a cow. Why not? Nobody can hear you.

You peel back the foil lid from the plastic orange juice cup and check the date. You don't know the date exactly, but you know it's not 2023. You gulp it down anyway. It will probably turn your guts, you think. You might vomit. But won't that be more proof that you do exist?

Your tray is suddenly empty. You have eaten too fast. You have an urge to get back to your room, but you are not allowed to go anywhere unless a guard tells you to. You tap your legs against the table and crack your fingers and try not to look at the other girls.

But you can't help it. You flick your eyes around the shed. The five girls are sitting at a table together. You look away. Maybe you will play the game they are playing and pretend they don't exist.

But then out of the corner of your eye you see Bambi get up. She is walking in your direction and no guard is apprehending her. Your guts churn. You search her hands to see if she is holding any sharpened cutlery. She stops on the other side of the table.

Bird? she says.

That's me.

You've been feeling no good?

I had an infection in my shoulder.

You got shot?

I did.

So where's your mob?

I don't have a mob.

Where's your country? she says.

I don't have a country.

Well, where are you from?

I grew up in Sydney, but I moved to Darwin about a year ago.

You Koori or what?

No. My mother's white. I think my father's Indian.

Indian? Like, from India?

Yep.

Is Bird your real name?

It is.

Don't you want to ask me what my name is?

I know your name. You're Bambi.

How do you know that?

I just know it.

Well, we've been asking around and no one here knows who you are. No one has ever heard of you.

I've never been in prison before.

Darwin's a small place.

I've only been here a year.

Bambi is looking at your empty tray.

You shouldn't eat the mashed potato.

Why?

It's how they keep us sedated. Sometimes they just stir that shit right in.

Thanks for telling me. I'm trying to clear my head.

Bambi sits down opposite you and places her hands on either side of your tray. She leans in, examines your face.

Bird?

Your heart quickens. You think she may have recognised you.

Is it a nickname or what?

It's just the name my mother gave me. She's a bit of a . . .

Hippy?

Yeah. How did you get the name Bambi?

It's what my nanna called me, 'cause of my big old brown eyes. 'Like a deer in the headlights,' she said. And it stuck.

Bambi scoops up her long black hair and ties it in a knot at her neck.

Can I see your scar? she asks.

You tug at your t-shirt and expose a waterproof patch that the nurse put over it.

What's underneath that?

You peel back the edges of the plaster. The skin is pink and purple, puckering around the wound.

I only know one other person who's been shot by the police. My cousin. And he's dead.

I'm sorry, you say. And then you both sit looking at each other, neither of you saying a word, until the prison guard yells that it is time to get back to your work groups.

Why don't you come and sit with us tonight? says Bambi. *You can meet the other girls.*

I'd like that, you say.

Mealtimes are the same every day, but aside from that, you don't know what you are doing from one hour to the next. There is no schedule, no bulletin board, no communication of any kind to tell you how your hours will be filled. There is only the pattern of days and repetitions that you must memorise for yourself with the understanding that any of it, at any time, can change.

In the afternoon, you are moved on from wrapping tissue paper around toilet rolls to working in the laundry. At first you think this job is about the worst you could do – handling other girls' dirty clothes with their blood and occasional shit stains that implicate all of you.

But then you are pulling the laundry out of the industrial dryers, untangling singlets from elasticised bras, shaking out static, smelling detergent, sorting things into piles. And there is a fleeting feeling that with your own effort and with your own hands, you can make something better than it was when you began.

Is this why women are always doing laundry? you wonder. To feel that things can be made better, even in tiny and insubstantial increments of cloth?

At dinner, you sit with the five girls at their table. You feel giddy to be so close to them again, to recognise them all and yet be so unknown to them. Amidst all their talking and their laughter, you want to say, *Don't you remember?* and *Why don't you remember?*

But then you feel the cost of remembering yourself – this cellular disappointment that things don't ever change, not in any way that matters. Life just repeats and repeats.

So you do not say a word. You eat and do your best to keep one life separate from the other. To take in their smiles, their small talk, their complaints about the food. This is all there is between you, this one shared reality. You tell yourself it has to be enough.

37.

HIMALAYAS, UNKNOWN YEAR

In the cart, the dry heat of the day and the cold of the night are your only measures of time, and the cramps accumulating in your body.

The drivers take turns to sleep. They only stop when they want to eat or piss and that is the only time you are allowed to relieve yourself. The drivers lift you out of the cart and you must squat awkwardly together with the girls, trying to balance on legs that are slow to get back their feeling. The drivers turn their backs to you but there is still the humiliation of being witnessed by each other, as you groan and sway, and then catch the smell of whatever it is coming out of you.

When the driver pulls up, you are expecting to be lifted out and lined up again. But they don't lift you out. They remove the strip of cloth still binding your mouth and tie them around your eyes instead. You guess this is so you cannot see where you are going, or how you might leave.

I'm so cold, says one of the girls.

The drivers finish blindfolding you all, and then you feel them stepping over you and a weight of blanket being dumped on your legs. It smells like a wet animal.

Beneath the tightly bound cloth, your eyes feel like hot orbs. The wheels creak over the road and you can feel the girl next to you shivering as she sobs. You wonder if you are being driven in circles.

When you wake, the wheels of the cart are clattering over cobblestones, and the air smells of something sweet. You can hear women's voices.

The cart jolts to a stop. Soft hands sweep over your face. Someone is touching your ear, your neck, your arm. You strain to get away from them, but you are wedged between a basket and another girl, and there is nowhere to escape.

Someone unties your blindfold and announces, *There are six of them.*

Another woman pushes her face into yours, saying, *And they are all in good health.*

And then there are many more faces, lit up by lanterns, appearing out of the dark and leaning into the cart. With their sudden presence, their closeness, you feel ashamed – ashamed to be one of six girls packed like animals, sitting in your own filth and stink.

But the women are all smiling as they hold the lanterns above their heads. You can see they are wearing long, thick cloaks. You think that they must be nuns. But they wear their hair long and look much better fed than any nuns you have ever seen.

Two of them help down the only other girl with a shaved head. She is sitting at the front of the cart. As soon as they hold her, she begins to sob.

You are safe here, the women assure her. *We will look after you.* They wrap their coats around her and lead her away.

The other women step forward in pairs, as if this is some organised ceremony, or something they have rehearsed, each of them helping a girl from the cart and leading her up the path.

You are the last one to be helped down. They reach for you, and you shuffle away.

We only want to help you, one of the women says.

I'll help myself, you say. And you move to the edge, but you are still not certain about your legs. You swing them over the cart and flex your feet until you can feel a strength returning to them. Then you plant your feet on the cobbled path and take your first step.

We are so happy you are here, says one of them.

It wasn't my choice, you say. The stones are cold on your bare feet, and you focus on placing one foot in front of the other.

I'm sorry your journey was uncomfortable, the other woman says.

You stop and regard them both. They are holding lanterns by their sides. With their long hair and cloaks, they are hardly distinguishable from each other.

Do you know we were drugged and then kidnapped? you say.

We understand, says one of them. *But you'll soon find out that you are one of the lucky ones.*

The women walk behind you as you shuffle along the uneven path. A monastery – or a nunnery, you suppose – looms on the right side of it, a terraced garden on the left. You can see rosebushes that are lit by lanterns hanging from poles. The scent of the roses is what you must have smelt as you were driven in through the gates.

You'll need to visit the bathhouse first. The woman points to a small wooden house beside the monastery. Steam is curling from its open windows. The thought of being clean, of washing away your filth and stench, has you hurrying along, ignoring the pain of your cold, bare feet.

Inside the bathhouse are deep copper tubs filled with hot water. The women have sprinkled rose petals on the surface.

Soak the journey from your bones, says one of the women as you peel off your robes. You step into the bath and the steam rolls up over you, concealing you from the others. You want to imagine that your body, your life will be so very different and distinct from these other girls. These girls who were all so compliant as they were helped out of the cart and led along the path, whose fate and yours have been mistakenly drawn together.

You sink into the water and remember Bird Springs. The fleeting peace when your mind and your body settled in the one place. The tinkling of sand. Your heart beating under water. How restored you felt in that moment. How different the world and everyone in it seems to you now.

You submerge, imagining every particle of dust, every fear you have felt, washed from you. You hold your breath. Whatever it is that is going to happen next, you want to delay it.

You soak yourself until all your skin is wrinkled, and a woman hands you a towel and a nightgown.

You must be hungry by now, she says.

You are. You look up from the bath. The other girls have gone.

Get dressed and follow me, she says.

The woman leads you inside the monastery to a dining hall where an older woman with long white hair is standing at the head of the table. She opens her arms wide as you enter and says, *Welcome, welcome.*

She invites you to sit down. Silence falls over the room as you pull out a chair. The white-haired woman nods and smiles as if she recognises you, but you are certain you have never seen her before. She joins her hands together.

Girls, she says. *You must all be wondering where you are.*

You look at each girl sitting at the table, and you take them in – the one with the shaved head, the one with the long black hair, the one with the curly hair, the small one, the tall one – but none of them will return your gaze. They are all staring wide-eyed at the white-haired woman, transfixed.

You will learn so much more in the coming days and weeks, she says. *But what you need to know is that you are safe. We are your sisters and we have saved you from the most awful fate. The men who kidnapped you trade in girls. And they will not stop their trade, not for us begging, not for anything. It is too lucrative a trade. We have used all the resources we have to buy you back, all six of you, to bring you here, safe with us.*

And then she pauses before she says, *Because otherwise, you would have been sold off as slaves.*

You consider the woman's words, her calm authority. You have never heard a woman speak like this. Even the silence in the room feels like it is hers to command.

You are our Little Sisters and we are your Big Sisters, and in that is our promise to take care of you, to help you grow your gifts . . . but surely you have all heard enough, she says. *Isn't it time we ate?*

The white-haired woman nods, and so begins a procession of food, the other women carrying silver trays out from the kitchen. It is more food than you have ever seen.

You say yes to everything offered to you until the food is spilling over your plate. Before the women have finished serving, you are scooping it into your mouth. And only when you have eaten everything on your plate do you raise your eyes to look again at the other girls. They keep their heads down. You wonder if they think that by looking at you or each other they will break the spell of what is being offered here, which is already so much more than they have ever known.

Some of the women stand up from the table to clear the plates and others begin to lead you, one by one, out of the dining hall.

Where are we going? you ask the woman who has linked her arm in yours and is steering you down the hall.

To your new room, Little Sister.

Down a wide corridor and up a narrow set of stairs. *Is this a nunnery?* you ask.

She laughs.

Originally it was built as a monastery, but now all the monks are dead and gone. We are not nuns as such, but we are devoted.

Devoted to what? you ask.

To our art.

To your art? you repeat.

We're painters, says the woman. *You will see we are painting every wall in this place.*

You are too tired to ask the woman anything else, so you walk in silence to the end of the corridor. Then she opens a door.

This is your room, she says proudly. *I prepared it myself.*

A lantern blazes on a desk, enough to light up the small room. You see a chair, a shuttered window, a narrow bed pushed against the wall. On the desk is a single rose. Its scent fills the room.

I don't have to share?

No. There are enough rooms for everybody.

You sit on the bed, turning your hands over the soft blanket. Such comforts you have never known.

Sleep well, Little Sister, the woman smiles. *I'll be back to wake you first thing in the morning.*

She closes the door and you slide under the blankets. You watch the lantern light trembling across the ceiling and wonder in what ways you will have to repay these women, what sacrifices they will surely demand of you now that they have saved you from becoming a slave.

38.

DARWIN, PRESENT DAY

Four days a week, you are assigned to a sport or physical activity, and one of those is gym group. None of your girls are in the group, but you do recognise the girl you accidently tripped over on your first day. Her name is Jackie, and she is bashing a medicine ball on one side of the shed. You park yourself far away from her and hide yourself as best you can behind an exercise bike. You don't want to be in Jackie's line of sight. But, with the pounding rhythm, at least you know where she is and where her fists are.

The prison nurse has given you a photocopied piece of paper with yoga exercises to help rehabilitate your shoulder. You roll out a yoga mat, and move slowly between the cat and cow positions and then stretch out in the child's pose. The antibiotics have helped and you now have full movement in your shoulder. You take yourself through the poses, keeping your face a few centimetres from the mat, because it stinks of someone else's foot odour.

You need to build your strength, in case Jackie, or anyone, comes after you. After you stretch, you begin your own repetitions of sit-ups and then you really test your shoulder with push-ups. You try for twenty.

You are face down, so you don't know how long Jackie has been standing over you. You haven't realised that her pounding rhythm has stopped.

You roll over, trying to look relaxed, and stretch your legs along the mat. She's like a wild dog, you think, and you don't want her to sense your fear.

What do you want, Jackie?

How do you know my name?

I overheard the guard saying it earlier.

Who gave you permission to say it?

Nobody.

So don't say it.

What should I call you instead?

Nothing.

Okay. Nothing.

And then she doesn't say anything, she just gives you a sharp kick in your ribs and walks away. You groan, nursing your side. Jackie is already pounding the medicine ball again by the time the guard comes over.

Everything alright here?

Yep, you say. *Everything is fine.*

After gym group you learn that Junk Food Day has been reinstated. And it's the first time since the flood and fire, or 'the riot' as the guards call it, because Junk Food Day is considered a privilege.

You are herded to one of two vending machines in the prison. You watch the girls in front of you step up and hold their heads still as a laser light trains on their eyes and identifies them. When it is your turn, you do the same. A digital screen on the vending machine tells you that in the three weeks you have been in prison, you have earned yourself nine dollars. You can see one packet of salty plums hanging in the top right row of the machine, and you have enough money to buy it.

You plug in the coordinates, A7, and watch a mechanical arm unfold and crunch its metal hand around the packet, and release it into a plastic trough. You crouch down to collect it. Your mouth is already watering. It has been so long since you've tasted a salty plum. But as you reach for the packet, you feel a weight pressing down on your back. It is Jackie pushing you to the floor with her knee.

Hand them over, she says. Her face is in your ear. She has your lobe between her teeth.

You squirm to get away from her. The other girls make an arc of legs around you so the guards cannot see.

The packet of salty plums is in your hand and you manage to tuck it down your shorts, but then Jackie reefs you up to standing and the packet falls straight out.

You both grab for the packet and there is a silent tug of war – silent because if the guards catch you, you will both lose your junk food privileges. But when the packet splits and the plums spill across the floor, the guards seem not to notice or care.

One salty plum rolls near your feet. You pick it up, brush it against your singlet and put it in your mouth. You don't chew it. You will savour it. You pass Jackie, who is scrounging for the rest of them, shoving them into her mouth and her pockets. You wonder who her last target was, and if this is really about you accidentally tripping her over.

You scan the courtyard for Bambi.

She's sitting on top of a table, eating cheese rings with Dev.

What'd you get? asks Bambi.

You open your mouth to show her.

Trade you, she says, wiggling the cheese rings on the ends of her fingers. *Three of these for one of them.*

You sit down beside her. *Sorry, Jackie nicked the rest of them.*

I think she's got it in for you.

I've noticed.

You can have some anyway, Bambi says, offering you the packet of cheese rings. But you are distracted by Jackie, who is now leaning against the fence, her eyes fixed on you, orange drool leaking from the corner of her mouth.

That girl is a beast.

Don't be too harsh on her, says Bambi.

Why? She just stole my salty plums, and this morning she kicked me in the ribs.

Dev and Bambi look at each other.

What? you say.

She's pregnant, says Bambi.

To one of the guards, says Dev.

Which one?

The Germ. She thinks he loves her. And she won't believe us when we tell her that he's tried to make a move on everyone.

That's why we flooded the place, says Dev. *The riot!*

I think he got the message, says Bambi.

Dev shrugs.

Well, he didn't come back after that, did he?

A guard blows the first whistle, which means you have two more minutes before you must stand in line again. You and Bambi watch Dev saunter to the bin and sweep her long arms at the crows congregating around it.

If you really were a bird, says Bambi, *what kind of bird would you be?*

I don't know. Some fidgety little thing with an angry-looking head?

Bambi laughs. *Like a little crimson finch. Yeah, I can see it.*

What would you be?

I'd be a gorgeous black kite. And I'd fly over this place and drop burning sticks into every nasty corner they've ever caged us in.

So you've thought about this?

Yeah. I think about it all the time.

The second whistle blows, and all the girls start tearing at their packets for the last lick of sugar and salt before they have to be in line. You line up behind Bambi, and a prison guard walks along the line counting you all. When they pass you, you lean into Bambi, your head resting in the middle of her back.

Bird! yells another guard, the one with the whistle, the one that everyone calls The Cow. *Straighten up, or I'll straighten up for you.*

All the girls laugh because nothing The Cow says ever makes any sense. She's glowing red in the heat, walking up and down the line, slapping her baton against her hand. Then somebody *moos* and everybody is laughing again. The Cow charges to the end of the line and whacks some unlucky girl across the back of her bare legs with her baton. You don't dare turn around to see who the girl is. But you hope it isn't Jackie.

39.

HIMALAYAS, UNKNOWN YEAR

You sleep a blank, exhausted sleep, and when you open your eyes, you don't know where you are. You are folded in so many soft blankets and only as you unwrap yourself do you remember the night before – arriving in the cart, the smell of roses, the women's faces appearing in the dark.

Out of bed, you flick the latches from the shutters and push your hands against them. They will not open easily so you shove your shoulder into them until you hear vines snapping and feel cold air on your face. Leaning out of the window, you can see the gates, and beyond them, a salt plain, the mountains.

Someone knocks on your door. You close the shutters and quickly move to straighten the blankets on your bed.

Come in, you say.

It is the same smiling woman from the night before who led you to this room, who said she had prepared it for you. She is hugging a pair of boots and a tunic.

Did you sleep well, Little Sister?

I did, you say. It was one of the best sleeps you've had in as long as you can remember.

Well, this makes me happy, she says, holding out the bundle. *These are for you. I think our feet are the same size. But we'll fit you for a new pair soon.*

You try the boots on and they fit well enough. They are warm, lined with some kind of fur.

I'll wait for you outside while you get dressed, she says.

And then what? you ask.

Her eyes light up and her wide smile broadens. *This is a special day for us all, Little Sister. It's the Feast of the Holy Man.*

And what Holy Man is that?

The one who gifted us this place and everything in it. We take him offerings.

I'd like to explore the garden instead, you say.

But it's decided, Little Sister. We'll all be visiting him together.

You sit on the bed, this strange woman's boots on your feet. Her presence in the room makes you feel claustrophobic.

Little Sister?

You can call me Bird.

Can I ask you a favour?

Depends on what it is.

Be like a rose. Open up and things will start to feel better for you.

She closes the door behind her. You wanted her to leave but now you feel stranded in the room.

You dress in the tunic. *Open up and things will start to feel better for you.* You pull up the hood and put your hands in your pockets and survey the room. Should you trust these women because they have given you a good meal and a bed? You contemplate this until the woman taps on the door again.

When you open the door, she claps her hands together and says, *Now you really look like one of us.* You walk along the corridor and when she tries to link her arm into yours, you snap your arm against your body.

The woman leads you back to the long table in the hall and instructs you to sit. The white-haired woman glides in. Her head seems to float far above her shoulders, and she reminds you of a swan. She tucks her arms into her wide sleeves as she surveys you all.

Little Sisters, she begins. *I hope you are well rested.* Her voice sounds honey-coated.

Today is an important day for us all, she continues. *It is the day we honour the Holy Man who first opened his gates to us when so many of us were not much older than you. He called us his Big Sisters. And now you are our Little Sisters, and, as I said last night, in that name is our promise to look after you. Starting with this food we have grown ourselves.*

The table is lined with dome-shaped lids. The Sisters lift them in unison, revealing platters of fruit so artfully arranged you wonder if you are allowed to eat them.

The Big Sister beside you pushes a platter towards you. There is only one fruit on it you can name. The snake fruit. You recognise it by its scaly skin. You take it from the plate and turn it over.

Do you know what happens if you eat too many of these? you ask the Big Sister.

I suppose it will give you a bellyache, she says.

Do you think it could ever make you see things? Cause hallucinations?

The Big Sister considers this while she piles fruit on your plate. *I know some food surely can. Some mushrooms, some herbs. But I've eaten a lot of snake fruit in my time and it's never made me see things. Why don't you try one of everything and then you won't have that problem?*

You peel the skin of the fruit, as the Big Sister points to each thing on your plate. *This one is wild apricot*, she says. *This one here is chutro, raspberries, harad, fig. Eat as much as you want but save one thing as an offering to the Holy Man.*

You make a face.

Is there something wrong, Little Sister?

My mother and sister worshipped at altars and listened to holy men all their lives, and it never did them any good. I think it harmed them.

The Big Sister nods as she chooses an apricot for herself and considers what you have said.

Of course, we can never really know what happens in someone's heart or head, can we?

After you have eaten, the white-haired woman stands and gestures for you all to do the same. The Big Sisters form a line behind her, and the girls – the newly named Little Sisters – form a line behind them. Everyone is carrying a piece of fruit as an offering, even you.

Reluctantly, you follow the line along the corridor, up a staircase that spirals for three levels, until you reach a small room.

As the girls enter ahead of you, you can hear their fast drawn breaths. When you enter the room, you see the walls are painted with intricate murals of the Big Sisters in a garden. The colours shimmer off the walls. Sitting cross-legged on an elevated wooden platform is a bald man in a red robe with rose petals sprinkled at his feet. You presume he is the Holy Man.

The Big Sisters kneel in front of him and you follow their lead, copying their movements as they raise their arms above their heads and move them in waves, in some kind of devotional dance. The Big Sisters rest their hands in their laps and begin to sing.

You stare at the Holy Man. You are sure he is smiling at you, so you smile back. His gaze is intense and you attempt not to blink, so you can catch him blinking. But he doesn't blink. He doesn't even seem to breathe. You trace his smooth face, his neck, his chest, his arms. There is not one hair or blemish on his skin. His palms rest upward on his knees. You follow the line of his crossed legs to his feet. And then you realise one of his toes is missing. It has been chewed off.

Then it dawns on you that the Holy Man is dead. You have the thought that the Holy Man is holey and then you start to laugh and you cannot stop. What is he even made of? Paper and wax? You try to stifle your laugh but it explodes out of you, and then all of the Big Sisters and the girls are turning to look at you.

You feel a hand come down on your shoulder. And another under your armpit. You are being guided by two Big Sisters from the room, back down the stairs and along the corridors in silence, until you are outside in the garden.

They tell you to sit down on a bench.

Why were you laughing? a Big Sister says.

Because the Holy Man is dead. Saying it makes you laugh again. *The Holy Man is holey.*

The Big Sisters widen their eyes, but say nothing.

You try to compose yourself. *Am I in trouble?*

No, Little Sister, says one of them.

It feels like I am. It feels like I'm about to be punished.

You will never be punished here, she says.

The other woman looks at her and then back at you. *Not unless you try to leave. But no one has ever wanted to leave, so why would you?*

The Big Sisters watch you for a while and you kick your feet back and forth against the stones. They tell you this is your time to reflect and then they leave you alone in the garden.

What is there to reflect on, you think, except this strange phenomenon of women worshipping men, alive or dead?

You boot the small stones in the direction of the roses. You do this until your legs ache, and you have the thought that even though you do want to be in the garden, you don't always want to be alone, and when a bell rings out from the monastery, you have an excuse to join the others inside again.

The Big Sisters corral you into a wide room that opens to a courtyard with a smaller garden. Glass bottles line the shelves on three walls, and there are more stacked in wooden crates covering the floor.

A Big Sister instructs you all to sit on the stools tucked under a high table, and then she takes a bottle from the shelf and hands it to the girl closest to her.

Can you read what it says aloud? asks the Big Sister.

No, says the girl, passing it to the shaved-headed girl beside her, who passes it to the girl with long black hair, who passes it to the girl who sits heads above you all. It is soon clear that none of you can read.

Tears of Virgins, says the Big Sister. *It's like holy water, only people will pay a much higher price for it.*

Who would ever do that? you ask.

Anyone seeking a miracle, she says.

We sell them at pilgrimage sites, adds another Big Sister. *That's where we learnt about the trafficking of girls. By talking to traders. We used to trade our Tears of Virgins to buy paints and brushes. But then we traded every last bottle we had to get you here, to save you. So we need your help to continue.*

A Big Sister orbits the table, placing a ceramic bowl in front of each of you.

What do you need us to do? asks the tall girl.

We need you to cry into these bowls. You don't have to fill them all the way. We dilute them with rose water anyway. But once you start crying, you will probably find your tears will keep coming, and some days it will be hard to stop.

At this instruction, you watch the other girls lean obediently over their bowls. Your palms turn clammy, all moisture leaves your mouth. You wonder if you might be able to sweat into the bowls instead.

Your face hovers over the bowl. You cannot tell the Big Sisters that you do not cry – that you have not cried since you were a child – when this must be the reason they have brought you here.

To farm your tears.

The room is silent. You glance around the table. No one is crying yet.

But how do we begin? asks a girl.

A Big Sister smiles and rests a hand on her shoulder.

Little Sister, you must bring to mind the saddest thing that has ever happened to you. And if nothing bad has ever happened to you then you must let yourself imagine it has.

We were all drugged and kidnapped, says the girl with long black hair.

Yes. Remember that.

What if I don't want to?

You have an imagination, don't you?

Yes, she says. *But what should I imagine?*

Your mother dying. Or your father. Or your favourite little lamb slaughtered and arriving on your dinner plate. Imagine that! And while you are thinking of these sad, terrible things, our Big Sister here will sing. And I promise you, soon your tears will flow like a river.

The girls all bend their necks over their bowls again and you do the same. You wish you still had your braids, or any hair at all that could fall around you like a curtain. You wrap your arms around the bowl and close your eyes. The Big Sister begins to sing. Her voice, full of feeling, cracks as it rises.

The other girls sniffle and sob. You don't look up but you can imagine tears rolling down their faces, one fat tear after another, all their tears filling their bowls. You work your tongue against your teeth and your palate until moisture springs into your mouth again. And when you are sure no one is looking, you spit and spit.

When the Big Sister finishes her song, you lift your head to see five blotchy-faced girls. You rub your eyes to redden them while the Big Sisters walk around the table, collecting the bowls. When they collect yours, they don't stop to examine it. They don't seem to notice the difference.

You've all done very well, says a Big Sister. *We will continue our good work tomorrow.*

But what if our tears dry up? says the tall girl.

This happens, says the Big Sister. *It has happened to some of us. We find chopping onions in the kitchen can work just as well. Because, as we say here at the monastery, 'Tears are tears. As long as they're the Tears of Virgins.'*

You know the Big Sisters are not going to want to clothe and feed you when they learn that you cannot cry into bowls, onions or not. So, in the afternoon, you scope the boundaries of the terraced garden. There must be a way to escape. You follow the roots of a fig tree through a tight nest of ferns, thinking that such giant roots could compromise a fence and break through any bricks or rocks. But closer to the fence, you can see the roots sinking beneath it.

You could dig your way out, but with what?

As you move towards the gate, laughter echoes up from the terrace below, and you see the girls through the trees. They are teaching each other a dance.

At the gate, you press your face between the bars, searching for any track or road that will lead you out of here. But all you can see is the salt plain, white and stark, throwing back a blinding glare that makes you squint. You hold your hands above your eyes to see beyond it. In the afternoon sun, the mountains seem to shift and leap.

You have noticed six dogs – tan, black and brindle – sleeping outside the gate. They look like hunting dogs, but earlier you saw the Big Sisters feeding them, no doubt to keep them close. You lean too heavily against the gate. It rattles and sets the dogs barking.

Retreating to the garden, you follow the laughter of the girls. They are now sitting together around a small pond with their feet in the water.

Come and join us, says the girl with long black hair. And you do want to join them. You are tired of feeling so alone.

You sit down. It is the first time you have sat with the girls outside of the cart and without the Big Sisters nearby. You still don't know any of their names.

I'm Bird, you say as you sit beside the long-haired girl.

I'm Bambi, she says.

The other girls introduce themselves too. Cleo, Dev, Kai and Reya. They are looking at you, all smiling, a warmth in their eyes. You feel guilty for judging them too soon, for thinking they were docile and compliant, and wanting to be separate from them and their fate.

Stick your feet in, says Bambi.

You take off your boots and follow Bambi's lead, plunging your feet into the water. Immediately, you understand why they were laughing.

The pond is full of carp, and the carp are nibbling at your feet. You are squirming, ticklish, you can hardly breathe for the laughter pealing out of your body. And then a whole afternoon passes in the garden with the girls, and you forget about wanting to escape.

40.

DARWIN, PRESENT DAY

Competition sport is another privilege that was taken from the girls after the flood and fire. But the girls have to exercise – prison rules – so the guards have set up a course of red traffic cones on the football field, and now you all must jog between them. Then you must perform ten repetitions of star jumps, push-ups and squats, but no girl must outdo or attempt to do more than another. No one can take score or play by any rules.

As you jog between the red traffic cones with Bambi, you notice Jackie sitting on the sideline near two guards. She's looking down at the grass, fanning herself with both of her thongs.

Do they know? you ask Bambi.

I reckon they all must know by now. But the problem is Jackie won't tell them who the father is. They're spinning this story that it's one of the boys from next door.

But how is that possible?

Well, it's not. Unless some kid could stick his dick through the hole in the wire fence, or something.

I suppose that's possible. You are both in hysterics at the thought.

And that's why they've put up all that black plastic over the fence. Like it's a big old condom.

You look over at Jackie again and stop laughing. She looks like one of the unhappiest people you have ever seen.

What's going to happen to her?

She'll probably have a kid in here. And then it'll be taken from her, and the whole cycle will begin again.

You zigzag between the traffic cones out to the edge of the field where the prison guards are training their dogs. The guards blow their whistles, which sets the dogs running after two life-sized dolls dressed in blue shorts and a blue t-shirt.

That's why they've really got us out here, says Bambi. *So they can put the fear in us with their girl-eating dogs.*

The dogs are no more than pups, but they are already huge. As you and Bambi do ten sit-ups, you keep your eyes on the dogs.

They're tearing after the dolls who are being moved along on a mechanical rail. The dogs latch on to their pillow flesh, ripping off the dolls' arms and returning them to the guard for a reward.

How do they train the dogs to tell the difference between a girl who's jogging between traffic cones and a girl who's running away?

I don't reckon they can, says Bambi.

41.

HIMALAYAS, UNKNOWN YEAR

They catch you pushing the head of a small hare through the iron bars of the gate.

What is it you are doing, Little Sister? You spin around, startled. You did not hear the two Big Sisters skulking down the path.

Feeding the dogs, you say as if it is the most innocent thing, and not part of a plan you are making to escape. *I found a dead hare in the garden this morning and I didn't want it to go to waste.*

Behind you, the dogs are jumping and snapping on the other side of the gate. The scent of the hare, the sight of its body dangling limp between the bars, has set them off. You force the rump and legs through to satisfy them. The hare's body doesn't even touch the ground before the large brindle has it in its mouth and is skittering out towards the salt plain, the other dogs in chase.

Have you fed the dogs before?

No. Just this once.

The two Sisters step closer, and already your back is pressed up against the gate. There is no room for you to step away.

You found a dead hare in the garden? asks a Big Sister.

Yes. Like I said, I didn't want it to go to waste.

What you don't say is that you ambushed a raptor in its hunt of the hare, as you have tried to ambush raptors in the garden every day since you have arrived. But this time, you had a long stick in your hand and you knocked the hare right out of its mouth as the raptor was flying away. The hare was not just stunned, it was dead. You ran your hands through its thick soft fur, along its back and its belly, thinking that this is the way the dogs will get to know you. Through your scent. And if you can find a way to feed them often enough, they will soon come to favour you, and make easier your escape.

I suppose that's the cycle of life, isn't it, Sister? one Big Sister says to the other. *And we're all playing our part in it.*

I know you want to keep the dogs close, to protect us, you say.

The Big Sisters smile and nod. You are eager for them to move away, for the interrogation to be over. But they continue to stand there, folding their arms inside their robes. You know they have more to say.

Little Sister, we wanted to speak with you alone today, away from the other girls.

Your arms behind your back, you grip the gate.

We know what you've been doing, says the Big Sister.

Feeding the dogs? You feign innocence again, futile as it is.

Little Sister, we know you've been spitting in the bowls.

No matter how much water you drink in the mornings, your spit is always viscous in the bowl. When the Big Sisters aren't looking, you try to stir out the bubbles with your finger.

What else can you do? You cannot suddenly make tears spring from your eyes.

You don't know what your punishment will be, what cruelties the Big Sisters are capable of, but you nod in admission. There is no denying it.

You are not like the others, are you? says the Big Sister. *You don't seem to be grateful to have been saved, or grateful for anything we have done for you.*

You have been kind, you say. *You feed us and clothe us very well.*

But still you won't give us your Virgin Tears? Even though it's the only thing we ask of you.

You decide there is no other way out now than to tell the truth.

I can't cry, you say. *I haven't cried since I was a small child.*

The Big Sisters glance at each other. It is curiosity, rather than anger, you see unfolding across their faces.

Don't you have feelings, Little Sister?

I do. But when I'm sad, tears don't well up in my eyes like they do for other people.

Well, I suppose that's nothing you can help, one Big Sister says, looking at the other.

But a girl should be productive, the other Big Sister says. *We must all make an effort to contribute and be a part of things.*

I do want to be a part of things, you say.

Then we'll think of something else for you to do, Little Sister, while the other girls are crying into their bowls.

We cannot have you wandering around the garden killing hares, can we?

The Big Sisters leave you holding the gate. You watch them walk back to the monastery, no doubt whispering about you. You wonder if they believed anything you said.

It is true you are grateful for their kindness, just as you are grateful for any kindness. But what is kindness really worth when the gates are always locked, and when no one ever asks what you want for yourself?

42.

DARWIN, PRESENT DAY

The guards have you digging ditches, for what purpose you do not know. The garden beds in front of the prison were all levelled by fire trucks. You want to believe there is some reason for your digging, some purpose. You want to imagine the ditches will train water into some new pocket of growth. But they probably just have you digging in the hot sun for the sake of it.

It doesn't matter, you think, because the six of you are together today. You have been allowed the privilege of choosing your working group, so you are with Bambi, Cleo, Reya, Kai and Dev. The guards have handed you caps to wear while they stand back and watch you from the shade.

Your short hair prickles against your neck, and you are not digging for long before you are saturated with sweat. The earth is hard, compacted, but at least you are with the girls. You feel safe with them, protected. You think of Mrs Whitehead, and her idea that you were drawing the girls because you wanted some real friends. Maybe that was true. Or at least part of the truth.

You dig. Beneath the topsoil you discover a bright red seam of ochre. You chip away at it with the edge of your shovel until a piece falls away. You are thinking that one small piece would be enough to make a drawing on your cell wall. Or you could grind it up and mix it with something oily to make paint. You rub it between your palms until it stains your hands. You hold your hands out to show Bambi.

She looks at you strangely. She drops her shovel and takes your hands in hers. *I remember . . .* she says.

What do you remember?

I don't know. I've seen these hands before.

You see the worry on her face, the confusion, and you want to protect her from it – from remembering it all. The kidnap, the cart, whatever is to come in the monastery. The burden of remembering.

A case of déjà vu? you say. *Too much sun?*

The guards yell at you both to get back to digging. But Bambi has said it. *I remember.* And in that glimmer into her remembering, you feel so much less alone.

You tell yourself again that whatever you had wanted, whatever great revelations you thought you would gain in meeting the girls, this friendship with Bambi is nothing you want to risk or burden.

The afternoon feels cooler. After lunch, the guards instruct you to shovel the dirt you have dug into wheelbarrows and then tip the dirt into one mound. You do this and watch the clouds sink lower and lower until the blue sky vanishes. A grey sky falls and splits. Rain pelts down and you are all soaked in a second. The guards call out, but you remain where you are, standing near the ditches you have dug, watching the rain turn them into streams.

The rain is so heavy, you lose sight of the guards and they lose sight of you. You all drop down into the muddy pools, sliding on your backs and bellies, squealing because you can.

The guards are still yelling, but it is as if they are somewhere else, somewhere far away. More urgent is this warm wet earth covering you. You roll in it, squealing untamed creatures, until a pocket of cold air sinks and hail begins to hit. Then you are all running for shelter.

Drenched, bedraggled, covered in mud, you are all laughing so hard you cannot stand up. You look at the girls, their bright, flashing eyes, and recognise in them what, for a moment, you felt in yourself – something limitless.

The guards, having witnessed this, are utterly spooked. Silently, they lead you back to your cells. Later they throw in a towel, and you wonder if there will be consequences.

You soon realise the consequence is no shower or dinner, but you do not care. From your small, barred window, you watch the sky light up as the storm builds and breaks again, as cool air tunnels through all the gaps in your cell.

At last, you don't feel like you are sinking alone in a swamp.

43.

HIMALAYAS, UNKNOWN YEAR

We are all sisters under the moon, says a Big Sister as she anoints your forehead with some stinking unguent.

Not the fucking moon again, you whisper to Bambi under your breath, but like the other girls, she is already tipping her head towards the sky and soaking in the moon. You don't understand how it is that the girls were drugged and kidnapped as you were, plucked out of their lives and wherever they were going, and yet you can feel no turbulence in them. You wonder if this is what crying brings, some release where they are not pent up like you are or always worried about what will happen next. Maybe they think the worst has already happened and being here in the monastery is as good as life gets.

The Big Sisters believe the moon is a cure for everything, and if you stand beneath it when it is full you will feel its healing power. You do not believe in the moon. You suspect this is a way for the Big Sisters to sync your menses, so it is just one week a month the Sisters will bleed, and all the rags can be thrown together into one boiling pot.

You don't want to think about the moon or your menses. You want to find a way to escape, and you want to convince Bambi to escape with you.

After the Big Sisters learnt that you could not cry, you volunteered to feed the dogs, as a way of contributing. You needed to win the dogs' trust, to let them grow used to you, so that when you were on their side of the gate they would not make a racket and give you away. But the Big Sisters would not allow it. *They are too temperamental*, they said.

So, you offered to chop wood because that was the only job you could think of that would help towards your escape – to make you stronger. Because if you were to survive crossing the salt plains and the mountains, you would need all your strength and more.

The Big Sisters agreed to you chopping wood. The cold weather was coming after all.

And so every morning while the girls cried into bowls, you chopped wood and walked around the rooms of the monastery, refreshing each basket with kindling and split blocks of wood, studying each mural for any clues as to how the women got here, and any evidence of the routes they took.

As the other girls soak up the moon, you can feel someone's eyes upon you. You look up towards the monastery and see the white-haired woman looking down. You meet her eyes, but she does not look away. She wants you to know she is watching you, always.

But then the dogs begin to bark, and all eyes turn towards the gate.

Two of the Big Sisters quickly step away from the moon-bathing circle, taking their lanterns with them to investigate.

Those dogs will bark at anything that moves, says one of the Big Sisters, to assure you all that there is nothing to worry about, that you are safe.

But their barking is insistent.

You think back to your arrival. Six girls in the back of a rattling cart, the wheels on the cobblestones, the women's voices.

So, why was it that when you arrived, you did not hear the dogs?

44.

DARWIN, PRESENT DAY

It is early in the morning. Already the humidity feels suffocating. There is a leftover stench from when the girls turned on the taps and flooded the place and now the big rain has brought it up again. The smell seems to be seeping up from the drain hole, the kind of putrefying smell that no amount of bleach or air freshener will disguise.

The morning alarm has not yet gone off. You sit on the edge of your mattress and wonder how the girls managed to get out of their cells that night. Did they know the risk of fire when they flooded the building? Did they do it anyway? Were they confident the doors of their cells would spring open?

You are still covered in mud from yesterday. You scratch at your skin. The bites on your arms and legs are bleeding. Your face stings from the number of times in the night you slapped it, trying to kill the mosquitos buzzing around your nose and mouth.

The morning alarm sounds and you hear the prison come to life – if life is what it is. Gates roll open, girls call out, guards' boots echo across cement.

And as the sun rises, so does the stench. You peel off your sweat-soaked singlet and stuff it in the drain hole. You can hear the guards moving along the corridor and you slip on a clean t-shirt before they bang on your door.

Rise and shine, Tweety Bird. It is a male voice. A voice that turns your heart to fists.

But how can it be?

Jerome is standing in your cell, dressed in a khaki guard's uniform. He is beaming at his success, beaming at you, a little bird who has flown again through an open window and is now trapped in his cage.

You clench your hands as they begin to shake. Then you clench every part of your body as he walks around you, tut-tutting. He shakes his head, says, *My little Birdy, what's this?* as he pulls your singlet from the drain and holds it to your face.

I think you've been avoiding me, he says.

What are you doing here?

I work here. I'm a correctional services officer.

Since when?

Since long before we met.

Does Mia know this?

Of course she knows.

She didn't tell me.

We didn't think you would approve.

I don't.

She hasn't come back from her yoga retreat. But I'm enjoying your house. I'm thinking the retreat was just an excuse and maybe Mia has flown the coop like you. Like mother, like daughter, they say. He begins to inspect your room.

Of all the times the guards have flushed your toilet, pulled back your sheets, looked under your bed, this is the one that feels most like a violation.

Are you done? you say.

For now.

At the shower block, you make sure you are not last in line and that you are nowhere near the cubicle visible from the door. You finish showering even before the water cuts off. You are second in line outside. At all times you must make sure there is another body between you and Jerome.

He leads the line to breakfast. Head down, you look at your feet the whole way. You are desperate to talk to Bambi.

You find her sitting at the table where she always sits. The other girls are still lining up, so you have a moment with her alone.

You look like you've seen a ghost, she says.

I wish it was a ghost. You sit close to her. *What's the name of the guard who's having sex with Jackie?*

We call him The Germ, but his name is Jerome. Don't worry, he got the message. He hasn't been back since our flood.

There is nothing in your stomach but you think you might throw up.

What's wrong? says Bambi.

Don't look now. But Jerome is watching us at the door.

Bambi looks.

The old pedo returns.

Bambi, he's my mother's boyfriend. He practically lives with us.

What?

I hate him, Bambi. I hate him so much.

We all hate him, Bird. Except Jackie. And that's the problem.

The other girls join you and Bambi at the table.

Where's your tray? asks Kai.

You cannot eat. And now, you discover, you cannot even speak. All moisture has left your mouth. You shake your head and sip on some of Bambi's water.

What's wrong with you two? says Dev.

Can I tell them? says Bambi. You nod. Bambi tells the girls about Jerome and Mia, and you watch their eyes widen and their mouths fall open, and you would like to shrink under the table for your shame.

After breakfast, your names are called out to join one line or another. You learn that today is Visitors Day, and you have been called into the line for a visitor.

I think there's been a mistake, you say to the guard.

No, she says. *You're on my list. You have a registered visitor. Margie Shapiro.*

You feel some clenched part of you release. Margie can help. Someone you can trust. An actual adult. You will tell her what Jerome has done. That you are not safe in here with him. That none of the girls are safe in here with him.

You watch Jerome and another guard lead the line of girls who do not have visitors outside to the courtyard, including Jackie. You follow the visitors line along a corridor and into a room you have never been and you did not know existed. The room is nicer than the other parts of the prison. The walls are painted dusky pink, the furniture looks new and there are plastic ferns in pots hanging from the roof. A guard points you to a table. You are given a fizzy drink and told to wait.

One by one, the visitors file in. They are being treated like prisoners themselves, having to keep in line and do what the guards tell them. You are suddenly nervous, self-conscious, feeling grotty in your bleach-marked t-shirt. You pat down the mess of your hair that you didn't even comb this morning. You wish you had known Margie was coming to visit you.

You see Bambi's mother and sister arriving. They are hugging Bambi. You can see how happy they are to see each other, and it fills you. A guard steps forward to remind them they cannot touch, and then she stands next to their table to make sure they don't. The lean in towards each other as close as they can.

There are other versions of this – parents, grandparents, maybe aunties, maybe siblings. While you wait, you look around at each table and try to guess what their relationship is.

There is a screen that separates the entry area from the visitors room, and you can see the feet of one late visitor. The guards are questioning them. You scan the room. There is one other girl still waiting. You look at the clock. It is 9.15 am.

You are ready to spring up and embrace Margie even though you are not allowed. But it is not Margie who walks past the screen. It is a woman, maybe a solicitor, maybe someone from social services, carrying a file and heading to the other girl's table.

The room grows loud with chatter. *Come on, Margie Shapiro*, you think. *Please don't let me down.*

You sip on your fizzy drink and wait.

45.

DARWIN, PRESENT DAY

Driving along the Stuart Highway, Margie is searching for the turn-off to the prison, so she doesn't notice the smoke streaming from the exhaust of her car. But then the engine dies, and she has to manoeuvre it off the highway and onto the side of the road. She manages to park it in the shade before she pops the bonnet.

The last time Margie looked, the engine was pristine. She'd taken the car to Len, her mechanic, for a tune-up less than a month ago. It was the third time she'd taken it to him since she arrived in Darwin. After driving 4000 kilometres from Melbourne and through the desert, she wanted to give the engine some love and attention, and so she had found Len, a mechanic and vintage car enthusiast with a peculiar passion for the Datsun 280Z.

But now the engine is covered with a dark, oily sludge. Margie runs her finger through it. It's like mayonnaise. She calls Len.

Margie! How's my car? he says.

Have you got me listed as one of your favourites?

You know I go to bed and pray every night you'll sell her to me.

I might give her away today, Len. I'm on the Stuart Highway and she just died on me. And I really need to be somewhere.

Not our fair lady! Talk to me, Margie, he says. *I'm heartbroken.*

I'm looking at it and the whole chassis is covered with grease.

You could have done a head gasket. Has she got oil, water?

Len.

I know. You're not a goose.

She just conked out on me.

Righto. Get her on a trailer and into the shop. I'll take a look at her first thing in the morning.

Margie looks beneath the engine.

Oh fuck.

Sorry, Margie. That's the earliest I can do.

No, it's not you, Len. There's oil pissing out of her.

Not good, Margie, not good. Stay with her until the tow truck arrives. They won't pick it up if you're not there to sign it over.

Thanks, Len. I'll call you first thing.

Margie closes the bonnet, gets in the car and reclines the seat as far as it will go. She looks at her watch. *Why now?* she says. *Why today?*

She calls roadside assistance, and the receptionist tells her the tow truck should be there within half an hour. She calls the prison number listed online but she can only reach an answering service. She leaves a long message explaining what has happened, that she'll be arriving late, but she will be arriving.

She pulls her car registration paper from the glove box and fans herself with it. This is her morning off. Already, she's walked Elsey, showered and double-checked the prison website before heading off to visit you. She thought she was going to be early.

She thought she was going to be sitting in the prison car park killing time.

She filled out the online request a week ago. She was thinking she could cook for you again, or bring you a hamper of fruit or art supplies. Anything. But reading the fine print, she learnt that visitors could not bring gifts, and if they did, they would be confiscated by a correctional services officer. She packed your sketchbook in her bag anyway. She has planned to make the case that she is returning something that belongs to you. And she could find no rules on the website against that.

She estimates that if the tow truck can arrive within twenty minutes, she will ask the driver to drop her off at the prison and she might just make the visitors' cut-off of 9.30 am.

The tow truck driver drops Margie at the prison at 9.35 am. She is hopeful and ready to unleash her charm on the guard sitting in the glass booth at the front gate.

When she approaches the booth, the guard does not look up. He keeps his eyes on the security camera monitors. Margie pushes her face up to the glass.

Hi, she says, flashing a wide smile. *My name is Margie Shapiro. I'm here to see one of the inmates.*

The guard turns to face her. *We don't call them inmates here*, he says. *They're detainees.*

Detainees then, says Margie cheerfully, pushing him a print-out of her pass.

You've missed the cut-off. Doors are closed.

Only by five minutes. I called and left a message. My car broke down.

Yeah, he says. *We hear that a lot. But it's 9.37 am now and there's nothing I can do for you. You'll have to reapply.*

Can I at least get a message to the detainee?

I'm a security guard, miss. Not a message service.

You're an arsehole is what you are, Margie says, and walks away.

Margie attempts to get out of the sun, but there is no shelter and there are no trees. She sits in the gutter, next to a flagpole that only partly covers one side of her face. She calls a taxi and waits.

An old Commodore screeches into the car park. A woman takes a small child out of a car seat and makes a dash to the glass booth.

Margie overhears the woman say, *What form online?* And, *Yes, I can read.* And then the woman is walking back to her car, the child kicking against her hip.

He's an arsehole, Margie yells out to the woman in solidarity, but the woman turns to her with a face so blank it makes Margie ache.

Margie watches the woman drive away, hitting the speed hump too fast, the sound of metal scraping against concrete. Margie puts her head between her knees and folds her hands around her head. Even her hair is hot to touch.

What are you even doing here, Margie? she asks herself.

And she is surprised to hear a clear voice answering her:

You are making right your wrongs.

It is Pema.

46.

HIMALAYAS, UNKNOWN YEAR

Autumn compresses, and soon it will be winter. Pema gets to work at Lhakyi's house, building up her food stores, collecting what remains from the garden. At night, she rides to the outskirts of the village and gleans fruit from her neighbours' trees. She collects wood wherever she can find it. She knows that this winter she must get used to her own company and depend only on herself.

When winter comes, it leans sharply into Lhakyi's house. Despite Pema wanting to feel the warmth of her friend, some lasting presence, she does not feel it. No matter how large a fire she builds, the house always feels empty and cold. Where else could she seek the warmth of her friend, she wonders, if not in her home?

Lhakyi was the village herb woman for villagers of the same caste. So, as Pema's winter aches arise, she searches for some tincture in the cupboards that she can use for herself. She finds baskets of dried herbs and jars of pungent ointments. In the cold house, she tries all of the ointments, registering their effect on her body and her mood. From their colour and their scent, she begins to trace the ointment back to each herb. And on some of the bottles, Lhakyi has helped with small drawings of the herbs that have gone into their making. In this way, Pema gets through the winter, tending to all the things that ail her, noting what symptoms and conditions each herb might ease.

And then Lhakyi begins to appear in her dreams.

Often, she is a vulture perched on the escarpment behind the house. She is eating her own human body, grinding down the last pieces of bone with her beak before flying away.

When Pema wakes, she thinks of her own suffering and what has been self-made. The conditions of her life that she has accepted because she never felt brave enough to resist them. And she wonders if all women become birds when they die, if they are not transformed into creatures of beaks and feathers so that they may finally rise and see the strange patterns they have made together in their human lives.

She thinks of you, your longings and instincts that she tried to quash. She thought she was saving you from some misery – of loving someone you could not love, of forever dreaming of a life that was not possible.

When the snow and the wind ease, Pema climbs the escarpment behind the house and sits where she has seen Lhakyi perched in her dreams. She watches a red, dense sun drape over the mountains and thinks of Lhakyi and all she has learnt from this season. She makes a vow to Lhakyi, and to herself, that as soon as the spring warmth returns, she will restore Lhakyi's garden. And she will continue to make ointments like the ones Lhakyi has left, knowing now what can ease aches and break fevers, what can stop bleeding or bring it.

She is thinking of the beauty of this garden as she climbs back down the escarpment and slips. A stinging pain as she scrapes skin from her hip.

And then it is not the garden she sees.

It is you, lying face up. But where you are, she cannot tell.

The warm weather comes, and strangers appear at Pema's door. They have come seeking treatment for their winter ailments. It is a small village so they know Lhakyi has passed, but they are hoping she has left supplies of herbs and ointments. They report to Pema that they cannot sleep, or all they can do is sleep; that they have lost their appetite, or they have too great an appetite. They are coughing, rashy, weeping, sore. And in their talking, Pema feels Lhakyi's presence at last, standing like a warm body beside her.

When Teshi rides a lame horse up the rise and stands exhausted at the door, Pema does not recognise him. Teshi introduces himself and Pema invites him in, worried for herself, of where she will go next, thinking this will be the last time she will boil tea on Lhakyi's stove. But Teshi has not returned to repossess his mother's house. He sips the tea Pema has made and tells her he has no intention of staying in the village. He has come here only to apologise.

He recounts that, arriving in the village, he learnt that Pema was now living in his mother's house, and that she had become the new herb woman for his caste. Then, in one breath, he tells her that he has travelled far, that he lost you on the Pilgrim's Trail, near the Holy Mountain, how he searched for you, how he found your boots, your tent with your name written on it in thick, dark letters . . .

Then he pauses, reaches into his pack and hands Pema what is left of your braids. All the amulets have been picked out. Pema smooths the strands across her knee and plaits them together in one piece as Teshi continues.

On the way, as he was leading his horse across the river, he had the strongest sense that you had passed, though he cannot explain it. He only hoped that he was wrong. He even hoped that Cho had been successful in capturing you because that would have meant you were alive and living with your sister. But he found Mida, and she assured him that Cho had not captured you and he believed her when she told him she had not seen you since the wedding . . .

Teshi talks and talks, unburdening his guilt onto Pema.

Pema listens and places the plait on the small altar she has made and lights a candle for you there.

When Teshi is done, Pema tells him that none of it is his fault. That your whole life, just as soon as you could walk, you had this instinct to run, to defy limits, to explore further. And she prays this instinct has led you somewhere safe, and somewhere good.

Having told Pema what he came to tell her, Teshi wants to leave the village while it is still light. Pema offers to treat his lame horse and gifts him her own good horse to ride.

Standing in front of the garden that has now begun to bloom, Pema watches Teshi mount the horse and ride away. She wonders why she has not let herself feel love for him before. He is, after all, Lhakyi's only child. She watches him vanish down the rise, and only in the space of his leaving does she hear again what he has travelled so far to say: that he lost you on the Pilgrim's Trail, that he believes you have passed away.

Words she cannot bear.

She sits down on a rock in the garden and begins to break the soil apart in her hands. She remembers the day before the wedding, how you had thrown rocks at the house and spun near the field until you fell down dizzy. How you had yelled out and clutched at the earth with your hands. The soil crumbles through Pema's fingers and she feels the terrible truth of it. All the ways she has failed you. All the wrongs that now cannot be repaired.

47.

HIMALAYAS, UNKNOWN YEAR

It must have life in it, the white-haired woman is saying. *It must have vitality. Because it is nothing less than the source of life you are trying to connect to.*

The Big Sisters have decided you have chopped enough wood and now you should learn to make paint so you can help them with their murals.

And so, you are facing a mural in the hall, and the white-haired woman is standing beside you as four Big Sisters paint the detail of another wild garden.

The white-haired woman leads you over to a table where she has arranged two roses in a vase and set out art materials.

Before you start grinding those stones into pigment, I want you to spend the morning with these roses. I want you to transfer their life to these pages.

She has laid out a small stack of paper and palm leaves, nubs of charcoal, fine-haired brushes, an iron nail.

I want you to find a relationship with each instrument and each surface.

What do you mean a 'relationship'? you ask.

I cannot tell you anything more than that, she says. *You will have to experience it for yourself.*

You want to tell her you have never drawn anything. You have only ever made indecipherable shapes with a stick in the dirt. You have memories of moulding lumpy figures out of mud and drying them in the sun. And then your sister Mida laughing when their arms and legs fell off.

But, somehow, the art materials in front of you feel perfect and alluring. You hold each of them in your hand. A quietness comes over you. If every Big Sister here has learnt to paint, perhaps it is something you can learn too, you think.

Don't be afraid, says the white-haired woman. *You have everything you need. Just begin.*

She leaves you sitting alone at the table. For a while you stare at the roses. You don't think so much about their life or vitality, but you can trace the lines of their leaves, feel the velvet of their petals, and decipher the shapes and shades within them.

With the nail, you begin to scratch into the surface of the palm leaf. And by the time the white-haired woman returns with a cup of tea, you have drawn something that looks unmistakably like a rose.

It is good, she says. *I can see the life in it.*

And this small encouragement fills you in a way you have never been filled.

Now draw me twenty more, she says.

Later—

The white-haired woman returns to see if you have followed her instruction.

Get up now, she says sternly, and you think you have somehow failed at this task, that as you have grown more confident, and your hand has freed up, perhaps the roses have come to look less like roses.

She leads you to the wall.

Little Sister, paint me one of your roses.

The Big Sisters have moved along to the right side of the mural and they are standing on chairs, painting the branches of a fig tree. The white-haired woman points to the low edge of the wall. *Just one rose, right there.*

What season is it? you ask. *What time of day?* You are wondering if you should add dew to its leaves, or if the petals should be shrinking in the heat.

These are good questions, she says. *They are the right questions to ask*, and she says no more before walking away.

You feel intimidated facing the wall. The Big Sisters' work seems to flow out of them. You chew on your nails, pace back and forth. What if your mark ruins the mural? Seeing you floundering, a Big Sister hands you a palette and shows you how to hold it.

Just remember, she says, *it's only a wall. Just hold the image of what you want to paint in your mind and breathe.*

The Big Sister has already prepared your paints. The palette she has handed you has daubs of red, purple, white and black. You dip the fine brush into the red paint and press it into the wall. And then you stand back.

It is just one red mark. But it thrills you. So you breathe, and you make more.

In the afternoon, having drawn twenty roses, painted one rose on the wall and crushed rocks into pigments that the Big Sisters turned into paint, you trudge out to the garden where the other girls have gathered. They sit around Bambi who is pretending to read their palms. You wait your turn and then you push your hands into hers, proud of their ochre-coloured stains and this thing you are learning you can do.

Bambi turns your hands over and holds them tight in hers.

Why didn't you tell us? she asks.

Tell you what?

That you couldn't cry. That you were spitting in the bowls.

Because I didn't know what the punishment would be.

Don't you think I can keep a secret?

You look into her brown eyes.

I think it's some kind of defect in me, you say.

Not to be able to trust or not to be able to cry? says Bambi.

You don't know what to say to her, so you deflect. *What do you cry about all day?* you ask.

Whatever comes into my mind. People I love. People I have lost. Have you really never cried?

My mother told me I cried when I was a baby, like all babies cry. But then an old monk performed a ritual on me and I haven't cried since. Sometimes I feel like I'm going to but then it gets caught up behind my eyes.

And now, says Bambi, *it is because you cannot cry that you are being taught how to paint.*

Yes, I suppose you're right.

Then maybe that old monk did you a favour.

You link arms with Bambi and walk through the garden, telling her about your first attempt at drawing roses, how it felt to make a mark on the wall, about the stones you ground down to make colours, the weight of a lump of lapis in your hand, how brilliant its blue. How you were told by the Big Sisters how much each lump of lapis costs and how you must not waste a speck of it.

No wonder they need us crying into bowls, says Bambi. *What else? What else?*

You want to tell Bambi everything. And not only about learning to paint, but all the strange things that have happened since you left the village. The girls that appeared to you on the trail, losing T at the Holy Mountain, the body you pulled from the lake. But you don't want to burden this new friendship with so many strange things.

That's all, you say. *Tell me about your day.*

Late in the night, the sound of the gates creaking open wakes you and draws you to the window. You open the shutters to see the Big Sisters carrying lanterns and running to the gates. They chain the dogs and lead them to the woodshed before the drivers approach. This is why you didn't hear the dogs on the night of your arrival.

Even from the shape of them you can tell they are the same drivers who kidnapped you from the Holy Mountain. They steer the cart through the gates and across the cobblestones. *Last delivery before spring*, you hear them say. You watch as the Big Sisters unload crates, while the drivers crouch under a lantern and smoke and eat. As the Big Sisters load more crates, these ones filled with bottles of tears, it occurs to you that this will be how you escape.

You will go out the same way you came in.

When the drivers return at the beginning of spring, and while the Big Sisters are chaining up the dogs, you will hide yourself behind the rosebushes and climb into the cart before it passes back through the gates.

The next day when you join Bambi in the garden again, after she has cried into bowls and you have prepared a section of the wall for the Sisters to paint, you take her hand in yours.

Escape with me, you say.

Escape where? Her eyes are following Cleo and Dev, who are in the upper terrace of the garden, devising a dance, stamping their boots into the first snow.

Outside the gate. To the world beyond the mountains. Saying it sounds like some whimsical idea that you have only just had, not something you have imagined every day since you could walk.

Bambi looks around at the garden, at the white-tipped mountains in the distance, and then back at you as if you are mad. *Why would you want to escape?* she says.

How can you explain your desire for the world when you have experienced so little of it? How can you explain your instinct to run? How you ache for vast skies, open fields and roads that unfold endlessly in front of you.

You watch as Bambi catches snowflakes on her tongue and copies the dance moves of Dev and Cleo. You wish you could take more pleasure in the snow, as they are, but it feels to you like another kind of closing in. Soon, the salt plain will turn into a sludgy lake that will freeze your feet if you try to cross it and the mountains will be impassable. Five more full moons, maybe more, before the winter will retreat, before you will have a chance to escape again.

You wipe away the snow and sit on a wooden bench seat, watching the girls dance. They radiate happiness and good health. You feel sluggish, overfed. Running is the only thing that will cure you.

You could run up and down the terraced garden, but you know that would draw too much attention.

Bambi gestures for you to join them. And you do want to join them. You want to learn their dance, to be a part of things. But something always stops you – your knowledge that this life, in the monastery with the girls, is not the life you chose. It is another life that has been chosen for you.

You stand and move towards the girls and begin to copy their dance steps. You are clumsy. You cannot match their pace. But they are patient with you. And they begin again.

I'll watch, you say, as they continue to dance around you, and you sit back on the bench seat.

You fear for yourself in this body, that you will be stuck here forever. That the snow landing on your skin is like daubs of paint, disappearing you and everything you have ever wanted for yourself.

You close your eyes. You can hear the girls singing and laughing, but you feel so far from them. This is what it must feel like to die, you think.

But you do not want to die.

Bambi tugs at your hands and raises them above your head. You stand up and she has a hold of you, and she is shaking your body, she is shaking you out of yourself. Your arms are waving with hers and you feel a warmth rising, a warmth that moves out of you and towards the girls. You feel snow melting on your face. Your skin is touching their skin. You feel their radiance, and for a moment you are happy, and their radiance is yours.

48.

DARWIN, PRESENT DAY

9.30 am. You are still waiting for Margie, scratching your name with your thumbnail into the soft plywood beneath the table. A guard taps you on the shoulder.

What? you say.

Looks like there's a no-show here. Follow me.

Just five more minutes. She might be trying to find a park.

There's plenty of car parks outside. Visitor cut-off is at 9.30. Your visitor will have to learn to be on time.

You fold your arms and shake your head.

Come on, says the guard. *Let's not make a scene.*

You push back hard on your chair. Its legs scrape against the concrete floor. You look at Bambi, and Bambi makes a sad face.

The guard leads you out to the courtyard where Jerome is talking to Jackie. Even from a distance you can see what is happening between them. He is playing her. No doubt using his words to bend her, the way he bends Mia. Maybe it was better, you think, that Mia got away.

But now this correctional services officer, this man of thirty-seven, is preying on a girl of fourteen, a prisoner who cannot leave.

You take a tennis ball from the bucket, and you want to throw it at his face. You want to crush his cheekbones and his jaw so he looks like the monster he is.

Instead, you pelt the ball against the wall and imagine it hitting him, over and over, bruising every part of his body until he is begging you to stop.

Bird! Dev calls out to you.

She is shooting hoops with Kai and they are both waving you over, but you wave them away. You are in the grip of your anger and you don't want to join them.

You continue bashing the tennis ball against the brick wall until you are in a rhythm, just you and the ball, and you are willing yourself far away from here. But then you see Jackie's shadow on the wall. You don't even turn around as you say, *Fuck off, Jackie.* Because no doubt Jerome has put her up to something. No doubt she has been part of his play this whole time.

Serve it to me, she says.

No.

But I want to play.

You bounce the ball hard in Jackie's direction. And back and forth you go, until Jackie does what she was always going to do – she holds the ball and pretends to throw it at your face.

You flinch.

Just joking, she says, and smiles. But then her smile freezes and she throws the ball away.

Woops.

You watch her sashay back to Jerome, and then Jerome laughing and passing something to her. You feel unhinged. You follow after her.

Go get my ball, you demand.

What? she says innocently.

You took my ball.

You missed my serve.

There's plenty more, says Jerome, pointing to the bucket and winking at Jackie. Jackie is now chewing on purple gum.

Where did you get that? you say.

Jackie smiles at Jerome.

Don't you know he's playing you? you say. *Don't you know he loves to play all the girls?*

Jackie swipes her fist at you. But you duck and wrap your arms around her legs and tackle her to the ground. You try to get to your feet, but she grabs your ankles, and she is flipping you over and pinning you down. She is shoving her thumbs inside your mouth like she wants to rip your face in half. Why is no one helping?

You grab her wrists and push your fingernails into them until you feel her skin break. She cries out and rolls off you, and then you are being dragged away by Jerome and another guard, across the courtyard and along the corridor. You think they are going to throw you in your cell, but they drag you past it.

Where are you taking me? you yell.

When they don't answer, you begin to kick and fight, but they keep dragging you down and down. A metal door slams.

And then you cannot see a thing.

49.

THE GHOST PLACE

You have heard the other girls call it the Ghost Place, but you never imagined you would have to experience it yourself.

It is hot and dark. If there is anything in it, a mattress, a toilet, you cannot see it. You lie down on your back on the floor.

All the strands you have tried to keep a hold on, to keep distinct and separate in your mind, they have all tangled around you and you feel one of the strands tugging hard – and at the end of it there is a wild, fighting fish and as it swims, and swims for its life, it only constricts you more.

It is the thing you have never wanted to face. It is your death.

It begins when you are alone in your room at the monastery. You are trying to map the sounds. The way the Big Sisters shuffle along the corridors, not in their boots but barefoot or in slippers, moving like they don't want to be heard, and gathering together in a room. Their soft humming gives them away.

You would like to sleep, but there is too much unease in your body. Unease that has you creeping past the other girls' rooms and stopping when you reach Bambi's. You want to raise your hand against the door, to gently tap on it and wake her, but you think better of it.

What if you are discovered? You don't want to get Bambi into trouble. And you are still not certain of what punishments the white-haired woman and the Big Sisters are capable of.

Even with their kindnesses, even though they have taught you to paint, you still don't trust them. You are not certain you believe their claims that they have saved you from a worse fate. Now that you know the cost of lapis, and how much of it they use, it makes sense to you that they would need to fill the monastery with crying girls. And how much longer will they want to keep you before they discard you, or better, trade you for another crying girl?

You can hear them, their voices fluttering in the hall. Gently, you push the door open just enough to fit your eye over the gap. You can see all the Big Sisters at work on the mural of the wild garden. How consumed with it they are. You have shared some of that sensation, the pleasure in the paint they must feel. Perhaps they are as devoted to their art as they say they are, working day and night as they do.

Some of the Big Sisters cluster around the middle of the wall and two others are working further away. You are lost in the detail of what they are painting so you don't immediately comprehend what it is you are seeing.

And when you do, your heart leaps. You squint. You think surely your eyes are deceiving you.

How can it be that two Big Sisters are floating halfway up the wall and there is nothing beneath them? They are painting the sky and painting clouds. They hold a palette in one hand and a paintbrush in the other. Their bare feet balanced on nothing.

You search for scaffolding, for ropes, a net, anything that would hold them up and suspend them at such a height. Then your throat tightens. You know you are seeing something you are not meant to see.

Quietly, you close the door.

The next day, you tell Bambi what you have seen.

I don't think it's my imagination playing tricks on me, you say.

And although you want to, you don't tell her about the times you think it may have played tricks on you before.

Wake me up tonight, she says, *and then we'll know for sure.*

So, in the middle of the night, you are up again and out of your bed, this time tapping on her door. She is waiting for you. You take each other's hands and quietly move along the corridor, dressed in your night clothes, but more alert for the cool, sharp air.

When you reach the hall, you whisper to her, *Are you ready?* She nods and you gently push the door. You can see the Big Sisters adding finishing touches to the mural they have worked on these past weeks. They are painting halos around the tops of the mountains.

Look, you say.

Bambi presses her eye against the gap. A sliver of light from the lantern-lit hall cuts across her face. She squints, just as you squinted. She is disbelieving, just as you were. She shrinks down, stands up, shakes her head. Then her whole body reels back.

But how? she whispers.

In your room, you light your lantern and both of you wrap yourselves in blankets and sit on the floor. You ask Bambi to describe exactly what she saw.

The Big Sisters were all floating, she says. *They were all floating up the wall and there was nothing there to hold them.*

You hug her, relieved you are not seeing things, relieved to share.

All this time you have spent examining the murals, you have been blindsided by your desire to escape. Never once had you let yourself wonder how the Big Sisters had painted such high walls, how they could execute the fine details of sky and birds and clouds. If you had let yourself wonder, would you have attempted to explain it away, thinking the Big Sisters were stacking chairs or dragging in ladders from the shed? Building scaffolding at night, only to take it away?

Your imagination was not playing tricks on you, Bambi says.

Do you think they'll teach us how to do it? Like they're teaching me to paint?

I don't know, says Bambi. *Maybe it's a power they want to keep for themselves. We have to tell the others.*

And then it is your body reeling back.

We don't have to, you say, realising how much you want to hold on to this secret with Bambi.

But they should know, Bambi says.

Why?

Because we've put our trust in the Big Sisters and everything they've said.

Can't we wait?

Bambi nods unconvincingly. You want to trust Bambi. But trusting all of the girls is too much. You fear the punishment the

Big Sisters will enact on you if they learn you have been spying on them.

Do you promise?

I promise, she says.

But even as she says it, you feel the secret slip away.

In the morning, the Big Sisters let you paint a small pond. But you are distracted, looking at the high halos of the mountains you glimpsed them painting last night. One of the Big Sisters tells you to sit at the table and sketch the pond in the garden, remembering how you first saw it and not as it is now, frigid with snow. You recall its surface rippling gold, how the gold broke into purples and greens when you stuck your feet in it. And the bright orange flashes of the carp beneath. You choose yellow, ochre and blue, and a Big Sister shows you how to mix a colour she calls pond green.

All the Big Sisters are busy putting the finishing touches on the mural and you wonder where they get the energy to work day and night. You wonder if they are not quite human, if that is what allows them to float. You wonder if there is something concealed beneath their robes.

You immerse yourself in painting the pond, in applying careful strokes. You paint the distortion on the surface as it ripples, and carp nibbling on the weeds beneath. You paint the pond fringed by lilies and tall grasses. And, at the end of the day, the Big Sisters step back from the work and examine it. They fold their arms across their chests.

You can paint, is all they say to you, and even if they do turn out to be not altogether human, you want so much for those words to be true.

In the evening, from your window, you see some of the Big Sisters proceeding to the bathhouse, so you sneak outside. This time you don't tell Bambi. First, you will find an explanation for yourself. All day, you have convinced yourself that there must be something under their robes, something that allows them to do what other humans cannot do. Quietly, you place a wood crate under the bathhouse window and watch as they bathe.

Inside, the Big Sisters move around uninhibited, filling their baths, keeping themselves warm by splashing water over their backs, water they are heating in large copper pots. And although each woman's body is different and unique, none of them are in possession of any wings, or anything unearthly – they all appear to be human.

What is there to think except that whatever it is that allows them to do what they do, they must all carry inside of them?

When you next join the girls in the garden, you know that Bambi has told them. They don't say a word. They don't have to. You can tell by the way they all flick their eyes to Bambi and the way Bambi looks to the ground. You are furious with her.

Will you show us? says Dev.

Bambi can show you, you say.

But that night, when you hear their doors opening, the girls whispering each other awake, you want so much to be a part of things, to not always hold yourself so separate and alone. So you get up and you tell them to take off their boots, their coats, anything that will make a noise as they walk, even a swoosh.

Then you and Bambi lead the girls downstairs towards the soft humming of the women. They are not in the hall where you last saw them. They have gathered in a new room to paint another mural. You push open the door a crack, and you and Bambi stand back as the girls take turns to look.

One by one, they shake their heads and shrug, but not in disbelief.

You peer in. The Big Sisters are painting and standing on nothing stranger than their socked feet.

Tonight, there is nothing to see.

You all walk back to your rooms in silence and each girl returns to her bed. Perhaps it is better this way, you think. Better that they doubt you and Bambi, and nothing more comes of it.

It is not until your next bath that you realise what is happening. When the girls undress, you see that all of them are covered with bruises. Purple and black splodges – as bright as paint – all over their hips and their legs. To you, the bruises are a plain account of how they are attempting to float themselves in the privacy of their rooms. They may doubt your version of events, but they do not doubt Bambi's. The idea has taken hold of them, and they are launching themselves from their beds, their desks, their chairs. And so is Bambi.

You wonder if they do this together in their rooms and why they have not asked you to join them.

In the bathhouse, you watch as panic falls over the faces of the Big Sisters. And then the Big Sisters turn their faces to you.

Why are they all looking at you? Why do they seem most disturbed at seeing your body unbruised? Through the steam and lantern light, you can feel their conclusion forming. That you must be responsible. The girl who doesn't cry, who kills small furry animals, who is deeply ungrateful at heart. She must be to blame for this.

The night passes and no Big Sister says a word to you, but in the morning you are woken early by a knock on your door. A Big Sister, unsmiling, instructs you to dress and meet the white-haired woman before breakfast in the hall.

The white-haired woman is waiting for you, sitting at the end of the long table. She gestures for you to sit in the chair in front of her.

Is it you who is doing this harm? she says.

No, it's not.

You wouldn't tell me if it was, would you?

Why don't you ask the other girls?

Why are you so unhappy here, with all that is given to you?

Because I didn't choose it.

Is choice the most important thing to you?

It is, you say.

Well, make your choice. You are free now to do whatever it is you please.

Can I leave?

She seems to contemplate this question as she runs her hands through her hair.

You are young, she says, standing. *You don't know what it is you are choosing.* And then she is gone and you are sitting alone in the hall, staring at the mural you helped paint.

It is a landscape that foregrounds a wild garden, flowers falling open, small ponds. Mountains fold behind it and the sky is washed with blue. But what you see clearest of all is your memory of the women floating up the wall.

In no time, the Big Sisters are echoing the words of the white-haired woman. *You are free to do as you please. Sleep all day if you want to.*

Since you have arrived, you have wondered what form their punishments would take. And now you know. They will isolate you. They will push you from the weave.

The winter turns bleak.

There is an endless need for wood. You retreat into your self-appointed task of chopping wood for the monastery, all the wood, with the renewed intention that you will grow your strength for your escape.

The woodshed becomes your domain. You keep warm by stacking and splitting, and carrying wood in basket loads to every room with a fireplace. You could do this all day, but you discover that alongside your need to be strong is an urge to paint.

So, you clear one wall of the shed and you begin to paint your own mural. You make your pigments from grinding rocks and sweeping up whatever the Big Sisters leave out on the tables. And if you need to do something you cannot do – mix a colour or create perspective – you wander back inside the monastery, with the apparent purpose of delivering wood, and you watch the Big Sisters working.

Mostly, they ignore you.

You sustain yourself in this quiet repetition of days, a way to bide your time through the winter. You eat your meals with the girls and the Big Sisters but that is the only time you engage, and even then you don't say very much, and they don't say much to you either.

Some days when you pass by the crying room, or worse, when you see the girls emerge with their arms linked, you get a pang for them, and you wish you were still friends. Especially Bambi.

But when you attempted to talk to her, she told you she had begun to think that what she thought she saw, she did not see at all. And it was only because you had put the idea in her head that she had thought it anyway. And so, she told the other girls that she had imagined it too. And since then, they have given up the idea and stopped leaping from their beds and tables.

Through it all, you keep picturing the spring that will soon emerge from winter. Spring being your time to escape. You tell yourself that outside, you will find other friends. But for now, you must chop wood and paint.

When you hear the Big Sisters talking of a new delivery, you think your time to escape is near.

It is so clear in your mind. When you hear the drivers coming through the gates, you will slip out into the garden and crawl along the hedges and hide and wait. And when the drivers have finished unloading their supplies and the Big Sisters are opening them, you will slip into the cart and into one of the empty baskets. Then you will travel as far as you can. You will stay quiet. You will give the drivers no cause to look and when the wheels stop rattling and the road turns smooth, because it is a well-travelled route, you will roll yourself out and you will run.

And so, every night you listen out. And every night you picture your escape, all through the last of the winter.

You are eating breakfast in the hall, with the other girls and Big Sisters chatting around you, when you hear a Big Sister calling out from the garden. *They're here! They're here!* And then suddenly all the Big Sisters are up from their chairs and running. Except the white-haired woman. She doesn't run. She glides, gesturing for you all to follow.

In the daylight, the drivers are steering the cart through the gates.

How had you not heard them? And how had you never imagined they could arrive in the full light of day?

The drivers pull up and the white-haired woman calls you over. You think you are about to be recruited to unload supplies, but as you move closer to the cart, you see the load the drivers are carrying.

Six more girls.

All in good health, a Big Sister is yelling.

The Big Sisters are circling the cart, fawning over this fresh batch of girls. They are coaxing them down, leading them towards the bathhouse, just as they led you. Each girl with two Big Sisters on her arms.

We're being replaced, you say.

In the privacy of your room, you attempt what the other girls have already tried but only you and Bambi have seen for yourself. You stand on the desk with your arms out by your sides and tell yourself you are weightless, that you are a bird, that you can hover above the earth, that you can rise up a wall.

You step off the desk, and no sooner have you stepped off than you are crumpled on the floor.

But then you are back up there, trying. You do this into the night, again and again.

The girls start calling themselves Little Sisters to remind the Big Sisters of the promise they have made, to take care of them, to grow their gifts – isn't that what they said when you first arrived? They name the new arrivals before the Big Sisters have a chance. They call them the New Girls, to remind them of their place.

The Little Sisters heard you when you said, *We are being replaced.* They thought it and feared it too. And now, they fill up their tear bowls easily.

Outside, the mist is starting to lift and the snow is beginning to melt. The Big Sisters are distracted settling in the New Girls. But you have discovered new worries. Wolves and leopards are prowling around the dogs outside the gate. One dog, a brindle, is already dead, so the Big Sisters have brought all the dogs into the woodshed until the leopards lose interest and move away. The woodshed is no longer your refuge.

A wind has blown in across the plain that tears off every delicate thing from branch and stem. In your room, the latched shutters rattle all day. With the onset of spring, the time that should herald your escape, there is a new feeling of being captive and alone.

You remember the ravines you walked through on the way to the Holy Mountain; how dangerous they would be now covered in snowmelt. And with this wind, pilgrims would be stripped from the trail that edged along the cliff as easily as a leaf from a tree. How can you know where the wind begins and ends? Small villages with their thatched-roof huts tied together with rope and twine, their mud-sealed walls – wouldn't they be made derelict by such weather?

You consider that you may not be able to return the way you came. And yet you know nothing of the world beyond it.

But then the wind does stop, and the water begins to trickle again through slate runnels and collect into ponds in the garden. The new growth that was prematurely stripped grows back, and you are able to walk up and down the terraces of the garden without wetting your boots. The leopards leave their patrol and the dogs are returned to guarding the gate.

You have stacked what remains of the wood to cover up your mural, and even though the weather is growing warm, there is still the need for wood to light the stoves. You tell the Big Sisters that the wood supply is low and they call the Little Sisters out to the garden. You are all to collect kindling, and when the kindling is piled high, you are to follow the Big Sisters down to the gates.

The Big Sisters leash all the dogs on chains and for the first time since you have arrived, you are led outside the gates. The Big Sisters instruct you to stay behind them and the dogs, and to follow them to a fallen-down tree. They have already done the work of sawing it into smaller pieces and now it is your job to carry it back to the shed.

The Big Sisters march out across the still-wet ground and the dogs tug on their chains.

Stay close, the Big Sisters yell as they lead you through the sparse forest.

The Little Sisters' voices chime with excitement in the crisp air. Sunlight bounces from their heads. The line of girls begins to fold around the Big Sisters and the dogs, and when you fall behind, nobody notices, or nobody cares.

You can feel your life beyond this one, glimmering, pulsing on the other side of the salt plain. You know the monastery is not your place and here you cannot be part of things. So, your choice is made.

You split out through the forest towards the plain, your eyes on your life ahead with its smear of shapes and colours.

The dogs notice you before the Big Sisters do. They lunge forward suddenly, their bodies large and strong, and the Big Sisters lose hold of their chains.

You run and you can hear the Big Sisters calling after the dogs. You know you can run so much faster, and you must, but the salt plain is soft under your feet, as soft as mush. Then one of the dogs nips at your heels. Does he think it is a game? You fall. You get up and with all of your strength you keep running. But in the end, it is no match for the dogs.

The cracking sound you hear is bone, your bone. And then all the dogs are upon you. The five dogs who are left. They are frenzied. They know your smell and they associate it with food. Their teeth and claws pierce your skin, and you can see it, but you can hardly comprehend it.

The Big Sisters are running towards you. They have grabbed sticks and branches, anything to beat back the dogs.

You cover your face. You can see your blood. You feel your body slacken and then go stiff. And that is the last thing you feel.

Not the end, but the beginning of the end.

You don't feel the girls stroking your damp head. But you do see them folding over your blood-stained body, the petals of a flower closing in as you rise and rise.

You are dying, yes. But you are not quite dead. There are still all of these invisible strands tugging.

Pema is the first to feel it. She is climbing down a small escarpment when she slips. It scrapes the skin from her hip and then it is you she sees lying in the snow.

Teshi is the next. He feels it as a sudden pain in his chest as he leads his horse across the river, the very same river you thought would mark your freedom, and maybe it did.

Something in Teshi knows you are passing. But he doesn't want to feel it, or the guilt he has that it is somehow his fault. He will never have the chance to explain himself, to tell you how he searched and searched. That he found your boots. That he found your tent with your name written in large black letters on it. BIRD. The only word he knows how to read and write, other than his own.

The Little Sisters, the Big Sisters, the dogs all shrink. Around them you see the country rippling pink and you think this is a colour you would like to make; this is a colour you would like to paint with.

Then you are sucked into a tunnel and it is upon you to remember what Pema told you when you were a child.

When you die, she said, *you must only go towards the peaceful deities. You must only go towards the light.*

But in the tunnel, you see no peaceful deities. You see no light.

You hurtle through as a tiny speck. At one end, the life you have left; at the other end, a future life, not yet visible.

In the Ghost Place there is one dim light that turns on before mealtimes, twice a day. This is how you measure time, by the dim light, by the plate passed through a small feeding window. You have counted three days. You yell to whoever delivers your meal: *How much longer do I have to be in here?* And they yell back: *How long is a piece of string?*

By the dim light you have discovered a short, thin mattress and a toilet. The only air that enters comes through the feeding window. You pass the time lying on the mattress or sitting in the dark, remembering.

He arrives without warning, when the dim light is off. You hear the metal door open and close and then there is the shock of his flashlight in your face.

My little Birdy, he says.

And seeing him in the Ghost Place, you know exactly who he is and who he has always been. He is Cho. And he thinks he can lay claim to you. He is who the girls have named him to be – The Germ – and he has pursued you through lifetimes, intent on possessing you, and seeking revenge.

I know who you are, you say, *and I know what you have done.*

And that's where the story ends, he says.

No, you say.

Do you think anybody cares what happens to you in here? He turns his flashlight off. You feel his arms around you. He is looping something around your neck. And you know what it is from the smell of it. It is your singlet, the one you stuffed down the drain in your cell to block the stench.

Nobody cares, he says as he winds it around your throat.

In that moment you think of the Holy Mountain. You had wondered then if silence was the better prayer and now you know.

In the Ghost Place you are not so far buried, not so far down, that nobody in the prison can hear you. You hook your fingers under the singlet, pulling it back from the force of Jerome's hand, and you scream:

Bambi.

Kai.

Cleo.

Reya.

Dev.

And each one of them hears you in their cells. They grab their tin cups and launch themselves from their beds and their desks, bashing the tin cups against their doors, their bedframes, the bars of the windows. They scream and howl. And the sound of their voices and your voice yelling back lifts them up and up.

And somehow every other girl in the prison knows she must scream and howl too. Soon their voices and the riot of their tin cups, tin on metal, tin on floors, reach every part of the prison.

You feel Jerome's radio buzzing against your back. You hear the officer's call: *Every guard report your position immediately.*

And then you feel his grip release.

In what you take to be morning, the dim lights turn on. The metal door opens. Two guards have come for you, neither of them Jerome. You are sitting in the middle of your cell, holding your singlet, and behind you on the wall with the nub of ochre you have kept in your pocket, you have written JEROME WAS HERE.

The guards walk you along a narrow corridor and out into the sun. You have heard that some girls being led out of the Ghost Place will suddenly faint as space and light expand too quickly around them. But you have never felt steadier on your feet.

The guards walk you to the shower block. You have it to yourself, and you choose the cubicle in the far corner. You undress, step under the showerhead and wait for the water to come on. The water teems down, pummelling your skin. You scrub every part of yourself, and when the water shuts off, you wrap yourself in a towel and step towards the mirror.

There is a red ring around your neck and a bruise forming at your throat. You dress in the clean clothes the guards have given you. You wrap the singlet in your t-shirt. It will be your evidence.

Outside the shower block, in the light of day, you make the guards look at your neck.

You say, *This is what Jerome did to me. He is my mother's ex-boyfriend. He is having sex with Jackie, and he knows I will report him. Hearing this from me now, you have to report him too.*

The guards listen and nod. They walk you down the corridor and past the cells.

All the girls are waiting by their doors. Their faces are pressed up against their small windows, their hands too.

And now the girls are calling your name. *Bird, Bird, Bird.*

All the girls who have saved you.

50.

DARWIN, PRESENT DAY

Margie walks around the inner-city streets, carrying your sketchbook, searching for more of your murals. She has found seven of them so far, four that T directed her to, and three she found herself. They are all of the girls, their bodies often cloaked, always standing shoulder to shoulder, under a bright moon. She is making a habit of it – finishing work, driving to the city, and then mapping every alleyway on foot.

As well as the murals of the girls, she has found two smaller pieces: on a transmission box, a boy meditating in a lotus position; on the edge of a building, a girl dancing, eyes closed, arms above her head.

Margie backtracks to the mural behind the supermarket, the first mural T showed her. She flicks through your sketchbook trying to find the origin sketch of the piece. It is giving her something to see the girls first drawn on the page and then to be rendered so large on the wall. It is giving her courage, she thinks. And more.

You have signed and dated the murals, so she thinks this must be the last one you painted before you were in hospital and then prison. In each mural, she has noticed the difference in the girls' postures and the direction of their faces – from staring at the full moon to this one where each girls' face is turned and looking over her shoulder.

As she did weeks ago, Margie has the feeling that their gaze is meeting hers and they are challenging her. They are asking, *What are you going to do now?*

Margie is walking back to her car when Lyn calls and invites her for dinner. T has caught a barramundi in the creek. He's going to bake it, and she's picked up a papaya salad from the market.

In her car, Margie connects her phone to the stereo and plays the new music T has introduced her to. She is driving out of the city thinking she will pick up a bottle of wine on the way when she turns off the highway and discovers the traffic is being diverted. She follows the arrows and yellow signs that direct her to an alternative route. The traffic slows and her car is still moving at a crawl when she drives beneath the underpass.

It is not until she is beside it that she sees it.

Another mural.

Margie slams on her brakes and the driver behind her sounds his horn and yells something out the window. She mouths an apology in the mirror and pulls over. Then she sprints back to the mural.

It is a portrait of you, but not only of you.

Your eyes are closed, your arms are wrapped around your body. One unbroken thread connects you to another woman's body.

Margie slides down the railing until she is sitting on the cement.

The woman is Margie. The unbroken thread an umbilical cord.

Margie feels this mural as a gift.

She has wanted to tell you that the moment she saw your body rolled into the hospital on a stretcher, the desire to always and forever keep you safe has overwhelmed her. But then when you woke and you looked straight at her, a terrible feeling came over her that she had already failed you.

And now the mural confirms that all of the feelings she had, somehow you had felt them too.

Margie takes hold of the railing and pulls herself to her feet. She walks back to her car and in its safety and darkness she hugs your sketchbook and sobs.

Somehow, in the chaos, she has found you.

Margie gathers herself. She places your sketchbook on the passenger seat and pulls out into the slow-moving traffic. She drives to Lyn's knowing that something has both ended and begun.

And this must be the time for Margie Shapiro to right her wrongs.

Epilogue

THE FUTURE

Margie will be the first visitor in line.

She will be nervous about whether you even want to see her. But you will be there at the table, waiting, sipping on a fizzy drink.

She will sit down. She will take your sketchbook from her bag and she will apologise for not getting it back to you sooner. She will tell you that she has found your murals, or at least some of them, and seeing them has made her feel braver.

And then you will notice a nervous red rash bloom from her neck and move up her face, and you will wonder if she will ever say what she really wants to say.

And then she will say it:

I'm sorry I failed you.

And you will hear it.

Her words will move into your body and something in you will shift, something no less than a universe. For a while, you will not be able to speak. But one tear and then another will roll down your cheeks.

But if you let me, she will say, *I would like another chance.*

Margie will organise a lawyer. Before your case goes to trial, you will turn fifteen in prison, and then you will be released into Margie's care and custody. By the end of the year, Bambi, Kai, Reya, Cleo and Dev will also be released. Jackie will speak up against Jerome, and two more girls and one guard will come forward, and eventually Jerome will be convicted and sent to prison.

Every Sunday you and Margie will cook a feast and drive with Elsey to the Nightcliff foreshore. Margie will help you spread out blankets in the shade and lay out the food. When the girls arrive, Margie will lead Elsey away and they will walk along the escarpment to meet Lyn.

Left alone and secure in the company of each other, you will all eat and laze and breathe in the sea breeze, and feel your troubles loosen.

It will look to you like something you would want to paint – six girls stretched out on blankets on the edge of a world, watching the sun streak the sky every shade of pink.

You will return to the school your grandmother chose for you. Art class with Mrs Whitehead will remain your favourite subject. Every class, Mrs Whitehead will tell you that you have a natural talent. And you will believe her.

And one day, Mrs Whitehead will introduce the class to a group of long-forgotten women.

They were muralists, she will say. *Mostly, they painted landscapes and wild gardens, and recently some of their work has been uncovered in a monastery in the Himalayas . . .*

THE PAST

Your body is still warm when the girls slip their hands beneath it and carry you inside the monastery. There is so much blood. Your robes are torn, your flesh is torn. For many full moons to come, each girl will wish things had gone differently.

Bambi and Dev take over your job of chopping wood and stacking it in the woodshed. Piece by piece, they remove the dry wood covering your mural. Your first mural. The one that gave you solace and taught you how to paint.

In the woodshed, light pouring through one window, Bambi and Dev take in the colours you chose, your deft lines and shapes.

They know better than to tell the Big Sisters what they have seen. But they parade each girl in front of it, Little Sisters and New Sisters, to show them what you painted: six girls rising up a wall, arms linked.

When the Big Sisters discover the mural themselves, they tell the white-haired woman. She instructs them to paint wings on each girl's back and to rub out her feet so that anyone in the future who sees the mural will think it is just another fantasy of angels.

But none of the girls who have seen it will forget.

They will carry it inside them. They will carry it through time.

Six girls rising.

No hand lifting them.

No force or power other than the one together they have found.

ACKNOWLEDGEMENTS

Thank you to my agents Thomasin Chinnery, Sharon Gallant and Benython Oldfield for your cleverness and commitment, always.

Thank you to my publisher Vanessa Radnidge, and the entire team at Hachette, for your belief in me and this book. Special thanks to Lee Moir, Maddie Garratt and Eliza Thompson. Thank you, Clara Finlay and Ali Lavau, editors extraordinaire. And thanks to Camha Pham.

Thank you Dr Adelle Sefton-Rowston and Dr Tracy Woodroffe, my PhD supervisors and first readers, for offering insight and encouragement.

Special thanks to Dr Kesang Youdon for being open to hours of interviews on village life in Northern India, and to Professor Neelima Kanwar at the English Department, Himachal Pradesh University, for your generous hosting.

And for encouragement, inspiration, and support, thank you to: Clare Atkins, Yo Bell, Mary Anne Butler, Chelsea Carr, Cheryl Collins, Rob Collins, Olive Faulkner, Jennifer Higgie, Angelina

Barda Joshua, Zoe Leaton, Lisa Madden, Carol Major, Jeanmarie Morosin, Phoebe Quilty, Simon Quilty, Kite Quilty, Stella Quilty, Katie Richardson, Holly Ringland, Amanda Roff, Karen Rogers, Walter Rogers, Jasmin Tarasin, Jo Taylor, Silas Taylor, Theo Taylor, Kit Taylor, Erica Wagner and Charlotte Wood.

And thank you to Jude Emmett, for all that and more.

Research and early drafting of this novel took place in Himachal Pradesh, India, with the support of an Asialink Fellowship. Special thanks to Devanshe Chauhan Lidgley and Michael John Lidgley for your hospitality at the Himalayan Orchard. And special thanks to Varuna, The National Writers' House.

This novel was mainly written on Ngalakgan Country, Jawoyn Country, Larrakia Country and Gumbaynggirr Country. I pay my respects to Elders, past, present and emerging.

Courtney Collins is an author, screenwriter and producer. Her first novel, *The Burial* (Allen & Unwin, 2012), was published in ten countries and shortlisted for numerous prizes, including the Nita B Kibble Literary Award, the NSW Premier's Literary Award for New Writing and the Stella Prize. *The Burial* is currently being adapted as a feature film. Courtney holds a Master of Creative Writing and is completing a PhD titled 'Working Against Whiteness in Creative Literary Production'. She lived in the remote Northern Territory for eight years before relocating to the Mid North Coast. In 2019, she travelled to the Himalayan region of Himachal Pradesh, India, to research *Bird*. She presents and co-produces @areyoustillworkingpodcast.

AUTHOR'S NOTE

Bird is a work of fiction but it deals with issues faced by many.

If you or someone you know is experiencing violence or abuse, you do not have to face it alone.

You can call 1800RESPECT on 1800 737 732.

If you are under 25, you can call Kids Helpline on 1800 55 1800.

If you are an Aboriginal person or a Torres Strait Islander person, you can call 13YARN on 13 92 76.

If you live in New Zealand, you can call the Family Violence Information Line on 0800 456 450 or Shine on 0508 744 633.